LEAST
EXPECTED

JORDYN GRIFFIN

Least Expected

Copyright © 2024 by Jordyn Griffin.

MILTON & HUGO L.L.C.
4407 Park Ave., Suite 5
Union City, NJ 07087, USA

Website: *www. miltonandhugo.com*
Hotline: *1- 888-778-0033*
Email: *info@miltonandhugo.com*

Ordering Information:
Quantity sales. Special discounts are granted to corporations, associations, and other organizations. For more information on these discounts, please reach out to the publisher using the contact information provided above.

Library of Congress Control Number:	2024911523	
ISBN-13:	979-8-89285-163-3	[Paperback Edition]
	979-8-89285-164-0	[Hardback Edition]
	979-8-89285-162-6	[Digital Edition]

Rev. date: 06/06/2024

Chloe-Lots of Leaving

alifornia has always been home, it was where I born, raised, where I went to school and college. It was also the place where I gave birth to my son, Colton. California has been home, but it has also been a place of heart break and pain.

I slam the back door to my black Cadillac suburban after placing the last of the bags in the back seat next to Colton's car seat. Climbing into the front seat, I start the car and turn around to look at Colton, sleeping soundly-not surprising. His dark blonde hair had gotten drastically longer than a month ago, and his sweet little cheeks were pink, he is my entire life, I could leave my belongings behind and be content for the rest of my life just having him. He may have not been planned out at the time, but I like to thank the good lord for placing this sweet boy in my life, the last 9 months have been the best of my life.

Because of his place in my life and the lack of family we have here, I need to do my job to provide a better life for him.

I push a strand of my blonde hair behind my ear and grab my sunglasses. Putting the car in drive, I head down the driveway to the main road.

Moving to Missouri was never really on my radar, at least not until my son was born. Being a single mom with limited family around, it has been harder to work and raise my son. My best friend Summer lives in St. Louis where she works for the St. Louis Wolves NHL hockey team as a physical therapist. Having grown up together since middle school through college, it has been awesome watching her achieve her goals and dreams.

After having my son, Summer offered me to move in with her. After some careful deliberations, the answer was a no brainer, not only was she my best friend, she was Colton's godmother and the closest thing the two of us have to family. We needed a fresh start. So Missouri here we come.

2

Chloe-Adjusting

I had spent 4 days on the road with Colton. We stopped when we both needed to stop, stayed in decent hotels and took in the sites along the way. Driving with a small child by yourself is not for the faint of heart.

I was less than an hour away from Summer's house and to say that I was excited would be an understatement. I hadn't seen her since the week after Colton was born, that was the end of October and this was now July. She flew out and stayed with me and was in the room when Colton took his first breathe.

As I was singing along to an Usher song my phone started to ring.

"Hey Love! I cannot wait to put this truck in park and tackle you into a hug" I giggled over the speaker.

"I would expect nothing less from you. Where are you at?" Summer asked.

"I am about 45 minutes out from your house. I am hoping the traffic is not disastrous as I enter the city". I responded.

"Traffic is a shit show half the time. I have dinner on the stove and wine on the counter ready for your arrival. I also am excited to see my godson" Summer excitedly responded.

After talking for about 15 minutes, we hung up; realizing that they could continue this conversation in 30 minutes in person with wine.

After 45 minutes on the road due to a 15 minute delay caused by a car wreck, I pulled into the drive way of Summer's home at 7:25 pm. Summer came rushing out of the house with her arms open and a huge grin on her face. I bailed out of the car with my arms open and a smile that mirrored summers. Both of us pulling the other into a bone crushing hug- the two of us finally felt whole.

After getting Colton out of the truck and our luggage out of the backseat, we made our way into the house.

Deciding that the rest can be unloaded later. Gently lifting Colton from his car seat, I handed him to Summer so she could get all her much needed baby cuddles in.

After handing my son over to his godmother, I graciously grabbed the wine glass on the counter and poured myself some, just needing something to relax the stress of the drive.

"So, tell me about this wonderful boyfriend of yours that I have yet to meet?" I asked while wiggling my eyebrows and making the kissy face at her.

"Ooh, Matt. Hmmm I do not know where to start. He is amazing, we met while I was working and when he walked into the trainer's room I knew I was a goner. He is a center for the St. Louis Wolves and he is damn good. He's 29 and he's from Colorado" Summer gushed while ticking Colton's stomach as he smiled at her.

Summer continued her rant about how amazing Matt was. The entire time I smiled and laughed along with what she said, but I also noticed how happy she was. I couldn't even remember the last time I saw her this happy.

Summer never really dated anyone through school and even into college. She had her fair share of boys throwing themselves at her feet but she never gave them the time or attention. Summer has beautiful black hair cascading down her shoulders and onto her back. Her eyes are the most amazing shade of blue. Summer also has the best olive toned skin that make her features shine through. I was happy to see her finally happy and with someone that I had no doubt about that she loved. I also felt a little envious of her but I was more happy for her than anything else.

We continued the conversation of Matt and Summer as well as her job for the team. The conversation coming to a halt when Summer's phone started ringing.

Summer smiled and apologized, handing Colton back to me before retreating to the living room. I smiled at her retreating figure and took another sip of wine. No doubt that it was Matt calling.

Colton was playing with the blonde strands of hair that framed my face. Looking at him, my heart swelled. His hair was a dark blonde and his eyes were the same emerald green color as mine. He was my little twin, for that I was thankful. I gave my sweet boy a big kiss on the forehead, where he started to giggle. His giggle, my new favorite sound in the whole world.

As I was playing with Colton and making him laugh, Summer came walking back into the kitchen, leaning against the kitchen counter watching the interaction between Colton and myself.

"That was Matt, he just got out of practice and is coming by. He did not want to impose since you just got here so he called to see if it would be okay" Summer said.

"Yay! I can finally meet the man you are 100% in love with. Please tell me he showered at the rink and is not walking in here smelling like a locker room" I responded back.

Summer laughed, "I also hope he showered there. As much as I do love him, I do not want to smell the locker room. He said he will be here in about 15 minutes".

I nodded. "Oh, can I see where our room is? I want to take my luggage into the room and change into something more comfortable, and Colton probably needs a change to."

"Oh shoot yeah. Sorry I was just so excited to have you here that I forgot. Follow me" Summer said.

The three of us made our way up the stairs, Summer had graciously grabbed our bags. As we got to the second story, we made our way down the hallway.

"Okay my room is here on the left, guest bathroom is the first door on the right and your bedroom is the second door on the right, it has its own ensuite bathroom and walk in closet. If you need to use the office it's the last door on the left and the linen closet is the door on the left between my room and the office" Summer pointed out. "Okay, get comfy. I'm going back down stairs to take dinner out of the oven and then we can eat."

"Thank you Summer. Not only for letting me stay with you but for being my best friend. I have a great feeling that this was the right move and I am just so happy to be back with you under the same roof" I said getting a little emotional.

Summer smiled and pulled me into a hug, "Chloe you are my person and having you here with me has been a dream. I cannot wait for what is in store for us. Had it been me in your shoes, I am 100% sure that you would have done the same, we can get through this together." With that Summer separated herself from me and made her way back down the stairs, leaving me to get settled.

Turning back into the room, I was greeted with a queen size bed, walk in closet and space for the pack-n-play I brought for Colton.

Placing Colton on the bed, I grabbed his bags and started to change him, making him more comfortable. Once done, I placed him in the crib with a toy so I could change as well.

Not wanting to fully unpack tonight, I changed into a pair of yoga pants and a crew neck sweater that said 'San Jose Fins'. I laughed thinking Matt is either going to find it funny or definitely judge me for it- either way I am wearing it. Taking my blonde hair, I gathered it and put it up into a messy bun. I found my makeup wipes and removed any makeup that had still managed to stick to my face.

I leaned over the crib watching Colton, poor guy has been through so much in his 9 months of life, but he is still so happy everyday. As he was holding his pacifier, he gave me the biggest smile ever. I reached down and picked him up, placing him on my hip. "Well buddy, let's go meet your someday uncle, shall we?" Colton tugged on my hair, giving me a sign that he had no idea what I was talking about.

I found myself walking into the kitchen where I saw Summer enveloped into the arms of a very tall man, Matt. I had not expected this man to be 6'2", for some reason I definitely thought he would be shorter. I had seen photos of him and Summer but they did not show his full height.

His Shaggy brown hair was covered by a backwards ball cap. He had grey sweat pants on and a long sleeve shirt. His arms were around Summer's stomach as her back was pressed against his chest and she was washing the dishes in the sink. I felt warmth spread through my heart seeing how in love the two were. I called it then that they would one day get married.

The two of them must have felt my presence as they both turned around with smiles on their face. Moving Colton to my other hip, I smiled at both in return.

"Matt, this is Chloe, my best friend and my roommate once again. And this sweet little stud is Colton, my godson and Chloe's son" Summer said smiling ear to ear.

"It's nice to meet the two of you. Summer has talked about you both so much, I'm glad you both are here" Matt greeted us.

I let out a little giggle, "I can say the same. She talks about you all the time when we are on the phone. It's nice to officially meet you."

Shortly after introductions, we had dinner and then retreated to the living room to relax. Colton was still full of life since the time change. He was crawling or trying his best to crawl on the living room rug with his toys that I had dug out of the car. I sat on the ground, my back to the couch. Summer was against the other couch on the ground, trying her hardest to get Colton to crawl to her, and in reality he almost did. Matt was perched on the couch laughing at Summer's antics and egging Colton on to do his best.

Only meeting Matt a few hours ago and I could already tell that he would be a part of Colton's and my life forever, and I was perfectly okay with that. Colton needs a male figure in his life, and Matt seems like the perfect guy.

An hour later, Colton was asleep on Matt while he sat watching ESPN and Summer and I were cleaning up the remnants of dinner.

I could honestly say that the first few hours in our new home felt more like home than the one I used to live at. Maybe Missouri wouldn't be so bad.

3

Reed- Sweetest giggles

The front door slammed shut giving me the pleasure of waking up early. With a loud groan of annoyance at my roommate for graciously slamming the door. I stood up, stretching before heading downstairs to get a cup of coffee.

As I walked into the kitchen I saw Matt leaning against the counter savoring a cup of hot coffee while scrolling on his phone.

"Hey dumb fuck why are we slamming doors this early?" I asked nudging him with my shoulder.

Matt let out a laugh, "Sorry didn't realize it slammed. Also it's like 8:30am why are you still in bed?" He asked.

"I went out last night with some of the guys since you abandoned me for a booty call with your girlfriend" I responded.

"In my defense it wasn't a booty call. Her best friend moved in so I went over to be the good boyfriend and introduce myself." Matt stated flatly.

"Is she hot?" I joked.

"She isn't bad looking. More your type, blonde hair, green eyes, petite build. But, she does have a young son" Matt said looking back at his phone.

"Oh, interesting. So you legit ditched me to have a weird best friend date night. Still find it rude" I joked again trying to make him open up.

But to say the least I was intrigued. I had known that Summer's best friend was moving in, but with a kid. That was new. Then again not my problem.

A few hours later, Matt and I were headed to the rink since it was early July and we were wanting to get some practice in since it was off season. Vacations were not much our thing, so having this extra time at the rink to work on skills was a better idea for both of us.

After lacing up our skates and grabbing our sticks and the bucket of pucks, we headed onto the ice, right when Matts phone starting ringing at full volume.

"Hey Babe, what's up?" Matt asked on the phone. "Reed and I are getting onto the ice to get some practice in and then probably hit the gym after, not 100% sure, why?" He moved his phone to the other ear trying to juggle everything in his hands.

"Let me talk to Reed, I think dinner wouldn't be a bad thing. I mean anytime we don't have to cook is always perfect. What time?" He questioned.

"Sounds good. Love you" Matt disconnected the phone from his ear, turning to face me.

"Summer said dinner 7:00 tonight her house, you're invited. We just need to bring some beer." He stated looking at me.

"Beer sounds good. Dinner sounds better." I voiced back.

Looks like I get to meet the best friend.

Roughly an hour later of doing drills, Matt came to a halt on the ice, turning to the benches.

Sitting in the stands is Summer, next to her is the most beautiful girl I have ever laid eyes on. Even across the ice I can see the warmth of her smile. Her attention is directed to the small child in her arms as she is holding him upright as he bounces against her legs. His attention seems to be on the ice.

Realizing I look like an idiot, I am snapped out of my daze by Matt hurtling past me towards the boards in front of our audience.

Skating forward I come to the boards next to Matt who is making the weirdest faces at the baby, who seems to be loving the attention. My attention then shifts to Summer's friend, her hair is the color of the sun and her eyes are the most beautiful green color, almost like emeralds. Her lips are plush and before I know it I am adjusting myself desperately behind the boards.

"Chloe, this is Matt's best friend, teammate and roommate, Reed Collins" Summer introduces us.

Redirecting my attention back to her, I am met with a shy smile across her face.

"Reed, this is my best friend Summer and this is my godson Colton" Summer gushes while tickling Colton, who has now turned his attention to her.

"Hi, it's nice to meet you, both of you" I responded gesturing to her and Colton.

"It's nice to meet you to" she said sweetly.

"Sorry about crashing your practice, we were heading to the grocery store and I remembered that I needed my work planner from the office, then well we ended up stalking the two of you" Summer explained.

"No worries love. Hey Chloe, can I hold Colton, maybe do a lap or two? I'll go slow I promise" Matt asked.

Chloe looked between Colton and Matt wearily. After a little internal debate, she stood up and handed him over the boards. Colton was kicking his legs excitedly reaching for Matt.

How could this kid love Matt already, they just met. Even when I met Matt it took me a few weeks to warm up to him.

Matt gave me a nod of his head, indicating for me to skate next to him.

"Since when are you the baby whisperer?" I jokingly asked.

"Honestly dude, last night sold me. This kid was cracking me up and watching Summer with him made me want my own." He smiled looking down at Colton who was smiling and kicking his legs.

"Don't go knocking Summer up. You have only been together a year. Calm down" I laughed. I reached over tickling Colton's foot, not realizing what I was doing or even noticing the smile form on my lips. Colton let out the sweetest giggle I have ever heard.

"Ok I take it back. Can you guys make one so I can hangout with it" I stated.

Matt laughed, "Dude, this kid is legit the coolest. Just you wait, give it some more time. I am already trying to get him to say 'Uncle' even though words are hard huh bud" Matt cooed over the kid.

After another lap of playing with Colton, we headed back to the boards where the girls were recording our interactions.

Matt handed Colton back to Chloe over the boards, she turned him to face us in her arms. As he looked back at Matt, he smiled and kicked his legs again, almost like he was trying to run out of his mom's arms. As his attention turned to me he let out the sweetest giggle once again, this time reaching his arms out to me as if asking for me to take him.

Summer tried redirecting Colton's attention, but after watching her struggle with getting Colton to change his mind, I reached my arms out.

"I'm okay with it, if you're okay with me taking him?" I asked.

"Are you sure? I don't want to impose. I think he liked being out there" Chloe asked sweetly. Now if only I could make her laugh or giggle, that might just be the next sweetest thing I've heard.

Chloe and I locked eyes, her green eyes embedded into my soul. I just met this girl and here I am, willingly taking her son to skate around the ice.

I nodded and grabbed Colton, placing him on my hip. Colton smiled and clapped his hands together signaling he was happy.

I skated a few small circles with Matt and the girls talked about what they should make for dinner.

Noticing that Colton had little shoes on, I held his upper body and placed his feet against the ice as I slowly skated forward. Giving him the feeling of skating. Colton continued to giggle and squeal while clapping his hands excitedly.

Well after 15 minutes of meeting this kid, I can definitely say he's my new favorite person. Looking up Chloe was watching with her phone out, her expression happy. I think we can both agree this is all ours favorite person in my hands.

4

Chloe: Cooking Chaos

After we left the rink to head to the store, Colton immediately fell asleep. Just my luck. In his defense he had a busy morning and then skating with Reed and Matt I think did him in. I am grateful that the people in his life seem to care for him, including Matt and Reed.

Reed. That man was a walking, or should I say skating, magazine ad for pure sex appeal. His eyes, dark pools of brown, they just sucked me in. He's tall, like Matt, and I am a sucker for tall men. His dark hair was shaggy and longer, but it was covered with a backwards ball cap. Again pure sex appeal.

Before I knew it we had pulled into the parking lot of the grocery store. "Do you want to wait in the car with Colton while I run in and grab the few things we need?" Summer asked while grabbing her bag.

"Yes please, if that's okay, he's a brute when woken up" I laughed.

"No worries, text me if you think of anything we didn't add to the list" Summer said getting out of the car.

"Thanks for reminding me, I'll need some of his baby snacks, I'll text them" I said smiling at her.

Fifteen minutes later, Summer was back in the car with the groceries and snacks. Heading home never felt so sweet.

After pulling into the driveway, Summer got out, grabbing the bags and heading to the door. I went around to the backseat, grabbing our Colton's diaper bag and my purse and setting them on the ground. Turning back around I noticed that Colton was still asleep. I take a deep breathe, trying my hardest to lift him from his car seat without waking him. When I say he's a brute, I mean like full on grumpy butt.

Successfully lifting him to my chest, I turn to shut the door as quietly as I can. Once the door is shut I reach down and grab my purse and then try to grab his diaper bag without losing the contents of my purse.

Usually, my purse doesn't leave the house, my wallet tends to get stuffed in the diaper bag, but for some reason I grabbed both today.

I started getting frustrated, I was not able to grab both bags without spilling my purse across the driveway, or waking Colton. I could feel my chest tightening, I knew the tears would pool in my eyes shortly after this feeling. I've experienced this feeling multiple times since having Colton, mainly it stems from the fact I am a single mother who has no one. I have to do everything on my own, yet deep down I feel like I can't, which makes me feel like a failure.

Taking a few deep breaths, I try to push the feeling away and gather my emotions. As my eyes are closed, my hand drawing circles on Colton's back, a deep voice startled me, "Chloe, can I help you?"

Opening my eyes, I am met with Reed who has a worried look on his face. "Oh umm, if you can please grab his diaper bag, that would be great" I responded trying to shake the anxiety from my voice.

"Yea, no problem, are you okay though? You seem a little nervous or upset" he asked sweetly reaching for the bag off the ground.

Giving him a small smile, "Yea I'm good. I was just getting frustrated at myself for having so many things"

"Hey, it's all good. How long has he been asleep?" Reed asked as he pushed the front door open.

"Since we left the rink. Thank you for taking him around the ice. I think that helped him fall asleep."

"Don't even worry about it. I had fun, plus I think I also need a nap after that." He laughed. "Oh, where do you want his bag?"

"Oh, umm if you can help put it on my shoulder, I'll take it upstairs. I need to take him up there anyways" I stated.

"You sure, I can just follow you" he asked again.

"Yea, it's fine" I smiled at him while reaching for the bag.

Reed helped place the bag on my shoulder. A smile gracing his lips. Giving me a nod of understanding.

After successfully placing the bags on the ground, I had gracefully maneuvered Colton from my chest to my bed.

This boy had been asleep so far a little over an hour, I guess today was a lot of fun for him. Propping some pillows around him to prevent him from rolling over. I quickly grabbed my suitcase and pulled out a pair of workout leggings and a light weight crew neck sweater, along with my slippers. Colton wasn't the only one drained.

Knowing I will eventually need to make my way down to the kitchen to help and to entertain our guests, I still removed the pillows from around Colton and laid down next to him. Just watching him breathe, watching his eyelids move every now and again and watching his little fingers extend. He is perfect.

His little lips are in a pout, his cheeks a light pink tint; 9 months after he was born and I am still in awe of how beautiful he is, and how thankful that I was graced with being his mom.

I reached over carefully, running my finger along his cheek, I could just be here with him forever and be ok. Studying his facial features, it's not a secret he's my kid, he took majority of my features, the only thing he got from his father was his dimples on both cheeks. As much as I resent those dimples on his sperm donor of a father, I absolutely love them on Colton.

Giving him a few more minutes I placed my elbow below me propping me up and got my phone out of my pocket. I took a sweet picture of Colton sleeping-knowing I can have a token to cherish in the future.

After another few minutes of scrolling on my phone, I noticed his hands and arms stretching out above his head. Placing my phone down, I directed my attention back to him, his green eyes staring into my own and large smile across his face. He's always a happy boy when he wakes up on his own accord.

After a quick diaper change and outfit change, we enter to kitchen to see Matt trying to help Summer cook while Reed is seated in a barstool chair against the eating bar- Watching and laughing at the struggle both Matt and Summer are dealing with.

I make my way next to Reed, taking the seat next to his, readjusting Colton to sit on my lap. "Well, what's the verdict, are we ordering take out?" I joked looking at Reed.

"Honestly I have no idea. I don't even know what Summer is trying to having him cook and honestly I have no idea how she has survived him for so long" he responded laughed at the two of them bickering.

"Do you want something to drink while we wait for our dinner verdict?" I asked.

"I'll take a beer if you have it" Reed responded.

I nodded my head, getting up from the chair. Moving Colton to my hip.

"Here hand him over. I'll take him while you maneuver around them" Reed offered extending his arms to Colton who was already reaching for him, babbling about something.

Smiling, I handed him over the rest of the way heading into the kitchen, bracing myself for what I was about to endure.

Opening the refrigerator I pulled out a beer and a sparkling water for myself before turning towards the couple.

"Matt, you have to wait for the water to boil before adding in the pasta" Summer scolded looking at the pot on the stove filled with dry pasta and ice cold water.

"You sure, I mean the pasta will just soften in the water and eventually it will get hot. It's fine" Matt tried reassuring her.

Summer looked at me with a pleading look, "So, how does Chinese food sound?" I jokingly asked.

"Chloe, the top drawer has all the take out menus. Can you get them out and have them on standby" Summer giggled.

I smiled back at her, shaking my head and walking back to the eating bar where the cutest sight graced my eyes.

Reed had Colton sitting on the counter, facing each other. Colton had Reed's hat on his head backwards, Reed was making funny faces at him as Colton giggled and placed his hands on Reed's face.

Getting closer I placed the unopened cans down on the counter, smiling at Colton I reached forward and tickled his stomach. His giggles were my favorite sound in the world.

"He is a cute kid. And I don't say that about any kids really, well also because I don't really know many" Reed stated out of nowhere.

Turning to look at him, he was looking at Colton as Colton was focused on him. As if the two of them had known each other since his birth.

"I mean I might be bias, but I think he's the greatest kid in the world. I was definitely blessed to have him" I said smiling at the two of them.

Reed turned and looked at me, smiling back. We just stared at each other, almost like looking deeper into the other person's eyes for information.

Our gaze was cut off by Summer walking up to the counter, "Okay, so Chef Matt has called it a loss with the pasta, so I'm going to call in a few pizzas. Any debates?" She asked as she reached for her phone.

"No debate here." I laughed.

"Same" Reed agreed, going back to playing with Colton.

Twenty Four hours ago I was on the road, slightly nervous about this new adventure. I had only one person I could rely on, but looking around the room I realized that Colton and I had more than we could have asked for.

5

Reed: Wanted

The time had been flying by, felt like I closed my eyes one second and when I opened them up we were already a week from our first preseason game.

In the month in a half that Chloe and Colton had joined the friend group, the five of us have spent almost every night having dinner or hanging out.

I found out early in August that Chloe had been an aesthetician or something like that in the beauty world. At dinner one evening, Summer and Chloe were talking about her opening her own salon or something around here. So Matt and I have taken it upon ourselves to look into buildings for rent as a way to help the girls out. It's what friends are for.

Matt and I have continued our routine of skating, doing drills and working in the gym almost everyday. Summer and Chloe bring Colton a few times a week and let us skate him around. Colton has gotten bigger, Matt and I joke that he will be a hockey player like us due to his love for the ice but also because of how big he is getting. Colton is constantly on the move crawling, but lately he's been pulling himself up to stand. Before we know it he's going to be running around, he's almost 11 months old. Words are fun, he hasn't said any other than baby words but we pretend like he's apart of all our conversations.

I have never had the opportunity to be around babies or kids, other than my teammate's kids; but even then I hardly interact. Something about Colton though drawls the two of us together. Every time we see each other I smile so big but he fights anyone and everyone to get to me. Crying included.

I think Matt is a little jealous of how much Colton loves me more than him. It's hysterical.

I'm currently on the ice in our practice rink, stretching and warming up along with my teammates. Todays practice is going to be brutal to get us back into the swing of things before our opening preseason game next week. As I'm practicing my puck handling drill, I can see Matt skating up next to me. "Hey, what are you doing Saturday?" Matt asked.

"Probably working out, napping, might hit the pool. Why?" I wearily asked. Hoping he didn't sign me up for something dumb.

"Summer, Chloe and I are taking Colton to the Zoo. We were talking this morning about favorite childhood memories. Chloe mentioned that Colton had never been to a Zoo and I about passed out. So I'm making us go. You wanna join us?" He asks.

"I haven't been to a Zoo since I was probably in elementary school. What time you guys going? I'll try and meet you there" I responded focusing back on the puck on the ice in front of me.

"Think they open at 9. Figured going right when they open before it gets too humid. Might just stay with them after Friday dinner so I can drive. Why don't you just crash at the girls' house? They have another bedroom" Matt explained.

I sat there watching the puck, pondering if it was a good idea. I had never stayed at their house. Let alone being invited to the Zoo with them felt like a family outing and I'm just Matt's friend.

"Dude. We all want you to be there. Think of how excited Colton is going to be. Plus he loves you. We all do" Matt said, almost like he could read my face.

"Yea, I, uh, I'll go" I agreed, looking back up facing him.

Matt nodded and skated off to the bench. I went back to the puck, the only thing I could control right now.

The truth is, since I met Chloe and Colton, they are all I seem to think about. Just something about the two of them has me drawn to them when they are in the room. When Colton starts crying I panic-because I want to help him.

When Chloe seems frustrated, I drop everything and assist the best I can without making her feel weak. When I'm not around them, I wonder what they are up to. If she has figured out her business plan, is Colton liking the new foods he's trying, did he nap today? All these questions, they are ridiculous to me- he isn't my son, he isn't my blood, but sometimes I forget that.

Noon finally rolls around and Matt and I are leaving the rink heading to our truck.

"The girls said that they need a change of scenery, so dinner at ours. You good with that?" Matt asked.

"Yea that's fine. We should probably clean. Not that Colton is walking, but he is crawling, do we need to baby proof? Maybe get those wall plugs. Oh, what about a high chair, do we have to get one or no?" I started rattling off these questions without really thinking about it.

"Calm down dude. If the girls didn't think that our house was safe, they probably would have recommended a restaurant. Why are you worried?" He raised a brow at me before turning his attention back to the road.

"Just never had a kid over at our house before. Just want them to be comfortable" I answered annoyed that I had sounded paranoid before.

Matt laughed shaking his head. "Can we please talk about the elephant in the room?"

"What elephant?" I asked furrowing my brows at him. "The fact that I can read you like a book and I know for a fact that you like Chloe and you love Colton. Can you just be honest with me and yourself and say that you like her more than a friend" he explained.

"I don't like her like that. We're just friends, you get that. And yes I love Colton, he's a cool kid" I said looking out the window.

"Reed, you know I'm not dumb and neither is Summer. You literally do everything you can when Chloe or Colton seem frustrated or overwhelmed. You literally panic whenever Colton cries or Chloe seems to be on the brink of tears. You even have gone so far as help with the grocery shopping if they don't have time" Matt said.

I turned and looked at Matt, "None of that means anything. My mama raised me to be helpful. That's what I'm doing, being nice" I responded back.

"Reed, when they are in the stands, you zone out staring at them. Anytime you get up for a drink, you always return with a sparkling water or a snack for them. You zone out when Chloe talks. Dude you like her. You like them" Matt directed.

I took a deep breathe, "Fine! Okay! Yes, I like her, I love Colton. I worry about them, I hate seeing either one upset or mad. But I can't like her, we know I'll never be good enough for either of them. I don't know much about her past since she won't open up, but I don't care that I don't know. I like her I do. But that's the extent. I can't act on it" I hung my head down with my hands on either side of it holding it.

"Reed, your past doesn't define your future. That goes for both you and Chloe. But you are good enough for her, for both of them. I wish you would see yourself for the good guy you are. What happened 3 years ago wasn't your fault." Matt said calmly, reaching out grabbing my shoulder.

"Matt, I couldn't commit then, what makes you think I can commit now?" I asked harshly.

"Reed, Jessica was not your person, hell I told you that multiple times. It wasn't that you couldn't commit, it was that she couldn't, she didn't leave you, she cheated on you" Matt truthfully stated.

"If I could have committed better than she wouldn't have cheated. I'm not good enough, she proved that" I harshly responded.

"Believe what you want. Jessica was the past, these two might just be your future." Matt whispered.

I just stared out the window. I hated thinking about my past, I hated thinking about the events that occurred. I hated that I hated myself, I also hated the fact that I thought Matt was right, but I couldn't bring myself to believe him.

No amount of therapy has helped me.

Before I know it 5pm rolled around, I was in our garage gym burning off the stress and anger that I had bottled up since the car ride home.

As I was cleaning up and putting the weights away, I was shook out of my zone by the sweetest giggle coming from the entry way. Colton and Chloe must be here. I wanted so badly to drop everything and run to them to see them. Doing that would prove to everyone how wrapped around their fingers I am. I can't have that.

I continued cleaning up and the giggles got louder and louder.

"Let's go find Reedy, what do you say Colt Man" I could hear Matt outside the door.

The door swung open, turning to greet Colton I was surprised to see him standing, his hands above his head holding Matt's fingers. The biggest smile on Colton's face, you could see his 3 bottom teeth poking out.

Colton was giggling when he saw me. My heart exploded. "What are you up to little man? Are you learning how to walk?" I asked kneeling down in front of him.

Reed babbled back, moving his legs to take a few steps, bringing Matt with him. He unlatched himself and reached for me. Scooping him into my arms I held him against my chest, soaking in the sweetest hug of my life.

"The girls are on dinner, Colton was trying to find you I think. He kept crawling around looking for something. I think he realized you weren't out there, because he started to cry. Once I mentioned your name he crawled over to me- so here we are" Matt explained, picking up the last weight off the ground, placing it back on the cart.

"Thanks man. Colt did you miss me?" I asked while tickling his stomach.

Once everything dangerous was put away and out of his reach, I put Colton on the workout mat, leaving out a jump rope for him to play with.

Matt and I sat on the ground, getting some last minute stretches in. Colton crawled all around, one hand holding onto the jump rope, dragging it with him as he scooted by. Matt and I were laughing, watching how he was interested in everything.

Colton would turn to look at me, his green eyes staring into mine, he has his mom's features, almost her twin.

Colton smiled showing off his little pearly white teeth, then babbling again.

I had an old hockey stick leaning against the wall, almost like it send out a beckon, Colton crawled over to it, dropping the rope he reached forward grabbing the stick.

Noticing that he was interested in it, I leaned over and grabbed it laying it on the ground, so it wouldn't fall on him. Colton crawled over, well over me, landing himself between my legs, one hand holding his pacifier the other touching the stick handle.

"I think we have a hockey kid on our hands" Matt laughed.

"I wouldn't be mad about it" I responded, looking at Colton examining the stick. "We should get him some mini sticks."

"His birthday is coming around soon, we should get a whole set up made" Matt countered.

I let out a laugh, "When is his birthday again?" I asked. "Let's just say he's going to have a killer birthday every year, especially when he turns 21" Matt laughed.

"Shit, Halloween? That's a hell of a birthday" I responded looking back down at Colton. As if sensing me watching him, Colton turned to look at me, holding out his pacifier to me, I took it. Colton directed his attention back to the stick, now with 2 free hands, he was grabbing it and trying to move it around.

"Can you imagine if we set up a goal, got some plastic balls and a mini stick for him, you think the girls would be annoyed?" I asked, running a hand over Colton's blonde hair. It's gotten longer since July, the kid needs a haircut or he's going to be matching me.

"Honestly I think they would love it" Matt responded. "And, I think it would be the perfect gift you could give him."

I nodded my head, I would buy this kid a whole rink just to see him smile.

An hour later, the door opened to the garage, Chloe poked her head in smiling at the 3 of us on the mat. "Dinner is ready boys."

Matt stood up, wiping his hands on his shorts, "Oh thank goodness, I was starving." He said bypassing Chloe and heading into the house.

I stood up, reaching down to grab Colton as Chloe came closer. She eyed the stick on the mat, "Were we having hockey 101 lessons in here" she let out the sweetest laugh.

"What can I say, the kid loves hockey" I said running my hand through my hair.

"I can take him, you have been nice enough to deal with him for the last hour" she offered, reaching for Colton.

"I'm good, I love hanging out with him. Plus you need a break every now and again" I smiled back to her. Colton took this moment to lean his head against the crook of my neck, pacifier in his mouth and his hand gripping the collar of my t shirt.

Chloe turned her head with a smile, watching Colton flutter his eyes open and close. She ran a gentle hand through his hair, "Once he sleeps on you, your trapped. Now's the time to run Reed" she laughed.

"Really, I'm good. I like having him, makes me feel wanted" I expressed.

Her expression changed from happy too confused, she took a second to find her words. "Reed you are wanted" she looked down, then back to me, cheeks flushing, she then turned and walked out the door.

'Reed you are wanted' the words rang through my head on repeat. I stood there, lost and confused. Did she mean she wanted me, or was she just making me feel better? Why did she seem nervous after, practically running away?

'Reed you are wanted'

6

Chloe: He said what?

Before I knew it, Friday was here and the boys were coming over for a sleepover in honor of Colton's first trip to the zoo tomorrow.

I love how 4 adults are commemorating this "milestone" in Colton's life, when Colton will not even remember it.

Maybe I'll start making a scrapbook instead of just taking photos on my phone. Something to look into.

"Chloe, I was thinking that we just order our Chinese food or Thai food. Maybe I will go to the store and stock up on candy and sweets and we can have a movie marathon tonight" Summer rattled on.

"Chinese sounds better. Sweets sound perfect. I will never turn down a movie night" I said while feeding Colton his lunch. Which consisted of some baby puff cereal and some sweet potato and carrot purée, sounds terrible but he's a fan.

"Oh my goodness, Colton look how cute you look post nap. Is that food good?" Summer cooed at Colton while sweeping her hand through his hair. He looked up at her giving her his toothy smile with baby food smeared all around his lips. Almost like he understood, he started babbling.

I let out a chuckle, I love when he's happy, I mean I love him regardless, but happy Colton was one of my favorite versions of him. His eyes light up, he loves to talk and he is always waving his hands in the air. My little bubbly party boy.

"Alright, I'm heading out to grab that stuff. The boys should be here soon. Colton you're in charge bud" Summer laughed walking out the door.

I looked at Colton, raising an eye brow at him, "Oh no, you're in charge. The house will surely burn down won't it big boy?" I laughed poking him gently in the cheek. A loud giggle emerged from Colton as his hands made a grab motion for me.

After a few more minutes of finishing his meal. I started to clean up his tray, hands and face. The front door opened and shut, indicating Reed and Matt had entered the house.

As their footsteps got closer, the butterflies in my stomach started erupting. I had told Reed that he was wanted the other night, but I hadn't realized I said it out- loud until it was too late. I had then ran and I haven't allowed myself to be alone with him since.

"Well isn't it my favorite people" I heard Matt laughing. "Wait till Summer hears that statement" Reed joked knocking into Matts shoulder.

I finished wiping Colton's hands, turning to see the two men. "Summer left about 20 minutes ago, she should be back within the hour. Something about Chinese food, candy and movie marathon. Oh also Colton's in charge, Summer said" I laughed picking up Colton from his highchair.

As I held Colton in my arms I felt the cold sensation against my chest, looking down I realized I had baby food all over my shirt. "Umm, can one of you take Colton? He just ate and is all cleaned up. Sadly I am not and I need to change."

Reed immediately dropped his bags and practically ran to my aide. Reaching out to grab Colton, our hands touches, sending bolts of electricity through my body, causing me to gasp for air. Reed slightly jumped at the contact, cheeks turning pink, "Come here little man. Let's let Mama get cleaned up. Wanna go play with the Dino toys" Reed tickled Colton.

Colton immediately perked up to the word toys and the dinosaur ones were by far his favorite. Watching Reed waltz out of the kitchen with my son on his hip, made me swoon. Since Colton was born it had been just the two of us. Since we moved months ago, he has taken a liking to Reed and I have as well.

A cough brought my attention back to my surroundings and my eyes off the retreating toned back of Reed. "You know, staring is said to be rude" Matt joked.

I glared at him, trying to hide my frustration of being caught ogling Reed, "I wasn't staring. I was just thinking. In that direction." Sly Chloe. Real sly.

"He's a good guy. Just so you know. You can trust him" Matt explained.

"I didn't think he wasn't a good guy" I responded confused.

"No, but he doesn't see himself as a good guy. His experiences in the past make him hate himself. But he really loves Colton, and I think he likes you" Matt said turning to head to the living room to play toys with the boys.

I looked at Matt with so much confusion yet questions plaguing my mind now. "Why does he think that?" I timidly asked. Why would he hate himself? Why would he not deem himself a good guy? He's been super helpful when he's over and he's been overly sweet.

"That's his story to tell. Just don't give up" Matt said. "Give up. When did I start trying?" I laughed.

"The two of you are so dumb I swear" Matt laughed walking away from me.

I quickly changed into a San Jose pull over and my comfy grey sweats before heading back to the living room. As I was turning the corner I stopped, wanting to spy on the boys. Peaking my head around the corner, I was met with the sweetest sight. Reed sitting with his back to the couch with his legs sprawled out in front of him. Colton was leaning his back against Reed holding up a dinosaur toy, his head looking up at Reed with his toothy smile. Reed ran a hand through Colton's hair, making baby small talk about the toy in Colt's hand. With one hand, Colton reached up towards Reed's face, Reed leaned forward knowing that Colton's arm span was too short. Once he leaned forward, Colton grabbed his nose, babbling and giggling.

I pushed off the wall and entered the living room, a smile across my face. Reed looked up smiling at me, then directing his attention to

Colton, "Look bud, mama changed and is ready to play. Only mama is wearing the wrong team's sweatshirt. How dare she" he joked.

My cheeks heated to hearing him speak so sweetly but also calling me mama, "Hey now, I haven't been able to add the wardrobe since I got here." I laughed.

Sitting on the ground in front of Reed and Colton, I clapped my hands together, trying to coax Colton into leaving Reed. Colton pushed himself up, wobbling slightly. He had been trying so hard to walk, I just wish time would slow down. Colton smiled at me, reaching both hands forward, "Mama" he babbled.

Tears swelled in my eyes as I leaned forward grabbing him into my chest. "Yea, baby I'm mama" I cooed giving him a large Kiss on his cheek. He has said "mama" before, but every time I hear it I get sad and happy. I kept kissing his little cheeks till he would giggle at me.

Colton pushed back and turned his head to Reed. Reed smiled, playing with the dinosaur toy Colton had dropped earlier. Colton turned and started to push off the ground again, once standing he stumbled forward onto all fours. "Da. Da. Da" be mumbled.

Reed and I stopped, froze. Did he say, "Dada", he had never heard the word before, maybe he was just talking.

Matt perked up, looking at Colton from the couch, "What did you say buddy?"

Colton crawled forward to Reed, pushing off Reed's thigh to stand, he placed his little hand on Reed's shoulder. Turning to look at Matt, he smiled and looked back at Reed, his other hand coming to Reed's cheek. "Da-Da" he said again. The air seemed to get sucked from my lungs.

Reed's eyes immediately snapped to mine, panic across his face. He shared the same expression I had.

Matt still sat gob smacked on the couch, his phone long forgotten.

The front door opened and shut indicating Summer's arrival. She shuffled into the room holding a few bags, her eyes scanning all of us in concern.

"Dada" Colton say again wrapping his little arms around Reed's neck, Reed's hand coming to Colton's back to support him.

"What did he just say?" Summer asked loudly.

I had stood up abruptly, picking up Colton and exiting the room. "We will be right back, he needs to change." I practically ran out of the room and up the stairs.

Getting to our room, I placed Colton on the ground on his play mat with toys. I hurriedly started grabbing out his pajamas and a new diaper.

I was upset, frustrated, sad, every and all emotions plagued me. I shouldn't be mad, Colton didn't know. Yet how does he know that word, we don't use it. He doesn't even know his dad- which I am very happy about.

This also wasn't fair to Reed. He hadn't made Colton call him that. He looked just as surprised as I was. He's probably also panicking.

I sat down next to Colton on the ground, his pajamas sprawled on the ground next to me. I leaned back against the bed, tears in my eyes. My breathing was erratic, I was panicking over nothing. Yet it was everything. This was dumb.

I had Colton changed into a new diaper, and we were fighting over the pajamas. He wasn't wanting to sit still enough for me to get his legs in the onesie. I was becoming frustrated more due to my emotions being all over the place. "Please baby, just let mama have 1 minute to get these on you and we can play some more" I tried to reason with him.

Colton started fussing when I would try to put his feet in the pajamas. I was bawling now.

I hadn't even heard the door open and close. I hadn't realized someone had kneeled down beside me. "Chloe, sweetie what's wrong" Reed quietly asked trying not to startled me.

I abruptly opened my eyes, wiping the tears away, "Nothing, nothing. I'm fine. Colton just doesn't want to help me get him dressed" I hurriedly explained.

Reed moved to sit all the way down next to me, Colton, crawling over to his lap. "Here, let me see if I can help" Reed grabbed his pajamas from my hand.

I sat there feeling like a terrible mother for crying, for getting frustrated and not being able to dress my own kid. I watched Reed interact with Colton, making faces, blowing raspberries, making Colton giggle. Before I knew it, my sweet boy was dressed in his all black footie pajamas that had little hockey sticks all over-a gift from summer.

28

Colton, crawled away from Reed back to his play toys.

Reed leaned back, his body lined up with mine, he placed his left hand on my right knee giving it a little squeeze, "You good mama?" He gently asked.

I nodded my head, "I, umm. I'm sorry if him calling you that made you uncomfortable" I quietly responded. I was watching his hand, his thumb rubbing back and forth along my knee. It was soothing, this was also the first time we have touched like this.

Just like earlier, the electric bolts were spreading throughout my body. His hand felt comfortable where it was. This was comfortable.

"Don't worry about it. I'm more worried about you though. What's going on in your head?" He leaned his head down trying to catch my eyes.

"Am I a bad mother?" I timidly asked, looking up to meet his stare.

His expression softened, "Chloe, why would you even think that? You are a great mom. Colton loves you so much" he tried to reassure me.

"I get frustrated easily, it's not his fault, but I feel like I'm failing him. I couldn't even get him changed just now. And him calling you, that word earlier, made me realize that he's lacking in that department. Does that make me a failure of a mom?" I started crying again.

Reed's brows furrowed together before they softened again, he reached his left hand across his body, gently caressing my cheek, turning it to have me face him. Once facing him he took both hands and gently started to wipe away my tears. "You are not a bad mother. It's understandable for you to get frustrated. I used to get on my mom's nerves all the time as a kid" he laughed. Making me smile at his comment. "Just because he doesn't have a dad doesn't mean he's lacking. I mean he has Matt and I and we are a lot cooler in my opinion." He smiled lovingly at me.

I kept my eyes locked on his, I probably looked like a disaster. I let out a shaky breathe, nodding my head slightly acknowledging what he said.

Colton crawled over during our staring contest, crawling into my lap. Reed's hands left my cheeks as I turned to face Colton. I ran a hand through my son's hair, trying to calm my breathing down. Reed's right, it's okay to feel frustrated I just can't stew on it.

Colton moved across my lap to face Reed. Clapping his hands together, giggling like we just said the funniest things in the world. This little boy didn't know what he said, he doesn't realize what he does, he's learning how to be human. And I love him.

Reed stood up, leaning forward he picked Colton up, extending his hand to mine to pull me to my feet, "Alright, how about the three of us go downstairs, grab a blanket, eat some food and watch a movie."

I grabbed his hand, allowing him to pull me. Once on my feet, I nodded my head agreeing with him smiling at the two of them. Reed dropped my hand, which caused me to feel almost disappointed.

"Come here" Reed gently said grabbing me by my waist. Pulling me to his chest in a hug. One of my arms went around his waist the other reached around to Colton's back.

Reed squeezed me, holding me tight against him. I felt him leave a sweet kiss on the crown of my head, "Remember Chloe, you are wanted."

The air left my body. My words fired back at me.

Reed released me but still kept me close, looking up I was met with his brown eyes, "Come on. Matt might eat all our food, we can't have that" I joked.

Walking towards the door, Reed kept his hand on my lower back, making me aware he was there, and that I was not alone. I would never be alone again.

The rest of the night was perfect. At 9pm, Colton was asleep on my chest as I laid down on the couch. Matt and Summer were asleep on the other couch and Reed was seated at my feet with my legs across his lap.

"Reed?" I quietly asked.

He turned his head, "yea" he whispered.

"Umm, I need to get up to put him to bed, can you uh, help me up?" I asked. Usually I would just help myself, but I didn't have the heart to risk waking Colton up.

Reed nodded his head and carefully moved from under my legs, reached down and gently transferred Colton from my chest to his. I slowly moved my body to a standing position, I was sore just from the 3 hours laying on the couch, I would definitely be sore tomorrow.

I reached forward for Colton, Reed shook his head, "I think he woke up when I took him, he just closed his eyes again. Let me follow you and hopefully he's out when we put him in the crib" Reed quietly said, leaving a kiss on Colton's head.

Getting to my room was the easy part, but Colton wasn't having the whole 'let Reed go'. Every time Reed went to pull him off his chest, Colton would fist his shirt and start to fuss. This rarely every happened-maybe when he was a new born but that was 11 months ago.

"You can just give him to me as he fusses and I'll stay up with him till he sleeps again, you need to go to bed" I tried to reason with Reed by taking Colton back.

Well, let's just say, my tactic did not work. Once Colton was moved off Reed's chest, he woke up crying screaming, "Dada".

I was getting frustrated again, this wasn't Reed's fault or even Colton's fault. I should have just slept on the couch.

"Chloe, this might sound weird" Reed mentioned getting my attention, "Can I just sleep in here with you? He isn't leaving me and maybe if I lay down, he will release me. Not that it will happen, his grip is pretty tight."

"Umm, yea I guess that's fine" I agreed timidly. I walked over moving the covers, Reed crawled in, laying on his back, Colton sprawled on his chest.

I turned to turn the light off, making my way to the bed.

This is weird right. Sharing a bed because MY kid won't sleep without him. It doesn't mean anything. Right?

Crawling next to Reed, I laid on my back staring at the ceiling.

"This might also sound weird. I uh, is it me or does Colton have the cutest expressions when he's sleeping" Reed whispered.

Turning on my side to face them, I was met with Reed staring at my son so lovingly. I reached over and lightly stroked my son's cheek, "Not weird at all. Sometimes I watch him sleep and I think about what a blessing he really is. I love how relaxed, how worry free he is. I'm envious that he can be 'free'. I love him more than my own life, but I owe my life to him, he saved me" I yawned. "Good night Reed. If you need me to take him, just wake me."

Reed shuffled closer to me, the best he could, he took his arm and forced it under my shoulders, pulling me closer to him. "Come here" he sleepily said, keeping me close to his chest.

Before I knew it, I was out.

7

Chloe: Chocolate evidence

All I could hear were hushed whispers and a "no, let them sleep" statement- definitely Summer. Wait. 'Them', whose 'them'? I started to question.

As I was slowly pushing myself to open my eyes, I felt my pillow start to move below me, that's new.

Opening my eyes I was met with Summer holding Colton who was playing with her hair. Summer gave me a 'we need to talk' kinda look. In my defense I am still very confused. As I was trying to have a wordless conversation with her, she turned to leave the room, taking my son with her. I pushed off my pillow and was met with a grunt.

"Chloe, could you not break me this early in the morning?" My pillow asked.

Diverting attention down, I was pleasantly met with a very sexy and tired looking Reed. "I am so sorry, I completely forgot you fell asleep in here." I hurriedly moved my hand from his chest-a naked chest I should say, pretty sure he had a shirt on last night.

Anxiously moving my hands through my hair, diverting my gaze to the window and now his chest.

I haven't woken up in a bed with a man since before I found out I was pregnant with Colton. That morning was not a pleasant one, it actually almost killed me. My breathing started to become strained as I remembered.

I felt a calming hand rub circles on my back, "hey, hey, Chloe, look at me. Breathe. You're okay."

I hadn't realized that my breathing had become labored and my body shaking. All I could hear besides Reed's attempts to calm me, was the far distance sounds of my past. The screaming, the yelling, the sound of a hand slapping across my face. This can't be happening. This hasn't happened in months.

I felt arms circling me, I felt my body being moved. I think Reed had me in his lap, I'm not so sure. I felt a hand caress my cheek, "Chloe focus on me love. Focus. Everything is okay. Colton is okay. You are okay. We are okay. Summer is okay. Matt is okay." he was trying to reassure me, without knowing what even was happening.

"I need you to look into my eyes. Can I see those captivating green eyes?" He sweetly asked. I felt his other hand massaging the base of my neck, and even running through my hair in a therapeutic pattern. I turned to look at him.

"That's my girl. Keep looking at me. Can you tell me 1 thing you hear?" He asked.

I studied his face as I struggled to find my voice, "I, umm, I can hear you" I responded.

He smiled, caressing my cheek lovingly, "What is 1 think you smell?"

"I can smell, I, coffee I think" I said furrowing my eyebrow.

He smiled, "Yea, Summer brought us coffee. What's 1 think you can feel?"

"I can feel you holding me" I shyly responded.

"Keep breathing babe. What's 1 thing you can taste?" He asked studying my face.

"I can taste, my tears" I embarrassingly responded, not realizing I had cried again. I went to wipe the tears, but his hand grabbed mine. Intertwining our fingers.

"What is 1 thing you can see?" He asked, playing with the rings on my fingers.

"I can umm, I see your eyes." I whispered.

He nodded, keeping our fingers intertwined a little while longer. After a few seconds, he released my hand from his. He grabbed my hips and moved me to where my back was against his chest, his left hand circling my stomach to keep me there. His right hand came across with a coffee in hand, "here, drink this and breathe. Summer has Colton, let's take this time to make sure you are okay" he said while playing with my hair.

I took a sip on my coffee, having him play with my hair relaxed me, this tactic always relaxed me. "I'm, I'm sorry about that. I hadn't had an episode like that since I found out about Colton" I tried to explain.

"Don't apologize love. We all have hurtles that we have to endure. Nothing wrong with them" he said sweetly.

I know he is just being nice, but the pet names like 'love' and when he said 'my girl' did something to me. I continued to sip my coffee, leaning my head against his chest, he felt safe, I felt safe.

"Colton's biological dad was not a good guy. He umm, he was the last man I shared a bed with. That was the day I thought I was going to die" I said truthfully. "I don't want you to feel guilty or sorry or even pity me. I was thankful to live that day, I was thankful that Colton has little to no features of that man. I survived, I am a survivor."

Reed continued to run a hand through my hair while his other arm pulled me closer. He leaned forward brining his face parallel with mine, "Where is he now?" He asked.

"I, um, I don't know. Once I woke up in the hospital, I never saw him. After getting out, there was no sign of him. I still have no sign of life" I sighed. I think the worst part is the unknown. Is he dead? I wish. Is he in jail? I wish. Where is he? Will he turn up? Will he fight for Colton? He didn't even know I was pregnant, so maybe I can play that part off. My mind started to get worked up again until felt a gently kiss on my temple.

"You're safe Chloe. Regardless of where he is now, he will not get close to you or Colton. Matt and I will make sure of that" he explained.

I nodded my head, taking in his words, I was safe, I moved away. I turned my head to look into Reed's eyes, leaning up I kissed his cheek, "Thank you for everything."

After a few minutes of silence we left the warmth of the bed and each other and made our way downstairs. Our ears were met with country music playing in the kitchen and the sight of Summer and

Colton dancing around while Matt laughed while eating his bacon. We were safe.

Reed left my side to go grab two plates, handing me one. Filling our plates with the food Summer cooked, dancing around the kitchen and singing, we were for sure wide awake and ready for the zoo.

About two hours later we were all piled into my suburban, Reed had offered to drive allowing me to sit shotgun while Matt and Summer were on 'Colton duty' in the backseat. Which consisted of feeding him snacks and making sure that all toys were easily accessible.

Shortly after our journey on the road we pulled into the parking lot of the zoo and paid our parking fee before we started to unload the car.

Successfully getting 4 adults, a stroller, diaper bag, our belongings and a toddler into the zoo was a major milestone for all of us. Pretty sure the only one not wanting to cry was Colton.

Colton's favorite exhibit so far was the ice cream stand that the boys visited while Summer and I ran to the bathroom. Returning we found both grown men with ice cream bowls and sadly, they don't know how to hide their evidence, because chocolate was all over Colton's face. Yet both very much unaware that their 11 month old best friend had unintentionally sold them out.

"So, how is the ice cream boys?" I jokingly ask, eyeing both of them, a smirk growing on my face.

"Oh it's great. We got enough for all of us to share. But we didn't give Colton any. Don't want him to be up all night you know." Matt tried to explain, well he tried to hide the truth. Let's be real he can't lie.

"Colton didn't even get a bite? How mean are you guys" I sarcastically responded, leaning down to wipe Colton's face with a napkin.

Hearing a thud, I looked up as Matt was rubbing the back of his head looking at Reed who was staring at him dumbfounded, "I legit told you 1. To not feed him any without checking. 2. Don't lie. And last but not least, check for evidence. You dumb fuck."

Summer and I both started laughing, reaching down I grabbed Colton out of the stroller.

"Well, now that we cleared that up, can we get moving? We need to burn some of his energy before we go home. I would like to sleep soundly tonight" I said walking towards the Safari Exhibit leaving the boys to push the stroller, well Reed, Matt legit walked past it.

"Hey buddy, you wanna feed a giraffe?" Reed asked coming up alongside me.

"Oh, that would be precious, can we?" I excitedly asked. "Matt, Summer will you guys watch our stuff, we are going to go feed a giraffe" Reed instructed while rolling the stroller to Summer.

After about 10 minutes in line, we got to the front and were given 1 piece of lettuce each. Walking up towards the side railing where they instructed us to stand, we waited a second before the giraffe walked over.

Colton's eyes became saucers watching the animal move closer to us. He eyed the giraffe as Reed showed him the lettuce, squealing and clapping his hands, loving the interaction. Okay so giraffes are a good animal.

As I was feeding the giraffe, I turned to look back at a giggling and happy Colton in my arms to see Reed standing back, phone out, snapping some pictures of us. Seconds later, my phone buzzed, message from Reed with the pictures he just snapped.

I smiled at him, "Thank you. Being an only mom, I never get pictures like this of him and I." I started to tear up.

"Hey, hey don't cry. This is a happy time" Reed tried to reassure me.

"I am happy. Gosh I'm so happy" I said turning back to Colton, placing a kiss on his forehead.

"Excuse me, would you three like a group photo with the giraffe?" A Zoo employee walked over having watching us.

"Oh that would be great, thank you" I gushed, handing her my phone.

Reed smiled and moved to my left, right behind Colton. His right arm coming around may waist, his hand landing on my hip pulling me close. Colton noticed how close Reed was and started to babble and clap his hands. This boy loves Reed.

"Okay, 1...2...3.. You guys make such a beautiful family.

Here you go. Have a great day" the girl said handing my phone back and walking away.

We didn't say anything, we didn't deny it. Taking my phone, I looked through the photos she took and was surprised, we did look like a family. My heart dropped.

Not paying attention, Reed applied pressure on my hip, "Let's get moving. They got a long line. Plus, we need to go see the Monkeys. Little man you will love the monkeys."

"Da Da Da Da" Colton babbled.

Reed smiled at me, it was genuine but you could also tell he was nervous with how I would respond to Colton still saying that.

Reed held his arms out towards Colton, keeping his eyes and smile on me, "Here, let me take him. You can sort through the good and bad photos."

Nodding my head I handed Colton back over, and did just that, only I stared and focused on how perfect we looked.

Guilt bubbled within me, I wish I could give Colton a family like that. That's something that will always eat at me.

We ended up catching back up with Matt and Summer and continued to walk around the different exhibits. I caught Reed on multiple occasions taking photos of Colton and I and then sending them to me. Almost like it was his day job to provide me with memories with my son.

We spent 5 hours, 5 long, grueling hours at the Zoo.

Matt ate all the junk food and splurged on the most expensive souvenir cup, because "Why not" as he said. Summer and I ended up with the best tan lines, hence the sarcasm. Reed ran all around making Colton laugh and have a good time-he will definitely be asleep before dinner. And Colton, well he decided to fall asleep right at the end, which was fine with me, at least a solid nap on the way home would be had by someone.

I offered to drive back, since it was my car. Yet I was gently picked up and placed in the passenger seat while being told, "Today you are the passenger princess" by Reed. Talk about swooning.

Matt and Summer relaxed in the back, pretty sure Matt was fighting all the crap he ate today. Summer closed her eyes and decided Colton had the better idea.

On the way home, I felt a hand on my wrist, a gently squeeze to get my attention, turning to see Reed, he studied my face before speaking. "Today was a good day. I think you are in the race for mom of the year."

I smiled and let a small laugh leave my lips, "I think giraffes have now taken the number one spot over dinosaurs after today. Maybe he can be a giraffe for Halloween" I yawned.

"He would be the cutest giraffe in my opinion. Maybe we can all be zoo keepers?" Reed excitedly asked.

"You want to dress up for Halloween?" I questioned. "Well it is his birthday and it is Halloween. Plus he is the only kid I would dress up for" Reed explained matter-of-factly.

"Shit, I need to plan his first birthday party" I let out an exhausted sigh, realizing I have another thing to do.

"Don't worry about it right now, rest your eyes. I'll get us home." He gently squeezed my wrist reassuringly.

Closing my eyes, I could feel his thumb rubbing my circles along my hand.

Today was a good day. Even if this man confuses the crap out of me.

8

1st Game Jitters

Who would have thought that 48 hours with Colton and Chloe and I would be feeling like I was the greatest man alive. When Colton called me "DaDa" the other night, it stirred up so many emotions, emotions I can't even decipher.

I couldn't get rid of the look on Chloe's face as he said it worried me. I knew she panicked. I knew that she felt guilty that he didn't have a dad. I guess that's why I ran after her when he fled the living room. I needed her to know I was okay with it and that she shouldn't feel guilty. She trusted me with a little information about the man who will only be referred as the 'Sperm donor' here on out. I decided to devote my time with them to be a positive experience for both of them so Reed can have a male figure in his life.

The pictures I took and sent to Chloe still remained on my phone, not only did I make one her contact photo but I may have set our "family" photo as my phone wallpaper. Call me a simp, I don't care.

After we got home from the Zoo, we ordered pizza and once again we crashed early. I ended up back with Chloe and Colton; again Colton refusing to sleep unless holding me. This kid has a choke hold on me.

The following morning, I woke up to Colton cuddling into my chest, his head placed in the crook of my neck, while Chloe faced me, my arm under her head. She was literally as close as she could be with Colton in between us.

I had carefully gotten out of Colton's hold and successfully moved my hand from under Chloe. Placing the two as one, allowing them to remain asleep but cuddled together.

I headed downstairs to get some coffee and wake up, as I entered the kitchen I was startled by two voices. "Well good morning sleeping beauty. How was your sleep last night in the GUEST ROOM?" Summer asked eyeing me, bringing her cup to her lips.

"I slept fine thanks" I mumbled reaching for a cup from the cupboard behind Matt.

"Yea, that GUEST ROOM is really nice. You should try it sometime" Matt laughed.

"Shut up. Nothing happened you pervs. Colton was having a hard night, literally slept with him attached to me like a baby koala" I joked. "I woke up before either of them and snuck out to give them some time together."

I grabbed another cup down, filling it with some coffee.

Turning to face Summer I timidly eyed her, "Umm, how does Chloe like her coffee?" I slid my hand behind my neck rubbing it embarrassed.

Summer giggled, "Just black."

I nodded, grabbing both cups, I eyed the two of them and exited the kitchen, leaving them to discuss my more than likely.

Quietly pushing the door open I tiptoed over to Chloe's side of the bed and placed her cup down. Looking over at the two of them, I noticed Colton starting to stir, I walked back around to the side I slept on and placed my cup down, ready to snag Colton to let Chloe sleep.

"Mama" I heard a sleepy mumble.

Looking up I watch Colton stretch his arms up, looking at Chloe with a smile on his face. He rolled over and got in her face, leaving a giant wet kiss below her eye.

Hearing a girly giggle leave her lips, I watched her eyes flutter open. "Well good morning to you to" she joked, kissing the little boy back.

Looking past Colton she locked her green eyes onto mine, almost like a leopard eyeing its prey. She smiled, then stretched, letting out the sexiest moans. Shit this isn't good.

"There's, uh, there's coffee on the nightstand for you" I said looking around the room, rubbing my neck.

"Thank you" she responded grabbing her cup. Colton had crawled across the bed for me, "dada". "No buddy, I'm Reed. Can you say Reed?" I tried to reason with the kid.

"I'm sorry if him saying that makes you uncomfortable. I haven't used that word around him, so I'm not sure if he is just babbling, but I don't think that's the case" Chloe sadly explained, cheeks getting red.

"No it's okay. He doesn't know any better. He's just learning, isn't that right little man?" I said tickling his feet as he laid on the bed laughing.

"Thank you. Well you and Matt. Colton doesn't have a single male figure in his life till you two. And, I, well, I'm glad he has the two of you. I am also happy to know and have the two of you" she sheepishly said, sipping her coffee.

"Well you're welcome. If I can be honest, I have never felt like a good guy. Not until the two of you showed up. I guess I want to be a good man for the two of you, make a good role model and someone you can trust, motivates me" I responded, finally sitting back on the bed, Colton climbing into my lap like a monkey.

We didn't spend that much longer lounging in bed.

Colton decided he needed to change and wanted breakfast. So, we worked together. She changed him and I took him downstairs for breakfast while Chloe changed and freshened up.

Colton and I enjoyed breakfast while Uncle Matt was scolded by Aunt Summer for dropping the carton of milk, all because he thought there was a spider. Turns out fuzz, scares Matt.

Matt and I had headed home later that afternoon to prepare for an early morning skate. We were a week from pre-season, usually I would be ecstatic but that meant time away from Colton and Chloe.

I really need to figure myself out, I can't have distractions, I'm not even dating Chloe, I'm not Colton's dad, but yet I felt like I was. Fuck I wanted that so bad.

A week of hellish practices, media schedules and PT had me worn out. Yet I made it, we were now 2 hours from puck drop.

Summer mentioned that she was bringing Colton and Chloe and that they were going to sit with the WAGs, so at least I knew where they were, but also at least Colton's ears won't hurt.

42

Summer walked into the locker room, "Hey Reed, got a second?"

"Yea what's up?" I said while taping my stick. "A really sweet kid made you something. Said something along the lines of "Babababa DADA". Not sure what he meant but here you go" She laughed while handing me an envelope.

I opened up the envelope and pulled out a folded piece of paper. Unfolding it, I was met with coloring squiggles. At the very top in the most beautiful handwriting said, "To: dada Reed From: Colton"

"Chloe and I were coloring today and he wanted to participate. So she helped him hold the crayon and not eat it. Once he deemed it was done, he grabbed it and crawled around the house looking for who we assume is you, because well your 'dada'" Summer explained while watching my face.

Tears pricked my eyes, I inhaled a large breathe and wiped under my eyes in hopes no tears fell. Looking up I saw Summer still looking at me, "This is the best gift I have ever gotten." I said honestly.

"Chloe wasn't sure if you would like it. She will be happy to know you do" she smiled. "You know, you two aren't so different; and don't take this the wrong way, but you've changed."

Confused, I furrowed my eyebrows while looking her, almost prompting her to explain.

"You're guarded Reed. Hockey is life, it's air, it's everything. Yet the moment Chloe and Colton showed up, your priorities change. I know Matt mentioned something before. Just know that you have my blessing. You are a good man, you're good for both of them. I'm going to go now before I get roped into working tonight. Good luck bud" She saluted while walking out.

Looking down I held the gift in my hands, my heart felt warm, tears once again swelling in my eyes. Fuck this feeling felt great. I smiled and I held the paper to my heart. I'm devoting myself to become the best man I can for the two of them, this is going to be my reminder.

I got up and placed the paper in my locker, making it to where it's the first and last thing I see when I open and close my locker door.

I skated around the ice during warm ups, Matt and I always end up playing tag, and right now he was it. As I skated by the glass, I did a double take almost falling on my ass.

Along the glass watching and waving at me was Colton, Chloe, Summer and a few other girls. Colton immediately noticed me and started clapping and reaching towards the glass. I skated over, forgetting about Matt; I placed my hand on the glass where Colton had it and smiled. Chloe smiled at the interaction between the two of us and started laughing when Colton started to clap and squeal.

I noticed a few of the other girls watching us, some with questionable looks and others with pure happiness.

Summer stood back and snapped some photos for Chloe to remember this moment.

Summer pointed at me and told Chloe something about turning, I guess group photo? As I was leaning against the glass taking a photo, I was completely knocked off my feet falling into the boards.

Opening my eyes, I see Matt standing back laughing, fucking great.

He reached a hand down to help me back on my feet, "What the fuck man. Could you not see that I was busy and not paying attention?" I asked angrily.

"Sorry man. I saw you and knew I had to win. Did I interrupt the family picture?" He asked mockingly.

I shoved him, looking back to Chloe who mouthed, "You okay?"

I nodded my head 'yes' and smiled. After a few more minutes of interacting with Colton, I motioned that I had to return the bench. As I was about to turn, she placed her hand on the glass and smiled. I removed my glove and placed mine against hers on the glass smiling back at her. Taking my hand back off the glass I kissed my finger tips and tapped them 3 times against my chest and skated off.

Not sure what the fuck that was, but I guess it was now our thing.

A hat trick a fucking hat trick. I haven't score a hat trick in so long, and to have one on opening night preseason was amazing.

As I exited the locker room, I was still buzzing. I held all 3 pucks and placed them in my bag.

Matt walked alongside me, both of us still jacked up on the high of winning.

A bunch of the other guys walked out "Reed, Matt. You both down for the bar?"

"Yea, text us the location and we will be there" Matt yelled back.

I hadn't decided if I wanted to go out, usually once games started I decreased my booze intake. Even though I was still energized, didn't mean I was going to keep it going to the early morning.

Walking into the family room, my world stopped, everything faded. The only ones present in the room to me were Colton and Chloe. Chloe was holding Colton, who was fast asleep, his head below her chin. She was standing talking to someone, probably Summer, she was swaying back and forth keeping Colton asleep.

Catching my eyes, Chloe turned and smiled at me. Her smile was breathtaking, it was perfect, it was mesmerizing.

Matt and I walked over to the girls, "Babe, you, me, some of the boys at the bar. What do you say?" Matt asked while wiggling his eyebrows.

"I'm down" Summer said smiling at Matt, "Also, good game tonight boys. You both played great."

"Thanks Summer." I responded.

"Oh shoot, Chloe, I don't want to leave you hanging." Summer panicked looking at Chloe.

Chloe looked up from having been adjusting Colton, who I knew was getting heavy. "No you go have fun. I need to get him home and then bed for the both of us. Plus I'm good to drive us home" Chloe reassured her, giving her the go ahead.

"I'm not going, I rode here with Matt. Chloe can you give me a ride home or I can sleep on the couch" I asked.

"Yea that's fine" She smiled.

"Okay, well we will get heading out. You two get home safe" Matt said while grabbing Summer's hand to lead her out.

I turned to look at Chloe, "Here, let me take him" I said reaching forward.

"I can't let you do that. You just played a long game and you have your hockey bag" she argued.

45

"Chloe, I'm fine. You need a break. Let me help love" I argued back.

I noticed when I called her 'love' that her cheeks went red and shit were they cute. She nodded slightly as I reached forward and took Colton from her arms.

Immediately seeing relief flood her face.

We headed out of the arena to the employee lot where she parked with Summer's pass. She opened the trunk and helped me put my bag in the back while I walked around to transfer Colton to his car seat. "Umm Chloe, I like to think I can do everything, but how the fuck does this work?" I quietly asked.

I could hear the sweetest giggle pass her lips as she opened the other door and crawled through the back seat to face me.

"Okay, I will walk you through it. Carefully lift him off your chest and carefully set him in." She instructed.

After 5 minutes of her teaching me the ways of the car seat and my realizing my hatred for them-yet I love them; we got Colton safely and securely strapped in.

Nothing makes you feel like a parent like putting a kid in a car seat.

Chloe and I made small talk on the drive, I noticed she was heading to her house and not dropping me off-which I am more than fine with.

Pulling into the driveway, she put it in park and stopped mid movement, "Shit I forgot to drop you off" she panicked.

"It's fine, I'm here more than my own home that I probably would have come here anyways" I answered honestly.

"You sure?" She shyly asked.

"Love, I am totally fine. Matt leaves clothes here I can raid. Plus I feel better knowing that you and Colton aren't alone" I responded reaching out and grabbing her hand. "Let's get inside and get ready for bed."

Once we got inside, I found a pair of Matts grey sweats and changed. Chloe took Colton to the kitchen to make him a bottle before putting him to bed.

Walking into the kitchen, Chloe was standing at the counter trying to get the lid on the bottle while holding a sleepy Colton in her arms. Walking over I grabbed Colton, allowing her to properly seal the bottle.

"Let me feed him, you go change and get comfy" I insisted.

"Are you sure?" She cautiously asked.

"Yes, now go. We will be fine" I reassured her, gently nudging her towards the stairs.

Once Colton was done with the bottle, I did what I had remembered learning and burped him-I wasn't sure if he needed to be or not, so I did it anyways. Once he was satisfied, I just stared at him, taking in his features, he was a cute kid, definitely his mother through and through. I leaned down a placed a gentle kiss on his head.

Colton's eyes started to flutter, telling me he was close to sleep. Chloe had yet to return so I started pacing around, just rocking him back and forth in my arms, hoping he would go to sleep.

Walking into the living room, I carefully leaned down to grab the remote and turned on the NHL highlights from tonight's game, making sure that the volume was not loud to wake the small kid in my arms.

After about 10 minutes, Chloe came into the living room while I sat there with Colton laid out across my chest. "Why is it that you are the one he loves to sleep on? I'm legit like jealous" she giggled.

"What can I say, everyone loves me" I smirked, trying not to laugh on accident.

Chloe moved closer to me on the couch, taking her finger and gently stroking Colton's cheek, a smile spreading across her face. "Do you want me to take him?" She asked, turning her attention to me. Her face closer than it has ever been.

"I'm good. Me and little man are bonding" I replied. "Well, I feel bad. Can I make you something to eat?" She offered, "You have to be starving."

"Anything would be nice, I'm not picky" I responded, allowing her to fuss over something. I had a feeling she felt like she needed a task.

She smiled, getting onto her feet, "I will be right back" she giggled. As she walked behind the couch towards the kitchen, her hand went through my hair giving my scalp a small massage. Pure Heaven.

A few minutes later Chloe returned with a quesadilla, a large quesadilla, apparently she felt like I could eat for a family of 4-she isn't wrong.

I grabbed the quesadilla taking a large bite, "Oh this is heaven." I moaned.

Chloe quietly laughed, placing the empty plate in front of her, "It really isn't much. I made them all the time when Colton was born. It was super easy and I could use one hand to make them while I held him." She explained, looking back at her sleeping son in my arms.

"You're a good mom Chloe" I stated flatly watching her intently.

She looked up at me, her eyes glossy. "Shit, Chloe don't cry." I pleaded.

"No, no they aren't sad tears. I just, it's always been him and I. Sometimes I feel useless or like the worst mom. But you always seem to know when I'm in my head and you reassure me. Thank you" She said wiping under her eyes.

Chloe was already seated as close as she could be to me to look at Colton, after watching her try to hide her tears, I placed my arm around her and pulled her into me so her hand rested on my chest. "Come here."

She willingly melted into my hold, "If I fall asleep you do understand you will be trapped" she whispered. Her fingers caressing her son's cheeks.

"Ehh I don't mind. There are worse ways to sleep" I joked, running a hand up and down her back, trying to calm her.

Having her this close caused my heart to beat fast. I was madly in love with this girl, even if she didn't feel the same, I was going to cherish the moments that she gave me. This being one of them.

I never thought I would ever be a "family man", but when these two entered my life, that vision changed.

While I was day dreaming, I didn't notice Chloe moving a blanket across her body and my legs, "Sorry I get cold easy" she stated.

"No problem for me. I love a good blanket" I responded giving her a soft smile.

Colton took this moment to shift in his sleep, moving his body to be more on my chest, his small hand lying flat on my chest and his head above my heart. Looking down at him, he has his lips parted, small snores leaving his mouth. His cheek pressed against my chest, the other bright pink- fucking cutest kid ever.

"I really love this kid" I blurted out.

Chloe moved her head from its place on my shoulder, studying my face, "I love him to. How could anyone not love him?" She asked placing her head back down on my shoulder.

"Thank you" I whispered into her hair.

"For what?" She questioned.

"The picture the two of you doodled earlier. I have it stuck to the inside of my locker at the arena." I explained.

"You're welcome, please don't take this the wrong way or freak out. But you are the only thing closest to a dad he has. And I don't want you thinking you have to be his dad, it's just you help so much with him that he loves you so much." She nervously explained.

I could tell she was afraid to say that, her words hit me in the heart. I wanted to be his dad in a way. I wanted to watch him take his first steps, say his first sentence, do all the milestones.

"Go on a date with me?" I blurted out.

Chloe lifted her head again, looking at me like a deer in headlights, "Wha-what?" She stuttered.

"Go to dinner with me. Both of you." I restated.

"You, you want to take me to dinner?" She questioned again.

"Chloe, I really like you. I might not a perfect man, but give me a chance, please. I want to take you out, both of you. If you decide on the date it isn't a good idea, then I'll back off, I promise" I stressed, my eyes pleading with hers.

She took a few seconds, her eyes connecting with mine almost like she was searching for something, then looking down at Colton and back at me, "Okay. I'll go out with you. Or, well WE would love to go to dinner with you" she smiled.

"Would you be free to go to dinner with me tomorrow evening? Say, 6:00?" I asked, my hand playing with the ends of her hair.

"6:00 is perfect." She smiled. Laying her head back on my shoulder, pulling the blanket up higher.

Leaning my head down against hers, I placed a tender kiss to her hairline. "Perfect, I can't wait."

Before I knew it, my eyes fluttered shut and darkness took over.

9

Chloe: Dinner and a good news

I woke up to a slobbery Colton kisses, opening my eyes I realized that Colton and I slept literally on top of Reed, on the couch.

Reed was still asleep, so I gently removed his hands off me, standing up and grabbing my happy boy off Reed before he was woken up.

I'm not sure what time we fell asleep, but it was no 8 hours of well rested sleep, that's for sure.

As I picked up Colton as his hands reached for me, "mama" he babbled with a toothy grin.

"Good morning baby" I cooed, kissing him on his cheeks.

Knowing I needed to start his bottle and get him changed, I headed to the kitchen. Where I was graciously met with a hangover looking Matt and Summer, both quietly sipping their coffee.

"Good morning party animals" I joked, bouncing my hips back and forth making Colton laugh.

"Shhhh, not so loud little dude. Uncle Matt feels like death" Matt groggily said, placing his forehead on the counter in front of him.

Summer laughed at Matt before turning her attention back to Colton and I. "Wanna explain why you 3 were on the couch and not in a bed like normal people?"

"Honestly, Reed fed him last night while I changed and when I returned the 2 of them were watching highlights and then Colton fell asleep. We were just talking and I think we dozed off not long after" I purposely skipped the part about the date, not wanting Summer to make a big deal about it in front of Matt.

Summer rubbed her temples as I spoke, she was also hurting but not as much as Matt.

"Can you make him a bottle? I need to go change him and I probably need to change as well?" I asked her.

"Yea I got you both" she agreed, standing up out of her seat, heading to the fridge.

After Colton and I were both changed and fresh for the day we headed back downstairs to grab his bottle. Walking back into the kitchen I noticed Reed was up pouring coffee, well 2 cups of coffee.

As he turned with both cups, he paused. I noticed the bottle tucked in his arm, "Oh, hey I was just about to come find you both."

I smiled at him, as nervous as I am for our date, and as much as he swears he isn't a good guy, I just know he's lying to himself. Because any man willing to think of me and my son before anything and let us practically drool over him, is a very good man.

"You didn't have to do that Reed. Thank you" I graciously said, extending up onto my toes, I placed a delicate kiss on his jaw.

As he placed the 2 cups on the counter in front of me, he reached for the bottle, which Colton also noticed, leaning out of my arms towards Reed, "Dada".

"Come here little man, let's go sit with Uncle Matt and terrorize him and having our morning snack." Reed placed him on his hip, handing him his bottle before grabbing his cup. Before leaving the kitchen he leaned down kissing the top of my head.

"Relax Love" were the last words he said leaving the kitchen.

An hour or so later, Matt and Reed went to their house, a place they hardly visit these days. On their way out, Reed announced he would be back at 5:30 to get Colton and I. Leaving me with a very interested Summer, lurking behind me at the stairs.

"So, what's at 5:30?" She questioned.

"Oh, ummm. He kinda asked me and Colton on a date tonight" I timidly answered.

"Oh shut up, no way?" Summer excitedly clapped. "It's not a big deal, please don't make it a big deal. It's just dinner. I don't even know if we will have fun" I mentioned, more like trying to not get my hopes up.

"Chloe, that man is head over heels for the two of you. I've never seen him give attention to anyone the way he does the two of you. Plus he practically pushed me out of the way to make Colton that bottle this morning. He's hooked" Summer reasoned with me.

I could feel my cheeks redden and my smile grow. He really is a good guy. I don't want to get my hopes up but I am nervous and excited. Colton loves him and deep down I think I could also love him. I am scared, but it's normal, especially with my past.

Summer and I spent the time between the boys leaving and me getting ready with basic house work and playing with Colton, while also trying to get him to take his first steps, he was getting very close.

While I was cleaning the kitchen, my phone started to ring, an unknown number, every person's nightmare.

Cautiously I answered, "Hello?"

"Hi is this Chloe?" The voice asked. "Yes this is she" I answered weary.

"Hi this is Mr. Johnson, I have the space on Olive Street downtown that you put an application in for 2 weeks ago" he said.

"Oh yes, hi, how are you?" I excitedly asked.

"I'm doing great. I saw on your application that you are an esthetician looking for a space to run your business. Are you still interested in the space?" He asked.

"Yes, I am still very much interested" I responded quickly.

"Well perfect, I know I listed the space for $2,000 a month but honestly, I was going to see if you would take the space for $1,000 a month" he explained.

I was shocked, I had a lot saved up from my time in California, but this would be another win for me today. That was a steal in this area.

"Yes, that would be great actually" I responded.

"Perfect, can you meet me at the space tomorrow mid-morning, say 11am. We can go over the contract and get you the keys" He eagerly said.

"Yes, I will be there tomorrow at 11. Thank you so very much" I gushed.

"Have a good day Chloe" He said before hanging up.

I was flabbergasted, this is the last thing I even thought about. I forgot I had put an application in for that spot, it was my dream layout and here I am, about to sign my contract.

I rushed into the living room where Summer was on "Distract Colton Duty", ready to share my good news, "Summer, you will not believe this. I uh, I got the space on Olive Street."

Summer stood up in a hurry with the same shocked face I had, "No shit. Really? This is amazing Chloe!"

"I'm like in shock. Holy shit. This is happening. It's really happening" I gushed.

Summer pulled me into a hug, rocking me back and forth, "I am so proud of you girl. I will help in any way I can" she offered.

"Thank you. I might need you to help decorate for sure.

Shopping will be in order" I laughed.

As we were hugging, I felt two little hands on my legs. Looking down, I see Colton staring at me, holding a black looking disc. Pulling away from Summer, I kneeled down to Colton's level, "what do you have here little man?" I asked, reaching for the disc.

Colton handed it over while bracing himself on my shoulder, giving me his toothy grin, his green eyes bright and happy.

Looking back at the disc I noticed it was a puck. It had the team's logo on one side, flipping it over I see white blade tape with writing on it. It had "9-23. #13" Yesterdays date and Reed's jersey number. Below it "C.L.M" those are Colton's initials. Still confused, the third piece of tape on it said "Love Dada". I choked on air.

He signed it "Dada", this was one of the pucks from his hat trick. He gave it to Colton.

My eyes were filling with tears again, this man hadn't even taken us out on our date and I was fully aware his presence in my life.

Summer placed her hand on my shoulder, kneeling down, "He gave that to him while he gave him the bottle this morning. He was telling Colton about what this puck meant to him-even though Colton had no idea what he was talking about." She explained.

I smiled holding it in my hand, "He's a good guy. Fuck I don't even know why I'm crying" I laughed. "I think I'm going to go place this in a safe place so Colton can one day have it as a memento and not try to eat it right now."

As I got up, I checked the time, 2:30. Deciding that I should take a 30 minute nap and then get ready, I reached down and picked up Colton. "Let's go power nap before we have to get ready buddy."

"If you need me call me" Summer yelled from the kitchen.

5:00 rolled around and I was staring into my closet and my unpacked boxes of clothes, letting a loud sigh leave my lips, I sat down on the edge of the bed. Needing a mental time out.

As I was stressing over nothing, Summer entered the room with a cup of coffee for me, "Figured you might need this and I wanted to see how it was going."

"Well, it was good, I mean Colton's still napping, my hair and makeup are done, but it went to shit when I went to get dressed, I don't know what to wear" I sighed again.

"Let me look" she disappeared into the closet.

A short time later she emerged with a pair of black trouser pants and Olive green scoop neck body suit. "Summer that's like business attire" I stated.

"Well I love the body suit, it makes your eyes and boobs pop" she laughed, tossing me the top. "Fine, I'll see if I can find a pair of cute jeans or a skirt."

A few minutes later she returned with a pair of light washed, straight legged jeans that had 2 slits at the bottom of the legs. "Here wear these, that top and here's a sweater I would pair it with. Oh and wear your black wedges."

Giving up with arguing with her, I hurriedly got dressed, as much as I didn't want to admit it, the look was perfect. "You are a life saver. I hope he isn't taking up to like a super fancy place."

"He called me earlier telling me his plans, which is another reason I came in here. I wanted to snoop on your outfit" she laughed.

Shaking my head and laughing, all I could think about was the fact he knew I was probably stressing, how does he know me so well?

Colton had woken up shortly after my attire situation was handled. He was now dressed in a long sleeved plain tan shirt, black pants, his boots and a green zip up jacket. By 5:25 we were both actually ready and no tears were shed. I quickly repacked his diaper bag and changed out my purse to a smaller one.

By 5:30 we were walking down the stairs and Summer was opening the door for Reed. Punctuality must be a quality of his, not a minute earlier or later.

As Reed entered, he looked up the stairs to see Colton and I descending. Coming to the bottom of the stairs, he reached for Colton's bag, placing the strap on his shoulder. He was dressed in dark wash jeans, a plain black button up shirt with the sleeves rolled partially up his forearm, his tattoos peeking out underneath. His hair was styled back out of his eyes, still hanging slightly over his ears.

"Well don't the two of you look amazing" he complimented, placing a kiss on my cheek before moving to place on Colton's head.

Colton smiled at Reed, giving him a peak at his bottom teeth.

"You look very handsome yourself Mr. Collins" I complimented him back, my hand naturally finding its way to his collar, smoothing out a wrinkle.

Locking eyes, we stared at one another, both smiling wide. We were shaken out of our trance by Colton giggling.

Reed looked down cleaning his throat, "Are you both ready to go. I got us reservations at 6:00" he asked.

"Yea, let's head on out" I responded.

I offered for us to take my car due to the car seat, which Reed agreed to, but quickly stole my keys and insisted on driving.

On the way to the restaurant, we made small talk while Colton played with his toys in his car seat, every now and again he would babble unknown words and occasionally you could hear him utter the words 'mama' or 'dada'.

Reed pulled us into a parking lot to an Italian restaurant in downtown. The place looked fancy, and expensive.

Reed ran around the outside of the car and opened my door, helping me down. Once I was out of the car, he ran back around and was unbuckling Colton and getting him out, placing him on his hip.

I grabbed the diaper bag, before meeting Reed at the front of the car.

"Reed, I hope you didn't bring us to an overly expensive place. They probably don't like babies in establishments like this" I honestly stated.

"Don't even worry. I've been coming here since I moved, this is a nice place but trust me it isn't like high end. Trust me, they are going to love Colton" he reassured me, reaching for my hand, intertwining our fingers.

As we entered the restaurant we were met with an older woman with greying hair, her eyes were a deep brown, as she recognized Reed, her smile grew large on her face.

"Oh my sweet boy, I haven't seen you in a while." She gushed running around the hostess stand pinching Reed's cheeks.

"I'm sorry Mrs. Romano, life's been keeping me busy" he answered turning to look at me, smiling. "I want you to meet Chloe and Colton, they are my dates this evening."

The words leaving his mouth caused the butterflies to erupt in my stomach.

I was quickly pulled into a bone crushing hug, "Oh my dear it is so nice to meet you."

"It's very nice to meet you as well Mrs. Romano" I responded, hugging her back.

As she pulled away she looked at Colton, who was eyeing her with a puzzled look of not recognizing her.

"This is my son Colton. Colton, can you wave 'hi' to Mrs. Romano" I asked while running my hand along his hair.

Colton lifted his hand and gave her a shy wave, turning his head to nuzzle into Reed's neck.

"I'm sorry, he isn't usually shy" I apologized.

Mrs. Romano turned her attention from the two boys back to me, "Sweetie don't apologize, he doesn't know me, also please call me Francesca" she responded, placing her hand on my upper arm giving me a warm smile.

"Alright my dears, let's get you three seated and well fed. I will also go grab Lorenzo, he's missed you Reed" she stated while grabbing 2 menus, leading us to a booth in the corner.

The restaurant was quiet, not many people occupied the tables or bar area.

Once we got seated, I offered to take Colton, but both boys refused my offer.

"Francesca and her husband Lorenzo have owned this restaurant for the past 30 years. At one time all their kids worked here with them, at least that's what I was told. This is true home cooked food, it's one of my favorite places to come" he explained while readjusting Colton on his lap.

"She seems really sweet, I really love the feeling here, it feels like home" I said while making funny faces at Colton.

After a few minutes of small talk and baby talk, an older gentleman walked over clapping his hands together, "Reed my boy. Where have you been?"

"Hi Lorenzo, I'm sorry I haven't been by lately. I want you to meet Chloe and Colton" Reed stood up, placing Colton back on his hip as he gave the older man a hug.

Lorenzo smiled wide seeing Colton before turning to see me, "Hello my dear, nice to meet you." Turning back to Reed, "You disappear for a month and you come back with a family. How did this happen?" he laughed.

Reed's cheeks turned red and his free hand rubbed the back of his neck, looking back at me he smiled before turning back to Lorenzo, "They walked into my life over summer and I haven't looked back."

His words were causing my stomach to have a volcano of butterflies dance around my stomach. My cheeks were definitely bright red. I got out of my seat and walked over to Reed, placing my arm on his, smiling at him.

"Hi Lorenzo, it's nice to meet you" I turned to face the older gentleman.

Colton reached his hands out for me, taking him from Reed, I placed him on my hip. Reed placed his arm around my waist pulling me in to his side.

Lorenzo cleared his throat, "It is so good to see you my boy. You played a great game the other night. I'm proud of you son" he said grabbing Reed in for another hug. "Don't disappear like that again though. You have me and the Mrs. worried." He let out a deep belly laugh.

"I promise I will not do that again. But I might not be alone here on out" he joked turning back to look at me and Colton.

Colton was getting antsy so I shuffled out of Reed's hold and went back to the booth, placing Colton next to me, pulling out a few toys and his snacks.

Reed returned back to his side of the booth after wrapping up his conversation with Lorenzo.

"Sorry about that. Tell me how was your day after I left?" He asked.

"It was good, I cleaned mostly" I answered. "Oh my goodness I don't know how I forgot. I got a call about that space for rent on Olive Street a few blocks over. The owner cut the price down per month and I meet with him tomorrow at 11 to sign my paperwork and get the keys" I explained.

Reed smiled big, reaching over to grab my hand with his, "Love that's exciting. Are you taking Colton tomorrow with you?"

"I think so. I don't have any other option. Summer has to go in tomorrow to the arena." I answered.

"I can watch him, or I can go with you and be on Colton duty if you need me to" he offered.

"Don't you have to leave for your away game tomorrow though? Summer was explaining how she was leaving with the team and she would be gone for a few days" I responded.

"I leave with the team around 3pm tomorrow. If you are meeting him at 11, I can be there" he stated.

"You really want to come with me and you really want to deal with this guy" I laughed pointing at Colton who was now standing in the booth, 1 hand holding cheerios and the other hand reaching for the display on the table.

Reed laughed moving the display away from Colton, "Duh, you need your full attention on tomorrow while you are there. I can take him to the coffee shop down the street or even wait in the car. Whatever you need, I'll do it" he answered tossing a cheerio towards Colton making him giggle.

"Alright, you can come" I smiled back at him, placing my hand back in his grasp.

Dinner went smoothly, over time Colton got used to Francesca and Lorenzo to the point, he was climbing over myself or Reed to get into their arms. At one point, I'm pretty sure they took him and showed him around the kitchen, I honestly don't even know, but they gushed over him like he was their own grandchild.

By the end of the dinner, Francesca came over while holding Colton, "Alright you 2, sit together. You guys need a picture" she handed Colton to Reed as he stood to move to sit by me.

I handed her my phone, opening the camera app. I scooted over some in my seat to allow Reed room, Colton laying his head on Reed's shoulder.

Reed's free hand went around my shoulders, bringing me in closer to him, my hand reaching back to hold his.

Francesca snapped a few photos before handing my phone back and collecting the plates off our table.

We left shortly after, making sure to hug both Francesca and Lorenzo, promising that we would return.

Colton was asleep before we left the parking lot, he had so much fun and loved all the attention that it wiped him out.

Reed reached over the center console, intertwining his hand with mine, bringing the back of my hand to his lips, "Well, I'm dying to know Chloe. Can we have a second date?"

The butterflies have permanent residence in my stomach from this man. The date was perfect, we got along so well, he thought about me and Colton. He tried his hardest and the effort showed, "I really had a good time tonight Reed. I think little man did as well. I won't turn down a second date."

Even in the dark, I could make out a little flush in Reed's cheeks. He kissed my hand again, "How about tomorrow morning, I take you both out for breakfast before you go to your meeting. I don't really want to wait a week when I return."

"Breakfast sounds good" I released my hand from his, reaching up and running my fingers through his hair, "I don't think either one of us could wait a week."

"How's 8am tomorrow?" He leaned his head into my hand.

"We will be ready." I whispered, turning to look back at my sleeping boy in the backseat.

Life was working out.

10

Reed: I hate goodbye

didn't kiss her goodnight after I walked them both into the house. I was afraid of rushing her. I just hope she hadn't gotten her hopes up and I let her down.

I was currently pulling into her driveway, it was 7:50am and I was 10 minutes early. To be honest I had been up since 4 am, I couldn't sleep, I kept replaying our date over and over in my head. It had gone so well, and the way home, her hands in my hair, it was perfect.

She had sent me the picture Francesca took of us, and it had already replaced my phone lock and home screens.

I was dressed in black joggers, a long-sleeved Henley and my green beanie. It was still warm but the weather was starting to cool down. I had make a quick pit stop by the store, grabbing her a fresh bouquet of flowers.

I knocked on the door, waiting patiently for someone to answer.

Summer opened the door smiling, "they will be right down. She's in their room. Colton isn't having a good morning."

I nodded, deciding to head up the stairs and see if I could help. As I got closer to the door I could hear Chloe trying to reason with Colton, "Colt, baby we need to finish getting ready. Reed's going to be here soon to take us to breakfast. Can you get ready for mama?"

Her pleading with him was the cutest thing I have witnessed. The best part was that Colton could hardly speak and he was trying to argue back with his baby babble. As I was about to knock on her door I heard Colton cry out, "No. Dada. dada."

I stopped, waiting, thinking, should I just wait downstairs, I was about to turn to walk away when I heard a defeated sigh from Chloe.

So, I knocked on the cracked door, peaking my head inside, "Hey you two. Summer said we were having a really great debate up here" I joked.

Summers shoulders fell, "Hey, sorry. Someone isn't really wanting their mom today." The sadness flooding her eyes as she turned back to Colton.

I walked over to Chloe, placing a kiss on her head, "I got these for you mama. Let me reason with the terror this morning while you relax." She took the flowers, nodding her head. She was dressed in a beige knit sweater that was longer, with black thick leggings and her black booties.

She looked so beautiful. Her golden hair was in 2 French braids and she had little to no makeup on.

"Thank you, these are beautiful. If you want to try with him, I will go put these in water." She stood up from the bed, giving me a peck on the cheek. Her cheeks turning red.

As she turned to walk out, I turned back to Colton who was playing with the giraffe toy we had gotten him from the zoo.

"Little man, my man. Work with me and mama here. You gotta put your jacket on." I held up the jacket as I sat next to him on the bed.

Colton dropped the giraffe, looking up at me, "Dada, Dada" he babbled.

"Yea buddy. Can 'dada' help you" I moved to pick him up to bring him in front of me.

With a little reasoning and handing him back the giraffe, he was fully dressed and ready to go.

Placing him on my hip, we walked back downstairs to Chloe and Summer talking by the door. Both girls turning to look up at us descending towards them, "I was just about to come see if you needed saving."

"We are all good. We just needed some manly talk" I laughed. "You ready to go?"

"Yea, let me grab my sweater" Chloe ran back into the kitchen where she left her sweater.

Summer smiled, grabbing her keys, "have fun you 3. I will be heading in early. Chloe, I will see you Sunday when we return."

Chloe came back around the corner, grabbing her into a hug, "Okay have fun, be safe. I love you."

"I'll FaceTime you both" Summer kissed Colton and headed out with her bags.

"Okay, you two, I am ready to roll" Chloe said, tickling Colton's stomach making him laugh.

We took her car once again, mainly for the car seat. I again, tricked her into letting me drive.

Not far from where she would be having her meeting was a small breakfast diner, a very family friendly place, which was also not going to be packed on a Wednesday morning.

Entering the establishment, we were seated in a booth along the front windows. Colton was eating his breakfast snack as Chloe and I looked over the menu.

"Okay, I definitely need a black coffee, and I think I'm going to go with the buttermilk pancakes with a side of bacon" Chloe smiled up at the older waitress while handing her the menu.

"Alright, and what about you sir?"

"I will have the biscuits and gravy with a side of fruit and bacon, and a black coffee as well. Thank you" I handed the menu to her as she left to enter our order.

Before long, Colton was seated in my lap while we played with one of his toys that lights up. This thing had me and Colton locked onto it, as I looked up, Chloe was snapping pictures of Colton and I.

Our waitress returned placing our food in front of us.

Chloe started giggling, placing her cup back in front of her. "Let me take him. His eyes went wide seeing your plate and I'm afraid you won't be able to eat."

"No he's good. You eat. We can switch him back when your full. Is there anything he can't have on my plate?"

"No, he loves bacon, but small pieces. I don't think he has had gravy though, but he loves bread."

Well, Colton loves gravy. We found this our when his tiny hand went straight into it and then into his mouth.

Chloe and I couldn't stop from laughing. "Here let me take him and clean him up. You need to eat."

I handed him over to Chloe who had finished most of her food. I looked up as she was wiping his hands while he tried to reach for the left over pancakes on her plate.

Before she could see me, I lifted my phone and snapped a few photos of them.

We left the diner around 10am, deciding that we were going to walk around and stretch our legs.

We had found a little park area that was empty, only a few older people sitting on benches.

Chloe and I sat down, Colton was trying to get free on the ground, I stood up, placing his feet on the ground while holding his hands.

Colton started giggling while looking at Chloe, "He's going to be walking soon"

"I hope I'm not on any away games when that happens" I looked up at her, watching her expressions as she watched her baby.

Chloe looked back up at me laughing, "I'll make sure to have the camera on him at all times in case that happens."

"What, um what are your plans for his birthday. I know it's Halloween, and I think Matt and I have a game the day after. But I would like to help with anything you need" I offered.

"I hate that his birthday is on a Thursday, but also, it would probably only be the 4 of us adults and Colton, so maybe we can just do dinner, some gifts and a cake" I couldn't help but notice how defeated she looked.

I didn't know much about her family dynamics other than her parents had passed away when she was barely in college. I wasn't sure if she had siblings or cousins, Summer only ever mentioned Chloe.

"Well, umm, I think my parents were wanting to fly in that week to come to a game. So, I mean you can say no, but maybe they can come to" I looked back down to Colton, trying to hide the flush of my cheeks.

No girl I have ever dated has met my parents. I'm not even dating Chloe and I want her to meet my parents.

"Your, um your parents? They would want to come maybe?" Chloe seemed nervous.

"I can ask, like I said they had just mentioned coming out that week, not sure if they are" I tried to reassure her and not make her feel nervous. "How about we do breakfast on the 31st, then that evening we do dinner with cake and then we go out trick or treating?"

"That sounds good, we could all be back by 9pm so you and Matt aren't dead the next day for morning skate and your game." She seemed less worried.

I checked the time on my watch, 10:30. "How about we head back to the car. Get little man in his car seat, he probably needs a nap and then I will drive you to your meeting and he and I will wait in the car."

"That sounds good" she smiled picking up Colton from the ground. Turning to walk towards the car, I placed may hand along her waist, bring her closer to me as we walked.

"Thank you for breakfast. Are you sure you don't mind the level of crazy that Colton and I bring to the table?"

"Love, there is no level of crazy." I noticed when I called her 'love' that her cheeks went pink and her breathing changed. Apparently, someone likes the pet name.

By the time I pulled up in front of the space that Chloe was renting, Colton had fallen asleep. Chloe turned to look out the window, seeing an older gentleman unlocking the door to the space, turning back to me she smiled. "I shouldn't be that long. Call or text if he wakes up or is fussy."

"Don't worry please. Go sign your lease and kick ass. I'm going to drive around so he stays asleep, call me when you're done." I leaned over placing a kiss on her cheek, nudging her out of the car.

"Ok, ok, I'm going" she finally stepped out of the vehicle, taking a large breathe. I could tell she was nervous but she had nothing to worry about. She quietly shut the door and headed for the rental spaces glass door, turning around to blow me a kiss and then stepped through the threshold.

I looked over my shoulder making sure no cars were coming before pulling back onto the road. I decided to go through the coffee shop drive thru and get her a coffee for when she was done.

The floral shop I usually go to isn't far from here, I know I had stopped at the grocery store this morning for flowers, so I wanted to step up my game and get her a better bouquet.

I went ahead and dialed the number to the shop, talking to the owner about what I was wanting and she agreed to charge my account and walk it out to the car so I didn't have to worry about Colton.

Once the flowers and coffee were secured, I called Francesca from the restaurant and ordered enough food for 2 days and she agreed on having it delivered to Chloe's home later this evening after I had left.

Knowing she was going to be on her own for a few days, I wanted to make sure that she was taken care of, I had already planned on having breakfast and the remainder of the dinners delivered while I was on the road.

Parking in front of the store front, I had music playing softly, Colton was still asleep. I took a good look at where I was and who I was becoming. I'm not the best man in the world, my ex proved that to me, but I am going to try to be the best man I can for Colton and Chloe.

A few minutes later, Chloe emerged with the older gentleman. They seemed to be wrapping up their conversation as she shook his hand and waved goodbye, heading towards the car.

She excitedly entered the car, practically jumping into the front seat, her smile was infectious as it span from ear to ear.

"Good news?" I couldn't wait to hear all about this space and her new plan.

"It's more than just good news. The space is everything I could have dreamed of. The location is perfect, the price per month is do able, the space is more than enough. I can bring Colton with me to work if I need to, there's a room in the back that would be perfect for an office/ nap area" I don't think she even took a break.

As she finally stopped talking she noticed the coffee in the cup holder, "Did you get me a coffee?" She asked shyly.

"I knew that the one this morning wasn't enough and it is your favorite drink, so I wanted to get you some. Oh before I forget" I reached behind her seat, grabbing the large bouquet of deep red roses. "I also got these for you as a 'congratulations' gift."

66

Her eyes started to fill with tears, "Oh Reed, these are beautiful. You didn't have to do all that for me. Thank you" she took a shaky breathe trying to calm her emotions.

"Before you ask, he hasn't woken up, except when I was in the drive thru he fussed a little, but his pacifier fell out. So I reached back found it and plopped that sucker back in and he's been good." I was beyond proud of myself for being able to handle Colton, even though he's not that much of a terror.

Chloe giggled, looking back to see him sleeping. "He's going to miss you and Matt and probably Summer while the three of you are gone."

"Well, I'll miss him and his mama more, that's a promise." Never in my life have I been so open about my feelings. "Ok love, one last stop before I have to leave you both."

I pulled back onto the road heading towards the arena. "Where are we going?" She looked confused looking out the window and back at me.

"Well, since I need to be at the arena to catch the bus in 2 hours, I figured we could go skating and then this way, I have to come see you when we return to get my car. It's my master plan" I laughed.

"Skating?! I don't have skates nor can I skate" she looked beyond nervous.

"Love, Summer took her skates this morning for you. And you will have me. You are going to be fine." I reached over grabbing her hand, bringing it back to my lips.

I could tell she was still nervous but I had plans to get her over any fears of falling.

When we pulled into the arena I parked in the player parking lot. Chloe exited before I had a chance to open her door, coming around to get Colton out.

Lucky for both of us, Colton was wide awake and he was making sure we knew it. I reached behind Chloe, grabbing Colton while she grabbed his bag.

I went around to the trunk of her car, grabbing my hockey bag and travel bag, slinging them onto my other shoulder.

Colton had a few yogurt bites in his hand as he snacked on them with his head on my shoulder.

Chloe walked next to me, opening the doors to the arena. Once we were in I headed for the benches, placing my bags down. As Chloe came closer, I held up Summer's skates that she left on the bench, wiggling my eyebrows in her direction. "Sit down here and I'll help you put them on. I'll give you Colton while I lace them."

She took Colton from me, sitting down on the bench. She took this opportunity to give Colton some more of his snacks to keep him happily occupied.

Once I was done lacing her skates, I grabbed mine out and quickly put them on.

"Here give me Colton, and then take my free hand and I'll help you onto the ice" I instructed, holding my free hand out, already scooping up my little buddy.

Chloe eyed me as we got closer to the ice, "Don't let me fall please" she pleaded.

"Baby, I promise to catch you, I'll always catch you. Do you trust me?"

She smiled, looking down at her feet, then to my hand and back to my eyes, "yes I trust you."

I finally got her on the ice and before long she was able to skate without needing to hold my hand.

Colton was loving being on the ice, I had leaned down and let his feet glide against the cool surface as I skated along. Colton continued to laugh and smile as Chloe recorded the moments.

I skated closer to Chloe while holding Colton up high, "Mama" he babbled, smiling at her.

"Hi baby. Are you having fun?" She cooed, coming closer so she could pinch his cheeks in a loving way.

"I think we have a future hockey player on our hands" I joked.

Chloe smiled up at me, as we came to a stop. "Well looks like you get to teach him because you have seen me out here, I will be zero help."

"I'll be his coach. Before we know it, he will be in the NHL killing it." I started to tickle his stomach, making him give me a big toothy grin. "So, 2 dates in 2 days. You, umm, up for a 3rd?"

Chloe smiled, tucking a piece of her blonde hair that had fallen out of her braid, back behind her ear. "Yea, I think 3rd date would be just fine."

"Perfect. I'll plan it out for when I get back." I shifted Colton to my other hip, making my arm closest to Chloe free. I snaked it around her waist bringing her closer to me. Her hands landing on my chest. I stared intently at her lips and her eyes, bouncing back and forth, she was breathe taking and she was in my hands.

"Reed" she whispered. Before I crashed my lips to hers. I could feel her hand wrapping around my neck pulling me closer, while her other stayed on my chest.

Pulling away, her cheeks were flushed and her lips were a little more plump. I tucked the piece of hair back behind her ear, "God you are beautiful." I leaned down placing a soft kiss back on her lips. Hearing the air exit her body.

Pulling back a second time, we stared at each other in a comfortable silence, not removing our hands from one another.

Our peace was ruined by Matt calling from the benches, "Hey guys, maybe get a room and not in front of the kid."

I really wanted to kill him.

Chloe hid her flushed face against my chest, as I turned my neck to look at Matt, lifting my hand and flipping him off. "Do you need something Matthew?"

"I hate when you call me that, and yes. We gotta get going here soon." With that he turned and walked away back to the locker room.

"Come on love, let's pack up." I skated back to the bench with both Colton and Chloe in my arms. Life was good.

After removing the skates and repacking my bag. Summer had retrieved her skates placing them in her office. I had taken my skate bag to the bus and put my night bag in the locker room with the rest of our stuff.

Chloe and I headed outside to the parking lot to get her back on the road.

Colton was having a hard time leaving my arms. "Come on bud. I gotta get going to work and you need to be good for your mama okay. I'll bring you some more pucks home and I'll score you a goal if you can be good" I really need to stop having debates with kids who can't talk.

Chloe giggled from next to me. She had taken him from my arms, placing him in his car seat buckling up. Once he was secured she hopped down, placing his blanket at toys in his lap. Tears swelled in his eyes as he sat there, he started to cry more, reaching his arms out for me, the word "Dada" leaving his mouth more than once.

I placed my hand on Chloe's lower back, sneaking in next to her, I reached forward and placed my hand on Colton's chest and stomach. "Hey buddy, I'll be back okay." I leaned forward and kissed his head. "Be good bub."

Chloe had tears in her eyes as well, not sure if it was from the interaction or from me leaving, I placed my hands on her cheeks wiping the few loose tears away, "Don't you cry either. If both of you cry I'm done for."

"I'm good. I'm good. I promise. I just hate when he cries."

I circled my arms around her body bringing her into my chest, "I'll text you and call you and face time you everyday."

She nodded her head. Taking in a deep breathe.

I placed a kiss on her head, slowly pulling away to look into her face, "Every goal I make this trip is for you and him, you got that? Every win, ever successful period is for you two. I have his picture in my bag."

I held up my phone to show her the screen, "I have both of you with me okay. Enjoy your time together the next few days."

She smiled, leaning up to attach her lips to mine. "Don't fight anyone unless they deserve it. I can't take care of you if you get injured away from here." She laughed.

"Oh and please send me pictures everyday, especially if he walks or talks more" I pleaded, I hated leaving. We weren't even dating and I was about to quit my job just to not miss a moment away from the two of them.

Chloe nodded her head again. "You better get going, I would hate for you to be left behind."

I kissed her again, longer this time, trying to put every emotion and feeling I have into it.

After releasing her, I quickly gave Colton one more kiss before shutting his door and helping Chloe into the front seat.

"I'll call you when we get to the hotel" I promised her. But I also wanted to hear her voice before going to bed. She kissed me again, harder this time. "Be safe Reed."

I shut her door, stepping back, looking at one another, I tapped the spot above my heart 3 times, she placed her hand on her chest and tapped it 3 times.

Turning around I headed back into the arena for the locker room. Ready to take on this road trip, but more than willing to leave it all behind and stay home.

11

Chloe: Meeting the parents

A few weeks had passed since the first road trip and me signing the lease to the building space. It was currently Tuesday and we were 2 days away from it being Colton's first birthday.

Reed had continued to take me and Colton out on dates and sometimes we just stayed in, usually ending in sleepovers, G rated sleep overs. Our relationship was progressing well and I was finding myself hating being away from him.

Colton has continued to call him "Dada" and every time, Reed reassures me that it's fine. Watching him interact with Colton warms my heart, caused butterflies and makes me want to jump his bones. Something we have yet to do.

While they have had a few road games, I have kept myself busy with setting up my new space to get it ready for opening in a month or so. Colton loves the shop, he has his own area and loves chasing after me well crawling after me as I move around.

We have also visited Francesca and Lorenzo a few times for lunch and an early dinner when we are working in the shop.

As I was moving my desk around in the office, my phone lit up, Reed, he was currently in Texas, they had a game tonight and would return tomorrow, perfect timing for Colton's birthday.

Answering the face time, I see Reed with his pads on and his hair disheveled. "Well hello hot stuff" I laughed.

"Well hello beautiful" he wiggled his eyebrows and smirked.

I moved to sit on the floor next to Colton, "Colt you want to say 'hi'?"

Colton looked up from his toys seeing Reed on the other end, "Dada" waving his little hand in the air.

"Hey buddy, you've grown in the 5 days I've been gone. What's that about? You got another tooth?"

"He does actually, it's been a B.I.T.C.H. of a tooth, he was running a fever this morning and hardly slept." I said running my hand through Colton's long blonde hair. He had some curls at the ends.

Reed's smile dropped, "Is that normal? How high was it?
Do I need to come home?"

I smiled looking back up at him, "It's normal, it wasn't too high, just enough to be uncomfortable. You're coming home tomorrow silly. We will be fine."

Reed nodded his head listening to me, "if you're sure then okay. You mind if I stay with you tomorrow when we land?"

I smiled, I loved when he stayed the night, he was so tentative to Colton that I usually got a little better sleep, but also I loved when he would hold me. "Of course you can stay. I'll cook dinner, you land around 6pm tomorrow right?"

"Ooh, what are you making? I loved that loaded Mac and cheese you made last week."

I laughed thinking about how he and Matt fought over the last scoop, only for Summer to get it when they were bickering. "Yes, I can make that. Oh, also I might need help Thursday for his birthday breakfast."

Reed's eyes lit up, "Sweet me staying allows me to see him first thing on his birthday I love this. Yea I can cook breakfast love, maybe get you some coffee in bed, maybe some long overdue kisses, whatever you need?" He looked into the camera seductively.

"I won't say no to any of that." I winked at him, getting an eyebrow raise from him.

Somewhere behind Reed, I could hear Matt say, "Colton doesn't need a sibling right now, keep it in your pants Collins."

My cheeks turned bright red, Reed turning a chucked a roll of tape at Matt. I knew it had hit him because he let out a whine of pain as Reed flipped him off.

"I wonder how he's my friend." Reed ran his hand through his long hair. "Well baby, I need to finish dressing and get out there, you going home soon?"

I stood up, picking up Colton, placing him on my hip, kissing his head, "Yea, I'm grabbing my bags now, I need to go see Francesca, she has my dinner for tonight." Grabbing the diaper bag and tossing my wallet in the bag, I snagged the keys off the table and headed out the doors, locking them as I shut the door.

"Good luck tonight Reed. We will get home and watch the game."

Reed smiled, "How's little man liking the hockey stick I had delivered?"

"I just love how you took his love for hockey and ran with it. Like you do realize he is in the stage where ankles are at risk right? That little hockey stick has about cut my leg off. But he does love it." At the mere mention of my ankle, it started aching.

"Has he really taken your ankles out?" Reed looked concerned.

"Oh maybe once or twelve times" I laughed, opening the back seat door, placing the diaper bag on the floor before placing Colton in his seat. Propping the phone on the center console.

"When I get home, I will rub your feet, I am so sorry Chloe." Reed offered, a hint of guilt in his voice.

"I don't need a foot rub babe. Having you home will be good enough" I grabbed the phone back, catching him turn red at the mention of the word babe.

Climbing into my seat and locking the doors, I started the car. "Okay, I need to grab my dinner. Good luck tonight hot stuff. Colton say 'bye'" Holding the phone up so Reed could see the back of his car seat, a little hand came out of nowhere, waving "goodbye", the words "bye bye" leaving his sweet little mouth.

Moving the phone back to me, Reed's eyes seemed glossy, "Shit that was cute. Caught me in the feels. Fuck. Okay bud I'll win just for you. Alright love, drive safe. Miss you."

"I miss you to. Call me later okay?"

Reed and I hung up after he told me he missed me 6 more times and promised to call me once the game was over.

Francesca ran out with my food, not giving me the chance to meet her half way. After catching up for a few minutes, I left and headed for home, I had a game to watch and I needed my bed.

Well, we lost. 3-4. Reed got 2 of the goals but it wasn't enough for us to make a comeback.

Colton has fallen asleep during the second period, we were both laying on the couch cuddled together.

Reed had called but we kept it short since it was late and he needed sleep.

I had woken up the next morning on the couch, Colton pressed against my side. I needed to start sleeping back in my bed because my back was shot.

I hated being alone in the house and I hated having to walk through the house and up the stairs to go to bed when it was empty like this.

My past still haunted me, especially in moments like this. The house was too quiet without Summer and the boys. I loved during the day when Colton was babbling, attempting to walk or giggling at anything and everything.

I picked Colton up, taking him to our room, he was slowly waking up while I changed his diaper and putting him in a fresh outfit. I quickly changed into a pair of legging, a sports bra and one of Reed's shirts, throwing on my fuzzy slippers.

Colton had his bottle while I cooked breakfast and made a fresh pot of coffee.

I had a few hours till I needed to start dinner and welcome my house mates. So I spent them prepping party supplies for tomorrow, wrapping Colton's birthday gifts, charging my camera battery and cleaning the living room and kitchen.

By 3pm the house was spotless, laundry was washing or done, dinner was prepped and Colton had a few good naps even while cutting teeth.

Colton was currently napping on the couch so I wandered over with a cup of coffee, deciding to lay down next to him and relax.

I started scrolling through social media on my phone, Reed had posted a story so I clicked on it.

It was a picture of Reed, myself and Colton at the restaurant from our first date with an emoji covering Colton's face to hide his identity, the picture had the caption, "headed home to these 2" with multiple heart emojis.

I liked his story, sending him a message with multiple red hearts.

I must have fallen asleep shortly after because I woke to the front door opening and closing.

"Shhh, I think they are sleeping. And you two are loud as fuck" Summer was scolding the two grown men.

I stretched my arms above my head, "I'm awake, not sure about little man though. What time is it?"

Reed laughed walking closer, leaning over the back of the couch to kiss my forehead, "5:30, how long you been out?"

I moved Colton to my arms, he was slowly waking up, "probably just an hour I think, he was out longer. I need to start dinner and he needs a bottle."

I went to move by Reed when his arm went out across my stomach, halting me from going pass him, "Let me take him, I'll make the bottle, you focus on that delicious dinner."

Colton was awake and fully aware of Reed's presence, practically bailing from my arms to his, a sleepy, "Dada" slipping out.

"Hey buddy, I'm home" Reed rubbed his back in a soothing way.

I loved how they loved each other so much, it warmed my heart watching them interact.

While Reed entertained Colton, I had finished dinner, Summer and Matt were unpacking and catching up on laundry.

We enjoyed the dinner and caught up on what was happening with my new business space and they talked about the games on the road trip.

We had made a game plan that in the morning the boys would cook breakfast while Summer and I decorated. We all planned on the zoo keeper and giraffe costumes for going out for trick or treating.

After cleaning up the kitchen, Reed and I walked upstairs getting ready for bed. Colton had fallen asleep not long after dinner ended, so Reed laid him in the middle of the bed before turning to look at me. "I love when you wear my clothes."

I turned to face him, my pj's in my hands, looking down I realized I was still in his shirt from this morning, "What can I say, it smells like you and its comfortable" I sashayed my way over to him, dropping the clothes in my hands to the floor. Placing my hands on his chest, slowly snaking them up and around his neck, "You know, I kinda missed you. I hate when you're gone" I leaned up kissing his jaw.

Reed seemed taken back by my confidence, "Shit baby, I missed you to and I hate being gone. I really wish we didn't have a roommate right now" he snaked his left arm around my waist, the other coming to the back of my neck. He crashed his lips to mine, pouring every feeling he has into it, kissing me with so much passion, I could feel my toes curl.

After a few minutes of the mind blowing makeup session, we slowly pulled away, both feeling hot and annoyed that we weren't alone.

I grabbed his hand, leading him to the bed, "Let's go to sleep before we are woken by the birthday boy."

Reed willingly followed me, crawling under the comforter, grabbing me by the hips, pulling me close to him. I turned my body to face his, appreciating the view of his chiseled chest. My hand resting on an ab while the other played with the hair cascading against his neck.

"Thank you for being here and willing to help me with Colton's birthday tomorrow. You are filling a void that you didn't have to do" I whispered, intertwining the hair with my fingers.

Reed let out a shaky breathe, "I wouldn't wish to be anywhere else." He leaned forward and placed a gentle kiss on my lips, "Get some sleep baby, tomorrow is going to be wild."

I snuggled up close to his chest, each holding the other close.

Wild was an understatement, Colton woke up at 5am, fully awake and fully ready to cause chaos. I bolted upright to hearing him talk, slowly getting out of bed to get to him before he had the chance to wake up Reed, who was sleeping soundly- surprisingly, cough cough, not.

I picked up the fussing toddler and rocked him against my chest, my hand on his back rubbing circles. Pacing around and trying to coax him into sleeping another hour.

As I realized that he was not going to go back to sleep, I adjusted him on my hip and quietly slipped out of the room to make him his bottle and breakfast while make some coffee.

While making his bottle, the realization hit me that he was officially a year old. He had his head laying against my shoulder and neck watching me prep the bottle in hand. His little hand was fisting some of my hair down my back and the other hand held the collar of Reed's shirt I was wearing.

I could feel the tears swelling up in my eyes, he was officially a toddler and no longer my baby. He has long since been the tiny 8lb 3oz infant that was placed on my chest at 3:46am on October 31st the year before.

I could feel the tears releasing, running down my cheeks, how could he be this big already, I hated and loved it.

I finished his bottle and handed it to him as he held it in place while eating. I busied myself with making coffee before plopping him down on the couch and putting on cartoons.

As I sat next to him on the couch, it's as if he knew that I was emotional and going to be a wreck, so to make it better, he abandoned his seat and crawled his way into my lap. Perching himself against my side, bottle being placed back in his mouth.

We lounged on the couch for a little while, I raked my fingers through his hair, noticing how long his blonde locks have gotten and noticed the curls that were on the end.

He was watching the cartoon intensely, every now and again looking up at me and smiling, his hand sometimes reaching up to play with my lip or nose.

The tears returned, I was for sure not making it through this day without crying a Nile's worth of tears.

I had long forgotten the coffee, but was quickly reminded of it when a large cup was handed to me from over the couch.

Looking up I was met with the sleepy smile of Reed looking down at Colton and me. "Thank you. Why are you up?" I graciously took the cup, taking in a large sip, appreciating the way it warmed my body up.

"I was until I reached over for you and found and empty bed. I don't like when you aren't there." He sat directly next to me, sipping his own cup and reaching for Colton's foot, tickling the bottom of it, resulting in a sweet giggle.

"I'm sorry, he woke up at 5, and he refused to sleep so we came down here" I leaned my head against his shoulder, feeling him leave a gentle kiss on my head.

"How about I get started on breakfast?" I could feel Reed's arm around my shoulders pulling me in, while Colton kept reaching a hand out for Reed to hold.

"Sounds good to us. Let me know if you need us to keep you company." I turned peppering a few kisses to his cheek, watching them turn a deep pink.

"I could always use company if it's the two of you?" Reed stood up, holding a hand out for me to latch onto, pulling me to my feet.

Colton was getting sleepy after his bottle, so I held him in my arms until he fell asleep. I didn't want to put him down, having the realization that one day there will be a last time I hold him or rock him; so savoring these moments mean everything to me.

Not long after we had Summer and Matt lazily moving into the kitchen, each pouring a cup of coffee and grabbing a plate of breakfast.

Reed's parents arrived into town the day before and today they were coming over to partake in the birthday shenanigans. This was my first time meeting them and when Reed offered to invite them I thought it over and decided that more the merrier. Plus, my parents died when I was 18, Colton doesn't know what grandparents are, I so badly wanted him to have that family dynamic.

I'm hoping things go smoothly, the last set of parents I met, didn't like me and well, toxicity ran in the veins of that family.

It was currently noon and Summer and Matt had left to pick up the lunch, we decided that Pizza was a good option. I had already made the cake the day before and frosted it; while Reed played with Colton I took the opportunity to grab his presents and put them on the table in the living room.

While setting the last gift down, the doorbell rang, alerting me to the realization that I am meeting his parents. Reed sprung up, picking up Colton and heading to the door. I was nervous, my hands came together, fidgeting. I needed something to do, but first I needed to breathe.

I could hear the pleasantries being said at the door and the cooing noises of Reed's mom towards Colton, with my son's sweet giggle gracing my ears.

I slowly walked towards the front, hoping and praying that my nerves and anxiety don't do me in before making it there, I need to feel Reed's hands or hold my son.

Turning the corner, Reed catches my eye and smiles wide, "Mom, dad this is Chloe. Chloe this is my mom Susan and my dad Dave."

His mom and dad both became excited seeing me, his mother meeting me half way, pulling me into a large hug, "Oh sweetie it is so nice to meet you, Reed talks about you nonstop and this sweet little boy of yours."

Warmth, Love and peace, my body relaxed into her embrace.

Letting go I met her smile with my own, "I am so happy to meet you both and thank you for coming to celebrate with us today, Colton and I both appreciate it." I moved over being pulled in by Reed's dad into another strong embrace.

I could hear Reed chuckling, watching me get passed from parent to parent, "Okay dad, she needs to breathe." Stepping back I felt Reed's arm slide around my waist, pulling me into his side.

Colton took this moment to reach for me, practically flying out of Reed's arms into mine.

"Please, come in and make yourself at home. Summer and Matt should be back soon with the pizza so we can eat" Reed, held me as we walked into the living room.

Reed had made himself at home on the floor between my legs as I sat on the couch talking with his parents.

Colton was sat near Reed playing with his large blocks.

Summer and Reed returned with the pizza and started unpacking it all in the kitchen. Reed stood up to help them set up, alerting Colton of his departure, "Dada" Colton cried, crawling after him. Reed stopped in his tracks, turning around to pick up the toddler, reassuring him that he wasn't leaving him behind.

I loved their bond, but I forgot that his parents were next to me. I turned to continue my conversation, meeting a shocked expression on both his parents' faces, "Colton calls you 'dada'?"

Reed turned, also forgetting they were there, "umm, yea he started before we started dating and we tried to correct him, but he refuses to call me anything else, I don't mind really" Reed said, turning to lock eyes with me, giving me his sweet smirk.

"And, Chloe you are okay with this? What about his real dad?" Reed's dad Dave asked.

"Colton doesn't know his real dad, umm his real dad wasn't or isn't a good man, he…umm.." I started to panic until I felt a hand on my shoulder.

Reed was there, "Colton's dad almost killed her, its best he isn't around. Like I said we tried getting him to call me something else, but he refuses. You can't change his mind and we, well we don't mind" Reed leaned down giving me a kiss on my head.

Turning and walking into the kitchen, leaving me with his parents.

His mom Susan seemed sad, "Sweet heart, I am so sorry, please don't think we dislike it, it just shocked us. And I am so sorry for bringing up and terrible memories" she laid her hand on mine.

"You're okay, you didn't know. I'm past that time in my life. Reed's helped me a lot. Honestly its second nature for us to hear Colton call him that, we completely forgot you guys didn't know." I gave her a reassuring smile to let her know that everything was okay.

We continued to talk until we were called to grab out food and eat. So far, I think they like me, fingers crossed they actually do.

12

Reed: Birthday Cake and Costumes

Chloe seemed to get along with my parents and they seemed to really love her-plus they couldn't get enough of Colton. This was the second girl I have ever let them meet and I am hoping she will be the last.

Lunch went smoothly, once we got passed the "Dada" mishap; but my mom seemed to light up every time Colton said it-almost like she had gained herself a grandchild, which in a way she did.

My dad and Colton couldn't get enough of one another, anytime Colton was close to him, he reached for my dad.

The last child my dad held was me, so watching him and Colton get along so well made me happy and released so many emotions within me.

As we were seated around the table, Colton was currently in my mom's lap, playing with her necklace and babbling to her about lord knows what. Chloe walked out with the most detailed, put together 3 layer cake I have ever seen. Usually homemade cakes I have seen are single layer with frosting slabbed on top. This was immaculate.

Chloe cut piece, putting a candle in the center of it and placing it in front of me, my mom had handed me back Colton so he could enjoy his first birthday cake.

Chloe sat down next to me, pulling her chair in as close as she could get.

Colton immediately wanted his cake, but once Summer started the 'Happy Birthday' song, poor kid became petrified, especially once Matt started singing. I think I also was a little scared.

Thank goodness his real job is hockey and not singing.

Chloe lit the candle, as the song was finishing; Colton drew his attention back to the cake, mesmerized with the candle this time.

Grabbing his hands before he snatched the lit candle, Chloe leaned forward, nodding to me as we blew the candle out for him. I loved that she felt the need to include me on that.

Everyone started to clap, resulting in Colton also clapping but not knowing why.

Once the candle was removed we let him have at it, turns out the kid loves vanilla cake. Although, after assessing his damage on the piece of cake it was concluded that myself and Colton wore most of the cake.

As everyone continued to enjoy the cake, Colton continued to take fist fulls and try to eat it that way, every now and again he would lift his little cake filled hand to my mouth wanting me to take some-then turning to the side and offering Chloe the same. From what I had received from his hand, the cake was the most delicious I have ever had.

As everyone was talking, I leaned into Chloe's side, bringing my mouth close to her ear for only her to hear, "Good job on the cake Love. Best thing I've tasted, besides you." Sealing my words with a kiss to her temple. I watched as her cheeks turned a deep red and watched her squirm in her seat. I haven't tasted her yet, but soon.

Chloe turned to look up at me, lust filling her eyes she leaned closer, directing her eyes to Colton before looking up at me, a smirk gracing her lips. She leaned closer like I had done to her, "You haven't tasted me yet Reed. But when you do, I'll be the best thing you have ever tasted, this cake won't even be on your mind." Unlocking her eyes from mine, she stood up grabbing Colton before heading to the kitchen to wash his hands. Watching her leave sealed my fate, she was swaying her hips more than usual, and there was no way for me to get out of this chair without everyone knowing what she does to me.

As I was stuck in the trance that her ass put me in and her words, I was shaken from my thoughts by my mother, "Reed? Are you good?"

I immediately turned to look back at her, watching Matt and Summer trying to hide their laughs knowing exactly what I had been doing. Turning to look back at my mom, her giving me the 'all knowing' mom look, "Yea I'm good, just thinking about the game plan for tonight. You know trick or treating. Oh and we need to do presents."

My mom snickered, "Uh huh, bet you were."

I gave her a looking making me seem confused as to what she was referring to, but deep down she knew and I knew that I had been caught ogling my girlfriend.

After we cleaned up lunch, we all headed into the living room where Chloe sat on the floor with Colton and Summer helped hand them the gifts.

Colton was more interested with the wrapping paper than the gifts, had I known this I might have just gotten him wrapping paper.

My parents had brought him a collection of dinosaur picture books, as soon as he saw the t-rex on the cover he smiled up at Chloe giving his best, "rawrrr" sound, making everyone laugh.

Summer and Matt had gotten him some new winter clothes for the Missouri winter approaching along with a few new race car toys-although I think Matt will enjoy them more.

When Chloe opened the gift I had gotten him she stopped, before looking back up at me, "You got him a jersey?"

I smiled leaning forward, "Turn it around"

She looked down at the St. Louis hockey jersey in her hand before turning it around, on the back read my number 13 with 'Collins' across the shoulders. "You got him your jersey?"

I smiled at her, giving her a nod, "This way everyone knows who his favorite player is when you guys come to the games."

She let out a laugh before getting Colton's attention showing him the jersey. Colton reached for it, interested in what it was. As if he knew what the jersey was for he took ahold of the jersey and waved it around saying "Dada" giving everyone a show of his tooth smile.

"There's more in the bag bud" I gestured to the bag in front of Chloe.

She gave me a raised eyebrow and continued going through the wrapping paper. She pulled out a wolf stuffed animal wearing a St. Louis hockey jersey and toddler sized hockey skates.

Chloe looked up at me, "you, you got him skates?"

I nodded my head yes, "You said I had to be the one to coach him, remember. I gotta start somewhere."

Chloe put the skates and jersey back in the bag, handing Colton the stuffed animal, she quickly stood walking over to me pulling me into a bone crushing hug. I wrapped my arms around her, pulling her into me. I could hear her breathing and I could tell she was trying to keep her emotions under lock and key.

"Thank you Reed" she whispered into my neck. "You're welcome baby" turning to kiss her cheek, my hand rubbing her back.

She pulled back giving me a small peck on the lips, straightening her posture and turning to return to the floor.

I watched her walk back to her spot before turning to look at my parents, my dad was smiling ear to ear watching Colton make this best dinosaur noises, but my mom was looking at me with a shimmer in her eyes and happiness on her face. She reached over and held my hand giving it a squeeze before giving me a kiss on the cheek, "You look so happy honey."

I smiled, bringing her hand up kissing the back of it, "The happiest I've been."

My attention was back on Colton and Chloe, she was opening the gifts that she had gotten him. The first one was a new dinosaur toy, the second was a strider bike and the third item she held up was a navy blue suit with white pinstripe down it.

I was taken back at first, "Did you get him a matching suit to one of my game day suits?"

She started laughing, "I did. I thought you guys would be so cute, especially on game day" her cheeks turning pink.

I laughed reaching for the suit, "Tomorrow is the next home game so why don't we wear it buddy?"

Colton looked over at me seeing the suit in my hands, "Dada" he babbled crawling over to where I sat. Standing up he placed his hand on my knee the other on the jacket of the suit.

"What do you say bud? Matching suits to give me good luck tomorrow?"

Colton started babbling nonexistent words and smiling.

Out of nowhere Matt sighs, "I want a little buddy now. Summer" he whined.

Summer laughed patting his leg, "Umm, not right now.

Just buy Colton a matching suit and share the kid."

I looked up, trying to seem offended, "We are not sharing my little buddy. Get your own Matt" I reached around and pulled Colton closer, pretending to protect him from Matt.

Matt rolled his eyes and threw his hands in the air, "See Summer, I told you Reed doesn't share."

Chloe was laughing watching us go back and forth, making eye contact with Summer she raised her eyebrow, "Wow Summer, refusing your boyfriend a little buddy means refusing Colton a best friend." I loved when Chloe joked around-only I don't know if she's joking here.

My parents entertained Colton as the rest of us cleaned the gift wrapping and refilled our drinks.

Walking towards the living room, I bumped into Chloe who was stopped. Looking up I notice her watching my dad and Colton reading one of the dinosaur books; Colton giving his best "Rawrr" and my dad copying him. My mom was laughing and tickling Colton making him giggle.

I snaked my arms around Chloe's stomach pulling her against me, "I think they like him" I whispered into her ear. Noticing that her eyes were glossy.

Spinning her around I walked us back to the empty kitchen, not letting go of her once, "Baby what's wrong?"

She reached up and wiped some tears that were beginning to fall, "Happy tears Reed." Taking a shaky breathe, "I always dreamed of my future kids having a close relationship with their grandparents, but I thought that dream sailed when my parents passed." I watched her take a deep breath in, running a hand through her hair, "But, watching your parents with him, reminded me of my parents when I was a kid and now how they won't ever meet Colton." The tears falling again from her eyes, "I just hope that he gets your parents for a long time, he already loves them."

I held her close, kissing her head, "Baby they are going to be in his life a long time, I promise. We aren't going anywhere, you're stuck with us whether you like it or not."

I felt her let out a small laugh, "I'm just emotional today."

I rubbed circles on her back, "I think Colton has both my parents wrapped around his finger Love. I think you just scored yourself some new babysitters."

Chloe pulled back a little bit to get a look at me, she leaned up on her tip toes bringing me into a heated kiss. I pushed her up against the marble counter top, my hands grabbing onto her waist right under her boobs. Her hands wrapped around my neck.

After a few minutes and 2 sets of swollen lips later, we were breathing heavy looking into each other's eyes. "We can't be doing that when I can't do anything about it Chloe. You're killing me."

She kissed me one more time, before seductively walking back into the living room.

I ran a hand through my hair trying to control my breathing but also fix the issue she left in my pants. As I was leaning against the counter top, I watched Summer walk into the kitchen with a sad looking Matt behind her, "Summer" he whined, "Just 1 kid."

I laughed watching Summer roll her eyes before turning to look at me, "Tell your friend I need a fat rock on my hand if he wants one so bad" then turning and headed for the living room.

Matt looked at me defeated, "Shit, I need to make sure the ring I bought is big enough now."

I felt my eyes get big, "You bought a ring?"

Matt made eye contact with me, cheeks turning pink, giving me a sheepish smile "Shit I forgot to tell you. Umm, yea."

"Holy Fuck man that's amazing. When are you asking?" I leaned against the counter showing him that I was invested in this for him.

Matt rubbed the back of his neck giving a weary smile, "I don't know yet, soon though. I think when we get a small break I want to take her out of town for a mini vacation."

"That would be perfect, she loves your guts vacations and I know she loves you. Dude I am so happy for you" I walked over pulling him into one of our rare hugs.

"Thanks man. I'm nervous as fuck." Matt let out a nervous laugh.

I would also be nervous if I was asking the woman I loved to marry me. Although I knew from the first moment that she was the one.

We lounged around the rest of the day before Chloe pulled out her homemade lasagna, prompting us that we had to eat before going trick or treating.

Everyone was seated around the table as Chloe dished out helping onto everyone's plate before taking hers.

Colton sat across from her and I, not giving two shits about us. We found out fast that he and my dad have an inseparable bond-so naturally Colton was sitting with him.

Chloe had tried to take him but both my dad and Colton said no. The look on her face was priceless.

Matt and I cleaned up dinner while Chloe went and got Colton's giraffe costume-the rest of us just wore safari hats and a khaki shirt and pants. Even my parents dressed up.

Matt, myself and my Dad were walking with Colton on my hip, the girls walking in front of us. Chloe would turn and snap photos every now and again. I so badly wanted her to have pictures of the two of them so I made it my mission to take as many photos of the two together.

My dad kept trying to get Colton to say 'Dave' but Colton kept babbling and laughing. Dad was relentless but this kid was stubborn. He refused to call me anything other than 'Dada'.

We had visited at least 5 houses when my mom stopped us in front of a home with a ton of Halloween decor, "Okay Chloe, Colton and Reed. You three need a photo."

Chloe turned to look at me as I nodded at her, walking over to her, we positioned so Colton was on my hip in between us. His head on my shoulder, his small hands around my neck. Chloe leaned in putting an arm around me the other on Colton.

My mom snapped a few promising to send them to us, "Okay this is my new favorite photo" she gushed. Showing the phone to my dad who smiled back at her.

Everyone decided to take turns taking photos with Colton, even though you could tell how sleepy he was.

Once my parents got to their photo, Colton perked up seeing my dad's arms out for his, "popa".

We all stopped my dad smiled looking at Chloe, "did he just say papa or something close to that?"

Chelsea took a deep breathe before looking at me, "I um, I don't know Dave. He's never heard those words before but he seemed to be calling out to you."

I snaked my arms around her body. Planting a kiss on her head.

My dad smiled back at Colton, "Colton can you say, 'Dave'?"

Colton reached up touching my dad's cheek, "Popa". My mom laughed, "Oh sweetie you are too precious" reaching out to lightly pinch his cheek.

Summer snapped the photos before handing the phone back to my mom.

Colton didn't say the word "popa" or even "papa" the rest of the night, because the kid crashed the second we headed home.

Once we returned, my parents said their goodbyes before heading out and promising to call Chloe before the game tomorrow to meet up.

Summer and Matt retreated to bed.

Chloe had taken Colton up to get him ready for bed and laid down.

I headed to the living room, sitting on the edge of the couch holding his tiny skates. His jersey laid across my knee and his little suit on the table.

Hearing Matt talk about marriage stirred something in me. I knew Chloe was the one, I know it's too early. I know she has a hard time trusting-especially when it comes to her heart and Colton.

I promise on this day forward I will be the best boyfriend/future husband in this world and that I will be the best father that little boy will ever have.

I want a family with Chloe, I want all 3 of us to wear the name on the back of the jersey.

13

Reed: I'm Yours

3 days have passed by since it had been Colton's first birthday. We did in fact find out that he meant the word "papa" when talking to my dad.

His jersey fits him great and he loves it. Our social media team and managed to snap candid photos of the three of us before and after games and now we are practically spamming all social media.

Summer and Matt had offered to watch Colton so Chloe and I could have a date- and tonight I am hoping that she agrees with staying with me. You know so that Matt and Summer can practice for the army of kids Matt wants.

I had sent Chloe a bouquet of flowers to her work space in downtown, not just a small bouquet but a very large attention grabbing bouquet with a very suggestive card with it. Thankfully I had ordered in person and I got to write it, because I want no woman or man knowing what is about to go down.

As I was leaving gym my phone started ringing, the Halloween photo we took pops up on my phone, sliding it answer I am graced with the sound of a Colton laughing and Chloe laughing along with him, "Hello beautiful, for what do I owe the pleasure of this call?"

Chloe giggles again, "I don't know maybe something about this floral bouquet the size of my car and the fact that this note has a lot of pent up energy with it."

I ran a hand through my hair, smiling as I threw my duffle bag in the bed of the truck, "Ohh and what does this note say love?"

"Oh please don't make me say it out loud?" She pleads. "Is anyone with you besides little man?" I asked getting into the front seat.

"No it's just him and I putting some decor up. I'm not saying it" she laughs again.

"That's fine, I will. I can't wait to taste you. Stay with me tonight, please." This time I'm the one pleading.

She takes a second before answering, "I can't leave Colton over night, I don't think."

"Baby, I'm going to tell you a secret, Matt wants kids, Summer wants kids, let them have one night with Colton to practice. And this way I can help you relax, more ways that you can count."

I could hear a hitch in her breathe, "Relaxing with you sounds good. Let me call Summer."

I start the truck, "No need I already talked her into it. I'll see you at 5 when I pick you up. Pack a bag babe."

I wish I could see her, but I know that her cheeks are red and she's breathing hard with anticipation. I have her, she knows it.

"I'll see you at 5 then." She breathes out, "And Reed?" "Yes baby?" I ask

"I can't wait to taste you either" she seductively says before hanging up on me.

She turned me on then hung up on me, this woman knows how to get me worked up and I love it. Fuck I love her.

I headed to the store picking up champagne, chocolates, some of her favorite candy, a few things for breakfast and some red roses. I even decided on grabbing a few things like a bath bomb, no idea what it's for but fuck it and then some Epsom salt and some tea light candles. I wanna make sure that my baby gets to relax.

Heading home, I unloaded the breakfast items in the fridge and then took the rest of the items upstairs to my room. Since this place has 2 master bedrooms, I get my own ensuite with a large tub. I placed the Epsom salt and bath balm on a little tray next to the bath, pulling out 2 towels.

I did a quick clean down of the tub since it's hardly used, along with cleaning any things else that didn't seem clean enough to me.

I grabbed a few stems of the roses placing them along the bath tub and adding a few tea light candles along the window behind the tub.

This morning I had changed my sheets and comforter, so my bed was freshly made and smelled heavenly. I took a few of the roses and tore off the petals, sprinkling them along the bed and a few on the floor.

Forgetting I had the champagne I ran down the stairs grabbing the ice bucket on our island, filling it with ice and 2 glasses before heading back up the stairs. Placing the Champagne inside I placed in next to the tub near the window, adding the 2 glasses next. I spread a few of the chocolates out next to the glasses.

Stepping back I admired my work, all I needed to do when we got back was grab the strawberries from the fridge and woo my woman.

I quickly changed realizing it was 4:30 and I needed to leave.

I sent Chloe a quick text, "On my way. Can't wait to see you."

She immediately texted me back, "My bag is packed, I'm ready when you are."

Fuck I love her.

I knew I loved her.

I just need to tell her I love her.

Before leaving I walked over to my bed side table, pulling out a long velvet box. I opened it to take one more look of the necklace. It was a gold thin chained necklace with 3 stones handing from it. One side had a Diamond to represent my birthstone, the middle was an Opal for Colton and then am Amethyst stone for Chloe. I wanted her to have something for all 3 of us, something that reminded her of me when I was gone on games. I closed the lid and pocketed the case.

At 5pm on the dot I was knocking on the door holding a bouquet mix of peonies and roses.

Matt opened the door, he had Colton on his hip who was holding his mini stick and a plastic puck. "Hey man, you look dapper. Come on in. Chloe will be down in a second. Little man and I were practicing our slap shot. Isn't that right Colt?" He turned to look at Colton who was smiling up at me.

"Dada" he squealed. Dropping the puck and mini stick.

Reaching out with my free hand I grabbed him, "My man. Are you going to have fun tonight with auntie Summer and Uncle Matt?" I gave him a kiss on the side of his head.

"Dude, I'm hoping this goes well. I'm kinda scared. This kid is great but like I gotta be on my best behavior because I want an army of these guys. So I hope we win Summer over."

I laughed, placing Colton on the ground so he can grab the stick and puck, "Matt you will be fine. Just keep him alive and you will be fine."

Chloe was walking down the stairs holding a small bag- full of clothes for our sleep over. Looking her all over I licked my lips. She was wearing a tight fitting small black dress landing mid-thigh and she was wearing the sexiest pair of black pumps. Her hair was styled in loose curls, as she walked down the steps her hair bounced against her body. The dress had sleeves to keep her warm, but her breasts were barely held in.

As she got to the bottom, she crouched down in front of Colton, bringing him to a hug and a large kiss, "Be good tonight for Uncle Matt and Aunt Summer. Remember you want friends, so be on Uncle Matt's side okay bud."

Matt and I laughed at her trying to plead with her toddler. As she stood up she turned to Matt, "Call or text if you need me okay."

Matt nodded his head then saluted her like the idiot he can be.

Saying one last good bye we walked hand in hand to the truck, I opened the door helping her up before placing her bag in the backseat.

Tonight I wanted to wine and dine her, so as I parked in the parking lot of the nicest most expensive steak house in the city, her eyes got big before turning to me, "Reed, this is too much."

"Baby I would buy you the restaurant if you wanted it. This isn't too much. You're my girl and I want you to only have the best." I reached for her hand giving her 3 kisses at her wrist.

We got seated against the back wall in a circular booth, the room was dimly lit, the candles flickered on the table. I decided my limit was 1 glass of wine because of the things I had planned for tonight, I needed it to go perfectly.

Chloe and I each got a glass of red wine, before agreeing on our appetizer and main courses.

After the waitress took our order and left, I reached for the velvet box with one hand, and grabbing her hand in the other. "I got you something."

She looked up from her wine glass, meeting my eyes, "You didn't have to get me anything Reed."

"I know, but when I saw it I knew I needed to have it. I needed you to have it." Putting the velvet box in front of her.

Anyone who saw the box would know that it wasn't a ring, so no pressure there. She carefully released my hand and opened the box, a gasp leaving her lips, "Reed, this is beautiful. Are these our birthstones?" She asked handing the stones in her fingers.

"Yes. I wanted you to always have Colton and I with you at all time. I hate leaving you for games, but now I will always be with you." I placed my hand on her thigh giving it three squeezes.

I could tell she was trying to hold back her happy tears, "I love it. Thank you. I hate when you leave to, but now I have part of you" she smiled leaning into me, placing a kiss on my lips. "Put it on me please?"

I grabbed the necklace, carefully unlatching it, Chloe turned her back to me, pulling her hair up.

I quickly latched the back of it, playing a kiss on the back of her neck.

"How did I get so lucky to have you in my life?" She asked, holding my hand in hers.

"I'm the lucky one love. I'll always be lucky with you in my life. I'm yours for as long as you want me" I laid it out without saying the words 'marry me' or 'I love you' hopefully she can tell.

She looked back up at me, cradling my jaw in her hand, "I'll keep you forever if you will let me."

I leaned into her kissing her again, pulling back I decided it's now or never, "I love you."

She opened her eyes, her searching mine for dishonesty or guilt, not finding any she smiled bigger, "Good, because I love you too."

Dinner went fast because we both wanted what was next. Quickly paying and getting to the truck we sped to the house.

Once we got in the house I ran to the fridge grabbing the strawberries, before grabbing her hand and pulling her upstairs. Before we got to my door I stopped turning back around to her, "Hang out here for like 2 minutes. I need to set something up."

She gave me a confused nod, allowing me to slip through my door. I hurried into the bathroom lighting the candles and placing the strawberries by the Champagne. Turning the water on warm letting it fill up.

Opening the door to the bedroom, I reached forward having her hold my hand, "I promised you relaxation love."

Her eyes found the petals on the bed before turning back to me, placing her bag by the closet door. "Rose petals, how romantic Reed."

I rubbed the back of my neck nervously, "Actually this way" leading her through the bathroom door. The lights were off, the only light was that from the candles.

Looking over at her, she studied the bath in front of her, "You did all this for me?"

"Of course baby. You deserve it. I love you." I pulled her into my chest. "How about we get out of these clothes and get into this nice warm bath. I got Champagne and snacks."

She let out the sweetest giggle, "Okay how about you get in first and open the champagne. I'm going to take my earrings off."

I quickly stripped out of my clothes, not caring that this was the first time she was seeing me naked. As I got into the tub, I could see her in the corner of my eye checking me out.

I'm proud of my body, my abs are like steal and don't even get me started on the size and girth of my cock.

I popped the Champagne, pouring two glasses. Turning around to face her, she stood against the counter watching me with a smile on her face.

"You getting in baby?" I asked raising an eyebrow.

She leaned forward, dropping the bath bomb into the water before looking up to meet my gaze, her tits were about to bust out of her dress. Her shoes were already off and she had placed her hair in a messy bun.

She slowly grabbed the hem of her dress, pulling it over her head, leaving her with no bra and no panties. I could feel the air leave my body, "You went commando all dinner?" I asked eyeing her stunning body.

She stepped over the ledge, placing her hand on my shoulder to steady herself. Once in the tub she kneeled down in front of me, grabbing the glass from my hand, "I didn't want to ruin any underwear knowing that you get me so wet." She leaned forward pressing a heated kiss to my lips.

She pulled back slightly, moving my head to kiss my neck, "Thank you for tonight."

I could feel her breathe hot on my neck, making my dick twitch.

I grabbed the glass back from her hand, placing it down. "Fuck baby. Let me make you feel good."

I could tell she was feeling confident tonight and it was sexy as hell, she moved closer straddling my lap, her hands running through my hair. "How about I make you feel good?"

Her hand reached below us, taking my length in her palm, I closed my eyes letting out a moan. She continued kissing me. One of my hands placed on her hip while the other massaged her tit. She let out a moan, pressing my lips back to hers to swallow the sounds.

My hand glided across her hip, placing it against her folds, rubbing her back and forth, slipping two fingers in and out of her heat.

"Fuck baby, I need you" she moaned.

"I need a condom baby, let me grab it out of my pants," I went to break us apart to lean over the edge when he hand stopped me.

"I'm on birth control if you're fine without it" Her green eyes filled with lust and desire stared into mine.

"I'm fine with it if you are." I leaned in kissing her again. She grabbed me again in her palm, lining me up with her center. As she eased herself down I studied her face, caressing her cheek and jaw, "God you're beautiful."

As she impaled herself with my cock, we both let out loud moans of pleasure. It had been so long since I had been inside anyone, and Chloe was tight.

"You fill me so good" she moaned out.

I leaned forward taking her breast into my mouth, swirling my tongue around her nub, sucking on her and grazing her gently with my teeth biting down. She let out a loud moan, "Reed!"

"That's it baby, keep riding me. God you take me so well. I want to hear that pretty little mouth say my name when you come" I kissed her neck, kissing down to her other breast giving it the same attention the other got.

She continued to buck her hips into me, my hand massaged the tit free of my lips while the other one held her tight at the hip.

I could feel her tight pussy clenching, her breathing becoming labored, she was close. "Come for me baby I want to feel you squeeze me."

My words did it for her, she quickened her pace before breathing out a loud, "Reed!" Before crashing against me.

I kept bucking my hips, I could feel my release on the edge, Chloe held my face with both hands, "Come in my Reed."

Her words did it for me. I quickened my thrusts, spilling my seed in her tight pussy.

Closing my eyes, catching my breath for a second. That was the best sex I had ever had. Clearly the bath agreed as well because our clothes that were on the floor were soaked with the water spilling over the side.

I grabbed the back of her neck, bringing her lips to mine, "Holy shit you are amazing."

She let out a giggle, carefully lifting up before turning around, sitting between my legs, her back to my chest. "I wish we had done that sooner."

I handed her the glass of Champagne, as she reached for a strawberry, taking a bite. I could watch her do anything and still be mesmerized.

She turned to look up at me, holding the strawberry out for me to take a bite, "I love you Reed Collins, don't ever forget that."

I took the rest of the strawberry in my mouth, not breaking eye contact, "I love you Chloe Murphy and I have never loved anyone as much as I love you... and Colton of course."

Her eyes were filled with lust as she took a sip of her champagne, placing it down, she stood up, giving me the best view of her ass.

"How about we show each other how much we really love each other Mr. Collins."

I quickly shot out of the bath, grabbing a towel and wrapping it around her. Picking her up bridal style I practically ran into the bed room, placing her on the bed.

She let out a laugh as she bounced on the bed, the view of her naked, happy and mine in the bed made me want to propose right then and there.

I separated her legs, settling in between them, I kissed her stomach, praying one day she lets me fill it with our baby. Kissing down her stomach I kissed the inside of her thighs, her hands gripping my hair.

"I promised to taste you baby" I said looking up to see her watching me as I drug my tongue from the bottom of her pussy lips up to the top bud.

Her eyes closed and her legs spread further apart. "Be a good girl baby and be as loud as possible."

Diving back in, I started sucking and licking, dragging my tongue in a circular fashion, her hips bucking against my face.

I continued to devour her as if she was my last meal. Her hands gripped my hair holding me in place as I slipped 2 fingers into her.

"Reed, oh fuck that feels good. Keep sucking like that."

Watching her come undone was one of my new favorite things to watch. I continued sucking on her clit as she opened her eyes watching me devour her. Her orgasm hit her hard, as I lapped up the sweet juices spilling out of her.

Her legs quivered, but I didn't want to stop until I had the last of the last of her sweet juices.

I moved forward placing my elbows on the side of her face, placing a kiss on her lips, "You taste fucking delicious baby."

She pulled me closer kissing me back, before she pushed me up and over onto my back. She placed her hand on my abdomen before giving me a smirk and leaning forward kissing my pecks, then my abs and then stomach.

As she got closer to where I wanted her, my cock kept twitching with anticipation. Her hand wrapped around the base of my cock, slowly stroking me, her thumb gracing over the tip wiping the precum down the base. Her eyes met mine, "It's my turn to taste you now baby."

Within seconds her lips were wrapped around me and her tongue swirled around my cock.

I could feel my cock hit the back of her throat and watching her take me was egging my release to come sooner than I wanted.

I gently pulled her off of me, "Damn baby I need to come but I need to come inside you."

She smirked while wiping the side of her mouth, I flipped us around so she was on her back.

I lifted one of her legs over my shoulder and aligned myself with her, pushing into her wet pussy.

Her hand dug into my shoulder and the other on my back. With every thrust I could feel her nails marking me and I loved it.

I leaned forward kissing her before moving down her neck and then taking her tit in my mouth like before. Her moans became louder and louder, "Reed harder, keep going I'm close."

I kissed my way back up her neck, gripping her hip harder to keep her steady, "Fuck I'm close to baby" I moaned.

"Come with me Reed. I need you" she panted.

I could feel her squeeze me before feeling both of our orgasms releasing, her pussy milking me dry.

I placed my forehead on hers, both opening our eyes, looking into each other's, I leaned forward kissing her, "You are amazing baby."

She let out a shaky breathe as I pulled out of her, laying my head on her chest. Her hand in my hair as my hands wrapped around her.

I kissed where the necklace fell on her chest, before taking a hand and holding the stones in my fingertips, "You know, we can always add more stones as needed right?"

She let out a laugh as she massaged my scalp, "I have a 1 year old Reed, how about we wait so there isn't any 2 under 2 happening."

I love that I can bring up kids and she is afraid of the talk. I just hope she knows the moment she gives me the green light, I'm knocking her up.

I kissed her chest again, "I love you."

14

Chloe: Dad Era

Reed and Matt had an early practice this morning, leaving Summer, myself and a very on the move Colton prepping and cooking the Thanksgiving meal. Since the boys had a home game last night and then another one Friday midafternoon, Matt and Summer are not able to venture off on their weekend cabin getaway until Saturday morning.

I have a good feeling that Summer is going to be coming back with some very shiny and large hardware on her ring finger.

Reed's parents are flying back in and should be here shortly, it's currently 9:30am and their flight was supposed to land at 9.

Summer was dealing with the 20lbs turkey while I was currently trying to keep Colton entertained by cartoons rather than going through every drawer in the kitchen. I really am hoping Reed's mom and dad get here soon, I need a break.

As I was chasing after Colton who had a ladle in one hand and a spatula in the other, the front door opened to Reed and Matt drenched in after practice sweat holding their gear bags. Both had large smiles on their faces as they watched the toddler run straight for them.

"Colton, sweetie, mommy needs those, can she have them back please?" I pleaded, crouching down to be eye level with my tyrant of a son. Who was currently hiding behind Reed's legs, giggling at me.

Matt tried to hold his laughter as he walked around me to find Summer.

Reed put his bag down, while playing with Colton's hair, "Hey buddy, how about you give mommy those back and we can go get ready before papa and meemee get here" Since Colton started calling Dave 'papa' we have been trying to find a name for Susan, apparently 'meemee' is the winner. Colton dropped both kitchen utensils before putting his hands up for Reed to take him.

Reed reached down grabbing the two items handing them to me, before reaching and picking up Colton, "Hey baby. I missed you" Reed leaned in placing a delicate kiss on my lips.

"I missed you to. How was practice?" Kissing him back harder.

Reed groaned as I pulled away, "It was nothing compared to kissing you."

Blush started creeping up my neck, "You know what would be so much better?" I winked.

Reed licked his lips, eyeing me as I bit down on my lower lip, "I have a few ideas, enlighten me though."

I let out a small laugh before reaching up on the tip of my toes, my lips centimeters away from his, "You taking a shower because you stink." Returning to the flat of my feet, I winked again before turning and heading back to the kitchen, making sure to sway my hips a little more than usual.

I could hear Reed groan and then whisper, "Colton, your mom will be the end of me."

Within an hour, Reed's parents had arrived and were engrossed in the life of Colton once again. I don't mind, it allows me to work on dinner and not chase my son all across the house. Reed finally showered, same with Matt, so now the house stopped smelling like a hockey locker room, thank the heavens.

Dave had whatever football game was one, the boys joining him in the living room drinking beer and eating whatever snacks we handed out, pretty sure a few were Colton's baby snacks, but no one needs to know.

Susan had joined Summer and I in the kitchen helping the two of us prepare the first ever Thanksgiving meal we have ever tried to cook.

Noticing that it was getting close to noon, I needed to find Colton and attempt to get him down for a nap. I had pulled his bottle out and was preparing it when Reed walked into the kitchen with a very heavy eyed Colton laying against his chest, "Oh good, I was just coming in here to make his pre nap bottle."

I smiled putting the lid on the bottle before turning to hand it to him, "Do you want me to take him and you can go back in there with the guys?"

Reed grabbed the bottle, leaning in to kiss my cheek, "Don't worry about it love, you worry about in here, I got him."

Reed retreated back to the living room, holding my entire world and heart in his hands.

Not realizing I had been staring, I felt a nudge against my shoulder, looking to my side I see Susan smiling at me, "I have never seen him act so domesticated, I love it." She let out a laugh.

I could feel the blush creeping up my cheeks, "I love how much he loves Colton and how helpful he is, thank you for raising a perfect gentleman."

Susan grabbed my hand with her, giving it a gentle squeeze before turning back around to work on the dinner rolls.

From the kitchen I could see Reed standing up with Colton in his arms, bottle empty and Colton's eyes closed. Reed is talking to his dad and Matt while using his free hand to gesture to the TV. Watching him in his dad era makes me want to give him more babies, I can literally feel my ovaries combusting.

Dinner went great, we let Matt carve the turkey since he was so excited to have a home cooked meal, he did need some help from Dave but it went well.

Colton loved everything I plated for him and only a few times did I have to wipe the mashed potatoes out of his hair.

I was in the kitchen cutting the pie into pieces to be plated and served when I felt two arms circle my waist, "Dinner was good baby" and a sweet kiss to my temple had my legs weak.

I smiled turning my head to look at Reed, "Thanks hun, it wasn't just me cooking you know that right?"

Reed leaned his head down, his nose nudging the side of my cheek, making me turn my head giving him access to my neck, "I know love.

But you are by far my favorite. What's for dessert, please tell me it's you." He continued to leave kisses along my neck and below my ear.

Trying my hardest to suppress the moan in the back of my throat, I closed my eyes, "You keep doing that and it will be."

Reed let out a small laugh, his breathe hitting my ear, "I wish we had some privacy baby, because it would be you on this counter with me devouring you."

I put the pie cutter down, spinning in Reed's arms, running my hands up the length of his arms to his neck, "I really love where this is going, and trust me I would love to be your 3 course meal, but your parents are in ear shot love" leaning up I placed a heated kiss on Reed's lips before moving to his neck, "maybe later."

With that I turned, grabbed the pie dish and waltzed out of the kitchen pretending that my panties were not completely dripping with my arousal. I need Reed and I need him the moment we get time alone.

The boys were in charge of cleaning the dishes and the kitchen, I mean it's only fair.

Matt and Reed had been whispering to one another the entire time and I was curious as to what the two of them could be gossiping about. But every time myself or Summer walked into the kitchen they would freeze up. Men are dumb.

Susan and Dave were staying in a nice hotel not too far from our house of the stadium, so they had left around 8pm to get a good night rest before meeting me tomorrow for the boys' game.

Summer and Matt had retreated to their bed right before 9 and I was currently trying to rock Colton to sleep. Reed was putting toys away while I was in our bedroom trying to transfer Colton to his crib.

Finally getting Colton down I headed into the bathroom to start the shower and go through my nightly routine, I still couldn't get Reed and his dirty words out of my head. I decided to entice him in a round of steamy shower sex so I sent him a text, letting him know just where I needed and wanted him.

Chloe: Heading into the shower, I could really use your tongue to make sure I'm thoroughly relaxed after today.

Reed: On my way

I let out a laugh as I imagined him flying up the stairs while unbuttoning his shirt and pants.

As I turned around to test the water the door flew open and a winded Reed entered, his pants were half on, his shirt was out of one arm and still around his neck.

I continued to giggle watching him look like a mess, "Are you good there handsome?"

Reed let out a moan, taking in my appearance, well the very bare view I presented to him, "I am now." Reed shredded the last of his clothes before pulling me in and placing me on the counter, his mouth assaulting mine.

"Reed" I whimpered as he broke the kiss moving onto my neck.

"What do you need baby? Tell me" he demanded.

I caught my breath, "You, I need you." The air was thick due to the sexual frustration as well as the heat from the shower.

"What do you need baby? Tell me. You want me to lick your tight pussy?" His hands were parting my thighs, while his mouth moved over my breasts.

I nodded my head, leaning back against the mirror, my hands coming to his hair and back.

"Words Chloe." He growled.

"Yes. Yes I want you to eat me" I moaned.

Reed dropped to his knees, pulling me closer to the ledge of the counter top.

He kissed back and forth along my thighs before licking the length of my cunt. I let out a deep moan the second I felt his tongue hit my nerves.

Reed continued to lick the folds, sucking and nibbling on my bundle. I continued to rock my hips and pull his hair, "Oh Reed, just like that."

Reed pulled back, bringing the fold between his teeth gently before releasing, "Quiet baby, we don't need the baby waking up." The words barely left his mouth before he had his mouth on me. His fingers pumping in and out of me, curling his fingers around. I continued to moan and move my hips riding his face, "Reed I'm close" I panted as the orgasm ripped through my body.

Reed continued to suck every last drop, my body continued to shake with the aftershock I was left in. My hand went limp in his hair.

Reed placed gentle kisses back on my thighs before standing up, meeting my eyes he took his fingers and put them in his mouth licking off my juices, "Fuck, you tase amazing."

My breath hitched in my throat watching him suck on his fingers.

I slowly pushed off the counter coming to stand before him, taking his free hand I led him towards the shower.

Once inside, I pushed him against the shower wall before dropping to my knees, "It's my turn now."

Desire and excitement flashed through Reed's eyes as I grabbed his length in my hand. Keeping eye contact I pumped his cock while running my tongue down the tip to the base of it and taking his balls into my mouth giving them a gently suck.

Reed's head fell back as he let out a breathy moan. I moved my tongue back to the tip before taking him in my mouth. I continued to run my tongue around his cock and over the tip, tasting the pre cum. Reed's hand was in my hair, holding it back.

I could tell he was getting close, his breathing was increasing and the moans were more frequent, "Baby I'm close."

I continued to suck harder, wanting him to release into my mouth.

Within seconds his seed was running down the back of my throat and I drank him dry.

I popped him out of mouth, Reed reached down grabbing my arm helping my up off the floor.

Reed placed his hands on my waist and his forehead against mine, "Fuck I love you."

I ran my hands through his hair, "I love you to." The rest of the shower we cleaned ourselves off, actually keeping things fairly PG.

Crawling into bed that night, Reed pulled my into him was he placed kisses at the crown of my head, "Move in with me."

My hands stilled from drawing circles on his chest, I moved my head to look at him, "What did you say?"

Reed continued to play with my hair, his hand coming to rest at the base of my neck, "Move in with me. Chloe I love you, I hate being away from you, hell I hardly sleep at home anymore. So, let's get a place together."

He could probably see the turmoil and the constant bickering back and forth in my head as I pondered the 'what if's', "You, you want me and Colton to move in with you?"

Reed's eyes met mine, his hand coming to move a piece of hair behind me ear, "Yes baby."

I really loved this man and he is there for not only me but Colton, he's everything I wanted in a partner. "Yes."

Reed's hands came to cradle my face as he leaned in kissing me, "You sure? Like 100% positive, I'm selfish and want you, both of you but if you aren't ready I'll wait."

I smiled, brining my hand to his cheek, "Reed there's no one else I want to wake up to and go to sleep next to. Yes I want to move in with you."

Reed's smile grew from ear to ear as he breathes a sigh of relief, "We can buy a house, whatever house you want, I'll buy it. We should call a Realtor tomorrow."

I let out a quiet laugh not wanting to wake up Colton, but also really happy that Colton can now have his own room, "Wait you want to buy a house? Why not rent?"

Reed's gaze met mine again, "Chloe for as long as I know I am not leaving the team or State, so buying a house makes sense. It's where we can plant our roots. Plus buying a house can allow us to figure out how many rooms we want and when we want to fill them."

I kissed his chest, "Think about kids again, aren't you?"

Reed's cheeks were turning a little darker shade of pink at my words, "Is it so wrong to want to have kids with you. I love the one we currently have, but we need more than 1 to make a hockey team love."

Shaking my head, my smile grew bigger, "How about one step at a time here Casanova."

Reed kissed the top of my head once again, "Fine. This conversation isn't over, it's just on hold. Let's get some sleep baby."

Kissing Reed one more time, I cuddled into his side while his hands possessively hugged me, keeping me locked in at his side.

"Good night Reed." "Good night Chloe."

The next morning I woke up to a hot cup of coffee on my bedside table and no Colton in sight.

Slowly getting up and stretching, I freshened up for the day and put on some leggings and a St. Louis Hockey sweater that I am pretty sure is Reed's.

I found Reed and Colton enjoying breakfast at the table with a untouched plate ready for me next to Reed. Smiling at the gesture, I walked over placing my cup next to my plate and kissing the top of Reed's head before moving to pepper kisses along my sweet babies face.

Colton was giggling and holding up his yogurt pouch, excited to see me and excited to wipe the excess yogurt on me.

"Good morning to my favorite boys."

"Hear that Colton, she thinks were boys and not men, how rude."

I let out a laugh as I moved to get seated, "Thank you for breakfast and coffee. What time did you guys wake up?'

Reed turned his head to look at me, a sweet smile on his face, "We got up at 6:30 with Uncle Matt and we went for a nice jog around the neighborhood. We decided that mama needed some sleep after yesterday."

I looked around the kitchen and living room, noticing the clock reading 8:30am and the absence of my roommate, "Where is Matt and Summer?"

"They headed to the rink, Summer had to meet one of the players on IRL for his knee and Matt wanted to get an ice bath in."

"Oh, do you need to go or want to go over there?" "Nope, what I want is to spend my next 2 hours with the two of you relaxing. The weathers nice, maybe after you eat we can take a walk to the park down the street." Reed reaches over grabbing the empty pouch out of Colton's hands, "Time to clean you up."

As I said yesterday, Reed in dad mode is excitingly sexy and hot.

As Reed mentioned, after we cleaned up Colton, we took a family walk down to the park in our neighborhood. The weather was surprisingly warm for November and there was no snow thank goodness.

We had put Colton on the baby swing and he had absolutely loved it, he wouldn't stop giggling and clapping his hands. "I think we need a jungle gym or a swing set in our house, hearing him laugh is killing me."

I giggled watching Reed swoon over the baby giggles and demand we get a swing set because of this, and I am not against it. "Speaking of houses, where would we even start?"

Reed looked over at me while he pushed Colton, "I already called my Realtor friend. Told him I want a gated neighborhood with security, a good size house that isn't a pain to clean, a big back yard, he said that he would have a list of houses before the end of next week and then we can tour them."

I walked over placing my hand in his back pocket, leaning into his side, "I'm really happy to be moving in with you Mr. Collins" leaning up I laid a loving kiss along his jaw.

Reed circled his arm around my waist, anchoring me to him, "No one else I would rather do life with than you baby."

After another half hour, we headed back to the house. Colton was fast asleep in the stroller before we even exited the park.

Once we got in the house, I took Colton while Reed started getting ready to head to the arena. Since the game was at 2:00, he needed to get into his game day suit and get out the door in the next hour.

Reed walked down the stairs looking for me, "Hey babe?"

Looking over the back of the couch as he walked in, my eyes deceived me as I stared at the man who was shirtless and wearing joggers very low on his waste. "Uh, umm, Yes hun" I cleaned my throat.

Reed smirked knowing I had been staring, "Do you and Colton just want to come with me. I know the games at 2, but I don't have to be there till 12:30 and you can hang out with Summer."

Looking at my phone it was not even 11am, which gave me plenty of time, "Yea, we can do that. Let me take him up and I will start getting ready."

Reed smiled picking Colton from my arms, before reaching his hand out for mine, "We'll let's get ready then family."

Pulling into the arena, some of the players were exiting their cars, some had their families in tow. Getting out of Reed's truck, I grabbed the diaper bag and walked around to Reed's side, helping get Colton out of the car seat.

The boys (mainly Reed) decided to wear their matching suits, with their black dress shoes. I had on my Collins jersey with a pair of black leather pants and my knee high black boots. My hair was tied up in a slick back pony tail with gold jewelry across my ears and neck.

I placed Colton on the ground, holding his hand as Reed grabbed his gear bag before we headed into the players entrance.

As we entered their social media team was doing their game day walk in pictures, so I steered my way to the side with Colton. Reed noticed and stopped, "Can umm, can Colton do the walk in with me?"

I smiled watching him get nervous, "Give me your bag and you can have him."

Reed smiled wide heading towards me handing over his bag that surprisingly didn't weigh as much as I thought it did, he took Colton who was mesmerized with the lights.

I walked to the other end while the social media team was eating up the cuteness that would be my boys. Colton was holding Reed's hand walking alongside him smiling at the cameras.

I took out my phone and snapped a few of them laughing as they were walking towards me. Reed's eyes met mine, giving me his flirty smile and wink.

Colton saw me and bolted from Reed, "mama" he babbled with his hands held high.

Kneeling down I held my hands out, "Colton you left dada"

Colton stopped and turned around before running back to Reed, "Dada". Pretty sure all the girls in the room swooned over the moment Reed kneeled down grabbing Colton, because I swooned and my ovaries combusted again.

After dropping Reed off to the locker room, Colton and I were in the family room, there were a few other wives and a few kids a little bigger than Colton.

Colton was playing on the ground at my feet with his dinosaur when another WAG walked over, "Your Chloe right?"

I looked up meeting her gaze, she was a little older than me, light brown hair and brown eyes, a polite smiled on her face. "Yes that's me."

"Hi, I'm Candice. I'm married to Luke Davies one of the defenseman. I wanted to introduce myself."

I smiled at her, "It's really nice to meet you. This is Colton my son."

Candice looked at Colton and her eyes widened, "Oh my goodness he is the cutest thing. How old is he?"

I ran my hand through his hair, "Just turned a year in October."

Candice took a seat next to me watching Colton before looking back up at me, "Mine is 5 and she is the sassiest trouble ever, takes after me but mainly her daddy. I miss when they are this small."

Almost like summons a small girl rounds the chair, her brown hair is pulled back into 2 braids, she's wearing a small jersey that is probably her dad's number, and a pair of leggings with her small ugg boots. Candice smiles pulling her daughter into her arms, "Brooke can you say hi to Chloe? This I Reed's girlfriend and her son Colton."

The small girl smiled looking at me and Colton giving a small wave and a soft smile before leaning into her mom.

We continued to get to know one another for the next hour, other WAGS joining us off and on and Brooke deciding to play with Colton.

Reed's parents walked into the family room, as they walked over Colton noticed them taking his time standing up before walking towards them babbling his version of "papa" and "meemee" with his hands up and a toothy smile on his face.

At warmups, we headed to the glass so we could see Reed and Colton kept smiling, clapping and pointing to the players on the ice.

Turning to head back to the main elevator to take us up to the section we were sitting in. I noticed a man lurking in the shadows down at the end of the hallway. He looked familiar, his brown hair was shaggy and he was tall and skinny. As he noticed me watching he turned and disappeared into the hallway.

He's back. I think it was Colton's actual dad, my ex. He's here. Why is he here?

I felt a hand on my shoulder causing me to jump at the touch, turning I saw Summer watching me, "Hey you guys ready? And are you okay?"

I shook my head to clear my thoughts, "Yea I'm good. Just thinking. Let's go."

I can't tell Summer or she will freak out and alert security and cause a scene. I can't tell Reed, he will only see red and seek him out.

Maybe it wasn't him.

The rest of the game I felt like someone was watching me, the hair on the back of neck was standing. I hated this feeling.

The game was brutal, by the third period we were tied 3-3. Reed had spent some time in the sin-bin, one for tripping and another for fighting another player.

As much as I hate when he gets put in the penalty box, he looks pretty hot fighting. I will never tell him though.

We had a minute left of the third period, Colton was asleep against my chest and I was holding my breath watching the time count down.

With now 15 seconds left in the period, Matt steals the puck from the other team, directing himself down the ice towards the other team's goaltender.

Getting closer to the goal, he passed the puck at the last minute, Reed coming out of nowhere slapping it in. Summer and I watched as the puck flew over the right shoulder of the goaltender hitting the back of the net. The goal alarm going off and the fans going crazy.

Colton stirred awake looking around before looking at me, "Colton, Dada scored. We won baby." Kissing his cheek.

Colton smiled up at me laying his head on my shoulder looking out onto the ice, pointing to Reed and looking back at me, "Dada!"

"Yes baby Dada. Dada won." Summer smiled at us before looking back onto the ice.

As the teams exited, our boys skated around raising their sticks in the air as a 'thank you' to their fans.

Summer and I stood up, I adjusted Colton better on my hip.

Reed skated to glass near me tapping his stick against it, catching my attention. Once my eyes were on him, he was smiling and holding a puck, the puck he scored with. Pointing at me then back to him, telling me to come closer.

As I got closer he tossed it up for me to catch.

Colton reached forward placing his hands on the glass, "Dada!!"

Reed placed his hands on the glass where Colton's were, his eyes tearing away from Colton to mine, mouthing the words 'I love you.' I mouthed the words back before he skated off.

Looking at the puck he had tape on it with the todays date on it and his name. Seems like it was written by the trainer. But below it sat another piece of tape that had todays date and the words 'I love you'.

We headed into the family area to wait for the boys, Reed's parents were already in the room talking to other parents and wives.

Once Dave saw me and Colton he abandoned his conversation and Susan. Making a mad dash to the two of us, "There you are my dear."

Seeing Dave get closer made me smile, Colton noticed Dave getting closer and got excited, reaching his hands out for Dave to take him, "Papa!"

I laughed looking at Dave's surprised face, "Reed might have been helping him work on words. 'Papa' and 'Dada' are his favorite so far."

Dave seemed excited looking at Colton then back at me, reaching out he gave me a big hug, "Thank you for loving my boy and giving us a chance to love yours."

His words hit me in the heart, he made me miss my dad so much, they would have gotten along so well. I took a deep breathe before plastering another smile on my face, "He's not just my boy. He's Reed's, which makes him your boy as well. We're all family Dave. Thank you for loving Colton as if he was your blood."

Dave gave me another squeeze and a kiss on the head as Susan walked over excited to see Colton and myself. "My sweet baby. Who has you?"

Colton clapped his hands "Papa!"

Dave laughed, "Papa is right. Who's that?" Dave pointed at Susan, "Meemee" he squealed

Susan took a big breathe, "I like Meemee. I can work with Meemee."

I watched them interact, getting lost in how much Colton loves his new set of grandparents that I almost missed Reed walking up behind me.

Placing his bag on the ground, one hand circling my stomach, planting a kiss along my cheek, "We should send Meemee and Papa with Colton to the house while Mama and Dada go celebrate."

His words instantly made me wet. I wanted nothing more than to rip his clothes off and straddle him.

Looking at him while raising my eyebrow, "As much as I love that idea, I'm exhausted and I know you need a good massage after that brutal fight."

Reed laughed, "Did you like that?"

I held eye contact, not letting him see how much he has affected me, leaning in to his ear, "Made me so wet, pretty sure I still am" sealing my words with a kiss under his ear.

I could hear his gasp for air, not prepared for my words.

His parents finally noticed his presence, "Oh honey, you did so good. But what did we talk about with fighting. You could get hurt." I loved when his mom scolded him.

Reed hugged his mom and then his dad, Colton reaching out and attaching himself to Reed.

Reed and I loaded up in my car that he had driven earlier, heading home to make dinner and enjoy a relaxing night. Summer and Matt had decided to leave now instead of tomorrow morning.

As we pulled out of the parking lot, I noticed a figure standing under a tree, lurking and watching.

I had no doubts anymore, he was back and he knows I know he's here.

Once we got home, I headed for the bedroom to change Colton and change into comfy clothes for myself. Reed had changed and headed downstairs to make dinner.

Peaking over the corner of the kitchen with Colton, Reed has his back to me, scrolling on his phone and stirring spaghetti noodles and the sauce, I loved when he looked like this.

Walking quietly up behind him, I covered his eyes leaning in to his ear, "Guess who" peppering soft kisses below his ear down his neck.

Hearing the sexiest primal groan leave his body, he grabbed my hand, spinning around.

"Well isn't it my favorite little boy and his amazing sexy mama." Leaning in to pepper more kisses down my jaw.

Colton reached forward for Reed, handing him over I peered around them. "Spaghetti smells amazing. Need any help love?"

"Nope, although can you get an ice pack out I think I strained my shoulder in that fight. I should ice it here soon."

I smiled turning on my heel to grab everything I needed to play doctor.

Dinner went well, by 8pm Colton was sound asleep upstairs.

Reed had been icing his shoulder on the couch, I decided to surprise him since he needed a stress relief. I changed into a brand new deep maroon Teddie, the lace barely covering my nipples and it falling right at the bottom of my ass. I added the matching thong before giving myself a twirl to make sure it looked good. I let my hair down and ran my hands through it giving it a messy look.

I quietly made my way behind Reed, running my hands down his shoulders and onto his chest, leaning down I kissed below his ear, "I think you need to relax baby" grabbing the ice pack and tossing it on the table. Removing my hands I walked around the couch watching Reed's reaction.

His eyes went into shock seeing what I was wearing-or barely wearing.

I took my index finger and glided it down his cheek and down his neck, "Do you like it?" I asked, meeting his gaze, biting my lower lip.

"Fuck baby, I'm speechless. You are the sexiest woman on the planet." Placing both hands on my hips, pulling me into him.

He leaned down kissing me, taking my lower lip between his teeth, "I'm going to fuck you so hard you can't walk tomorrow"

A breath hitched in my throat at his words, "Is that a promise or a threat?" I placed my hand on his groin, feeling him harden under my touch.

Reed stood, picking me up, my legs winding around his waist, "Be a good girl and be quiet, we don't want little man waking up while you are being royally fucked."

I whimpered as I kissed him back, his hands squeezing my ass as he carried me to the empty dining room table.

We haven't done it on the table, so I was excited to add this spot to our list.

Reed placed me on the edge of the table, moving my legs so be in between them.

Reed kissed me down my neck, once he got to my chest he grabbed the hem of the teddy and lifted it over my head, leaving me bare chested with only a small thong on.

He took each breast in his mouth one at a time before moving south, getting on his knees in front of me, he moved the thong down my legs before tossing them aside.

I was anticipating what was next, grabbing his hair in my fingers as he started to lick me at my heat. He held the outside of my thighs, before placing a hand on my stomach, telling me to lay back.

As I was laid back on my elbows, he grabbed me under the ass pulling me closer to edge.

The sensation of his tongue over my folds and darting inside me, feeling him fuck me with his tongue had me close.

I had one hand in his hair as he lapped at my core, sucking on my clit and biting gently on my pussy lips. He was eating me like I was his last meal.

"Reed, fuck I'm close" I panted.

Reed gabbed my thighs pulling me closer as he sucked me hard, causing my orgasm to crash over me. As I was shaking with the aftershock, he continued to lap up my juices.

Standing to his feet, he dropped his shorts and boxers, pulling me closer to him as he slipped into my wet core.

I laid back on the hard wood, placing both legs on his shoulders.

His eyes went wide watching both legs in the air, giving him better access to me and getting deeper, "Fuck baby this is hot."

He continued to thrust into me, holding me at my ankles, this position was getting me closer to my second release. "Reed don't stop, keep fucking me like that."

Reed groaned a deep aroused sound, "Fuck baby I'm close too, cum with me baby."

Within seconds my second release shook through my body, I could feel the way my body squeezed around Reed. Reed quickly came behind me, feeling him fill me.

He gently released my legs and pulling out of me, turning to grab a wet wash cloth and coming back to clean me up.

Once cleaned up, he pulled me to his chest, "I fucking love you Chloe."

"I love you to Reed. How about we go to bed now." As I turned to find my thong and teddy, I felt a squeeze and a smack on my ass.

Turning to look at Reed, he bent down to grab his clothes, "Don't look at me like that unless you want more." A smirk gracing his lips.

Walking away from him, heading for the stairs, naked, I looked over my shoulder, "If you're a good boy, maybe in the morning."

I could hear Reed's footsteps becoming more rapid as he got closer, before I knew it I was over his shoulder, his hand on my ass and he was taking the stairs 2 at a time.

Fuck I love this man.

15

Chloe: Road Trip

I t was Friday night, Reed, Summer and Matt would be back tomorrow evening from their road trip. Tonight the 3 of them were currently in Florida.

Summer and Matt returned last Sunday from their trip the cabin and surprise surprise, they are engaged. I knew it had to be happening soon, I am beyond exited for them and this new step. Plus Reed and I will be moving in together shortly, it feels weird being at this stage in our lives.

It was the start to the December and a week since I saw whom I believe to be my ex lurking in the shadows.

I can't say that I have been relieved to not see him, but that's what scares me. When I'm at my shop, I feel eyes on me through the large glass windows, sometimes I think cars are following me to and from home to work. I haven't seen him but I feel him.

Reed has been a godsend, I had mentioned to him on the phone vaguely that I feel watched, I can't bring myself to tell him the truth. Since he left on Tuesday, I have had breakfast and dinner delivered like clockwork, each day it's a surprise as the last. Each having a note along with the meal, "Don't forget to eat. I miss you and Love you both.-Reed" This man, I swear.

Plus along with the food, each afternoon there has either been a flower delivery for me or a toy delivery for Colton. Each coming from Reed.

We have FaceTimed each day, sometimes Colton and I are waking up and still in bed or it's towards the end of the night.

Colton has been running rampant, I can barely keep up with him I feel.

Each morning and each night, he looks around for Reed, the words "Dada" coming out as a cry.

But each time we FaceTime Reed, Colton claps, smiles and giggles.

Currently I am in the living room with Reed and Matt's game on and Colton is laying against my chest facing the TV. Every night that the boys have a game, I have put the game on to watch and Colton joins me.

There were 3 minutes left of the third period, Florida was winning by one point, making the score 2-3. Reed had gotten the first goal for our team, as I watched the camera move in closer, its as if he knew because he tapped his chest 3 times-our sign.

With a minute left, Reed had gotten a penalty putting him in the sin-bin where he will stay till the game ends; I knew he was beating himself up over this, especially if they cannot tie the game.

As the time ticked down my heart was racing, I really wanted them to win. With 10 seconds left, Matt caught a breakaway, racing towards the end of the rink, at the last possible second he shot the puck, bypassing the goalie and hitting the back of the net. The team going wild.

Overtime. 3 on 3. If I thought the 3rd period was going to kill me, I was not prepared for OT. They ended up going into a shootout. Both teams had 1 point on the board for the shootout, and we were down to the last guy-Reed. If Reed made this, we win.

Reed skated down the end of the arena, moving his body to the right, the goalie moved with him, at the last second he turned left fast sailing the puck above the goalies right shoulder, sinking it into the back of the net.

Reed lifted both hands in the air, a huge smile across his face. His team skating to celebrate the win.

I grabbed Colton's hands, clapping them together and waving them around. "Yay Colton, they won. Dada did it. Yay."

Colton started giggling, clapping his hands on his own.

About an hour later, I had successfully gotten Colton down to sleep, grabbing his baby monitor I shut his door and headed downstairs to the couch. Waiting on Reed's call.

Speaking of Reed, my phone lit up as I was grabbing some water.

Answering the FaceTime I was greeted with not only a happy Reed, but a freshly showered Reed. His hair was wet, some strands hanging over his forehead and his eyes.

"Well hello there hot shot" I smiled at the screen, setting my water on the table and getting comfy on the couch.

"Well hello there beautiful. Where's Colton?" "He's asleep. He stayed up for your game, but he crashed shortly after" I explained.

"I miss that butter ball. But I also miss you" this man can flirt with a brick wall and make it fall. It's me I'm the brick wall.

"What time will you be back tomorrow?" I moved the blanket around me, allowing it to swallow me whole.

Reed watched me intensely, his eyes lighting up and the remembrance of coming home. "I think we land around 5pm tomorrow. You miss me or something?"

I leaned my head against the couch, "Me, miss you? I don't know about that haha." Reed stuck his tongue out making me laugh at his antics. "Yes Reed I miss you. There I said it."

"I gotta get my truck from your house tomorrow, maybe, just maybe you want to get dinner with me?" He ran his head through his wet hair, his muscles flexing. The air has left my lungs, I am so done for.

I stared a little too long before answering, "Oh umm, how about, I cook dinner for you. This way you can relax, plus funny thing, Colton has all these new toys that he would love to show you." I smirked.

Reed laughed, "Toys, wow, someone must really love him to be sending him gifts."

"Haha, I know it's you, they come with notes you doofus." I caught him trying to hide.

"Okay fine, I just happened to be online bored and they popped up and I was thinking he would like them." Reed felt the need to explain himself, he didn't need to think.

"Well he loves them all, and I think he misses you, he keeps looking for you. But you never answered me, would you like me to cook dinner?"

"Chloe, I would love dinner and I miss him to" Reed smiled not the camera. "I love you."

"Can you do me a favor?" I asked

"Yea what is it?" Reed looked a little worried, almost like he crossed a line.

"Can you stop spoiling us, I haven't had to cook in days and the flowers are beautiful but you don't have to spend money on me or Colton, we are going to be buying a house soon and I don't want you wasting money on me like this." I didn't want him to feel like he had to, I make my own money, I don't want him thinking I am only with him for financial reasons.

Reed shook his head No, "Cannot do that."

My mouth opened as I was in shock he told me no, "What do you mean you can't do that?"

"Chloe, you are home alone with a toddler on the move, it's only the right thing to do on my end. You need a break from things like cooking. Plus why can't I spoil you. You deserve to be spoiled, and I want to be the guy to do that." He almost seemed offended I would ask him to stop.

Taking a shaky breathe and looking away from the camera, I collected myself, "I don't want you to feel like you have to do it. I'm not one of those girls who's with a guy for material items. I've been on my own for so long and every time a guy spent money on me in the past," I took a breath, "They wanted certain things in return. Things I. I wasn't comfortable with."

Looking up at the screen, he could see the, moisture pooling in my eyes, his jaw clenched. "Baby. The only thing I want in return from you is your happiness and love. I just want to take care of you and Colton."

I nodded my head, indicating that I had heard him, I still had some tears in my eyes, I felt a little choked up from remembering my past, looking at Reed, I gave him a small smile, "I miss you. A lot."

Reed smiled at my words, "Can we cuddle when I get back, the three of us of course."

"We would really love that" I whispered.

We continued to talk for a few more minutes before I yawned and he insisted I get some sleep.

As I pushed the door open to my room, I quietly made my way to the bed, hearing movement from Colton, I tip toed over to the side to check on him. He was laying on his back with the wolf stuffed animal that Reed gave him in his grasp.

Needing to change, I shimmied out of my shorts, being left in my panties and I picked up a shirt I had found on the floor, putting it on, I realized it was Reed's from one of the nights he had stayed. It smelled like him.

Crawling into bed, I cuddled the collar of the shirt up taking in his scent, being lulled to sleep.

I was awoken by my phone ringing, shortly followed by a crashing sound coming from down the hall, the sound of feet on hardwood making their way towards me.

I grabbed Colton quickly and my phone running to the bathroom, locking it before I could hear the door handle to my bedroom start to turn.

16

Reed: Break-in

After having up the FaceTime call with Chloe, something told me I needed to go home. Walking down the hallway to my coach's room, I knocked twice.

Coach Benson opened the door, confused why I would be knocking at close to midnight.

"Collins you good?"

I nodded yes, "I need to head home now. I have a gut feeling that I need to get back."

I wasn't sure what or why I needed to get home, but I needed to be there.

"What's going on Collins?" Coach was trying to process what I was going on about.

"My girl and son are home. I just hung up with her, and well something feels off. I'm worried coach, it's not like a 'I'm worried she's breaking up with me' but more like a 'something bad is going to happen'. Coach I can't wait around, I need to get home" I pleaded.

"Alright, I'll book you the soonest flight, go get packed, let Matt know your leaving."

I thanked coach sprinting back to my room, before reaching my door, I knocked on Summer's.

Summer sleepily answered the door, "What Reed?" "I need your house key." I held my hand out.

"Why do you need my house key?" She put her hands on her hip, clearly mad I woke her.

"I'm heading home, Chloe seemed sad and I have a gut feeling something bad might happen. I need to get there, please can I have the key so I can get in."

Summer pondered my words before turning and walking into her room, shortly returning, handing me the key, "Make sure they are both okay please."

I nodded. Turning and heading into my room, grabbing my bags and walking back to coach's door. All flight details were squared away.

Getting out of the Uber at the airport I sprinted in, getting through security and finding my gate. I should be home by 4am.

I slept the entire flight home, feeling the need to be well rested.

Grabbing my luggage I made my way outside, my Uber pulling up and heading toward Chloe.

I kept checking my phone for any updated, phone calls or texts. Something was off.

As we turned down the street, I noticed flashing lights in front of the house, at least 4 cop cars spread out. My Uber driver got me as close as he could, letting me out.

Grabbing my bags I ran towards the house, dropping them as I got to my truck, going under the police tape, my heart was racing, "Chloe! Chloe! Colton!"

"Sir, Sir please calm down. You can't be here." A younger cop stood in front of me.

"You don't get it, that's my girl and my boy in there. I need to see them. Chloe!" I was panicking, this wasn't good.

A cop came out of the house, I caught a glimpse behind him, Chloe was holding Colton, both looked scared. Chloe turned towards the yard, seeing me. She bolted past the cop, running towards me, throwing her arm around my neck, immediately sobbing into my chest.

I held her tight, Colton reached out of her arm, wrapping his arms around my neck, "Dada".

"Hey love, dada's here. Ssshh, it's okay, I'm here. You're safe." I kissed the top of her head.

I looked at the cop who tried to stop me from entering, "Can you tell me what happened, and why my family is scared?"

The cop shook his head no, "I can't but let get the detective in charge."

I thanked him as he walked away into the house. "Chloe, baby. What happened?" I ran my hand down her head, trying to sooth her. Her sobbing had calmed down, she was breathing hard still.

"I woke up around 3 to my phone going off. I was so tired I thought maybe you were calling so I didn't look at the screen. when I answered-" she took a deep breathe, squeezing her eyes closed, "all I could hear was Heavy breathing, I keeping saying 'hello'-but there was no one responding."

She took another breather, trying to calm herself, "When I hung up, I heard a loud crashing noise from down the hallway and the sound of someone walking on the hardwood. I panicked and grabbed Colton and my phone, locking us in the bathroom. Reed I think it's my ex. I, I should have said something when I thought I saw him at your game last week. I think he's following me."

She took another shaky breathe, she placed her head back on my chest, sobs left her body.

"Shhh, baby I'm here. I had this bad feeling so I caught an early flight, I'm glad I'm here. I'm not leaving. I got you, I got both of you."

The detective quickly walked over, "I'm detective Brown, I'm sorry that you three are having to go through this. My detectives have checked the house thoroughly, from the looks of it, it looks like the person had entered through the second floor office window, we believe he entered and exited through the same window. The loud crash you heard was from them knocking items off the desk. Nothing seems out of place, we have been checking for microphones and cameras and so far nothing. I understand if you do not want to go back in, but it is clear and he is not in the home. I will also be sending detectives to your shop to make sure no one has been there and that there are no devices hidden as well."

I nodded my head, "Thank you for the update, do you know where he is or why he's here? Anything at all?"

The detective slightly frowned, "We don't know any of that. From what we can tell based on some broken sticks in the backyard and a few footprints, he came through the back, we think he hopped the fence. I have cops in the woods behind your fence and a few patrolling along neighboring roads and streets looking for anyone who seems out and about. I did make a few calls to the cop who handled your case in California, they said after you were admitted in the hospital, they had taken your ex into custody, but his lawyer got him off. After that they couldn't locate him."

Chloe stared at Colton's face, then back at mine before turning to look at the detective, "What do I do? I don't feel safe alone. He almost killed me once, and now I have my son. It would be different if it was just me, but it's not. What am I supposed to do?" She took a shaky breathe, leaning back into me.

"We are going to put a State wide warrant out for his arrest, we have sent off his picture and his demographics. I will have some more cops in this neighborhood and even around the arena for your safety Mr. Collins."

I was taken back that he knew who I was. But I was more happy to know that they were taking this seriously, "I could care less about my wellbeing, all I care about is these 2 and their roommate Summer when she returns."

"We will keep you updated on any news we find. I really am sorry Miss Murphy that you are living this all over again." The detective handed me his card and told me to call if I had any more questions or concerns.

Looking back down at Chloe, Colton had fallen asleep at some point, his head tucked under my chin and neck. "Baby, do you want to go back in to get some sleep? Or do you want to go back to my place?"

She grabbed my hand, I could feel her hands shaking, "Can we go to your house? I need to grab some things for Colt and I."

"Yea baby, let's go inside and I will help, let me throw my bags by the porch so they don't walk off."

Chloe quickly packed 2 bags, throwing a variety of clothes in both, throwing some Toys in another. I grabbed the bags in one hand while following her down the steps. The cops had left, so we locked up the house and walked over to the vehicles parked in the driveway.

"Reed, can we, um can we take your truck? We just need to put the car seat in yours, I think he has been following me, so he knows my car."

I smiled at her, throwing the bags in the bed of the truck, "Yeah baby, why don't you do that, let grab my bags. And then I'll be right back to help you."

She nodded her head, opening the back seat of her car, moving things around.

Before I knew it, I had a car seat in my backseat, a sight I never thought I would ever see. Pulling out of the driveway, I reached over and grabbed her hand. Pulling her hand up to my lips, "I love you."

She leaned her head against the head rest, turning to look at me, "Thank you, for coming home early."

"I mean it when I say, No one, and I mean no one, will touch my family. You two are my family." I kissed her hand again.

Chloe seemed to calm down with my words, "I need to call Summer. I know you and I are going to be moving soon, but I think she needs to as well."

I watched her pull the phone out and call, I listened to the story over, my heart breaking more. Hearing her choke up as she retold the horror, I felt her pain when she said she locked them in the bathroom. I looked in the rearview mirror, looking at the little mirror on the headrest that showed a sleeping Colton. If something happened to him or Chloe I think I would have lost it. I wouldn't survive.

After hanging up, Chloe looked at me, "Summer said that when she gets back, her and Matt will stop by the house to check on it and grab somethings and then she is staying at your guys house for a few days."

"There's no question to it now, I am buying a house in a gated communities with 24/7 security, and I can hire a body guard for when I am not around."

"Well, let's table all that for a later time." Chloe giggled, the sweetest sound I had heard all morning.

We got home a few minutes later, unloading the truck and getting Colton inside, "So, our guest room is complete shit. So Colton gets to have a sleep over."

Chloe picked up Colton from the carrier, "I would love a sleep over after the night I had."

I placed my hand on her lower back, bringing her in closer, leaning down placing a delicate kiss on her lips, "I've wanted to kiss you since I left you baby. Let's go to bed."

I picked up the bags, directing her to my room. After getting settled, I crawled into bed, placing Colton in the middle of us, my arm reaching over him and pulling Chloe as close as I could get her.

"Go to sleep love, I got you."

Chloe ran her hand through my hair, "Good night Reed."

I could hear the faint snores leaving her and Colton's mouths, knowing they could sleep allowed me to close my eyes and welcome sleep. The last thing on my mind before drifting off was the mere thought that if I ever see this bastard in person, he will die.

No one, and I mean no one touches my family.

17

Chloe: New Roommate?

I woke up the following morning to Colton laying against my side and Reed's arms draped over our bodies, keeping us pressed to his.

I moved the hair out of Colton's face, dragging a finger down his cheek; how could something so precious be in so much danger. I could feel the emotions bubbling up, I was trying to hold back the sobs, as I parted my lips, a deep shaky breathe exited. What if he had hurt me or worse, Colton? Reed would have been a wreck.

Reed's hand found itself along my cheek, carefully turning me to face to him, he looked tired, but awake. His hair was disheveled, which during a time like this I shouldn't be thinking how sexy he is.

His voice was groggy but raspy, it was pantie dropping good, "Baby, like I told you last night, he is not going to get close to you or Colton. Let's focus on happy things today and when Summer and Matt get home, then we will focus on this." He sealed his words with a small kiss to my lips.

Only this small kiss, left me wanting more. I snaked my hand along his neck, pulling him in, kissing him harder.

Reed pulled back slightly parting our connection, a pout graced my lips as he laughed, "Baby as much as I want to further that, maybe not right now, let me just hold you."

Having forgotten I had a Koala attachment this morning, my cheeks started flushing, I ran a hand down my face, "I'm sorry. I'm not used to him in my bed most mornings."

Reed let out a small laugh, taking my hand off my face, I noticed that his hair was getting longer, it was hanging over his ears, I reached up and ran my hands along his scalp, pushing some of the hair back.

Reed watched me study him, his hand tracing circles on my thigh.

My hand resumed moving through his hair, the circles on my thigh have stopped and have been replaced with his firm hand squeezing me lightly.

Colton started to stir, he rolled off my chest in between Reed and I, stretching his arms high above his head. He slowly opened his eyes to see me and Reed both smiling down at him.

His eyes focused on Reed, a smile spreading along his face, then he would turn to me and his smile would grow bigger. Almost like he couldn't tell who he was happiest to see.

"Buddy are you hungry?" I moved the hair out of his face.

The happiest sound of a baby giggles left his body, Reed placed his hand on Colton's stomach, moving his hand back and forth, "Oh no are you hungry buddy?" Reed laughed.

Colton started laughing harder at Reed, placing one hand on Reed's and the other at his mouth-his pacifier missing.

I shifted out of bed, searching under the covers and on the floor, I need to find this pacifier or nap time will be hell.

As I was on the floor, looking under the bed, more likely in a very unskillful yoga pose, the laughter got louder, before Reed's words startled me, "Love I don't know what you are searching for under there, but all my playboy magazines are in Florida."

I lifted my head and sat down on my knees looking back up at Reed who had Colton standing on the bed, his small hands perched on Reed's head, Reed's hand held the pacifier. "Where did you find that?"

Reed winked and looked back up at Colton, "I had it on my night stand. He spit it out middle of the night, very cold against my chest by the way. When he didn't search for it or wake up I placed it there." Reed gave Colton a raspberry on his stomach, enlightening us with another round of laughs, "Colton look how funny mommy looks down there."

Reed smiled wide, coaxing me back in bed, "You make me the happiest guy on this planet" placing a kiss to my lips.

Pulling back, I decided to stretch, walking over to look out his large windows. Across the street was a large park, towards the far end it had more trees, it looked like a beautiful place to take Colton to enjoy the weather. But maybe I'll wait till this whole stalking thing gets handled.

I must have zoned out, as I stood there my arms wrapped around my midsection, I felt both arms of Reed's snake alone mine, pulling me back against his chest. I could feel Reed peppering kisses along my head down along my cheek to my jaw.

"What's in your pretty head of yours love?" Pressing another kiss to my neck.

"Just that the park across the street would be a great place for Colton when the weather is good" I intertwined out hands together and placed them back on my stomach.

"When all this blows over and that creep is behind bars, we will do a whole outing together in that park."

I hummed in agreeance, enjoying having his body wrapped around mine. "What did you do with Colton?"

Reed and I both turned to find Colton on the floor of Reed's room holding 2 pucks in his hands, clapping them together. "Gave him those pucks from my game last night and I was forgotten about. I'm kinda hurt about it" he laughed, placing another kiss on my cheek.

We stayed there a few minutes longer watching Colton play in his own little world. "I should change him and then get him some breakfast." I unwillingly unraveled myself from Reed, leaning up to kiss him, "Thank you for coming to save us and for bringing us here."

Reed's hand found mine as I turned to walk to mine and Colton's bags, turning to face him his facial features were serious, "No one touches the two of you. Ever. I would quit my job, risk my life for the two of you."

Tears were filling up in my eyes, I quickly wiped them away, I let out a shaky breathe, before plastering a small smile on my face, "Well it's a good thing we have you then."

Reed smiled, letting go of my hand, "You get little man ready, I'll go start the coffee and breakfast."

I looked up from where I sat on the floor, Colton's clothes and diaper laid out next to me, I watched Reed exit the room, still shirtless and I was not complaining.

"Alright Colt, let's get changed and you can play with those pucks with Dada."

Colton smiled, going back to focusing on the pucks in his hands.

After getting ready for the day, Colton and I headed towards the kitchen for breakfast. I fished out the bottles and items for Colton's breakfast from the bag I placed on the counter last night.

Not long after, Reed had the dining room table set with everything we needed. I had just finished making Colton's bottle as we sat down to eat. I had Colton back on my lap as he laid in my arms holding his bottle while he let me eat.

Reed took a long sip of coffee before returning the cup back to the table, "After breakfast, let me take Colton, and why don't you go through your bags, unpack and make sure you have everything you need. This way when Summer and Matt head over, they can get anything you forgot."

I smiled at Reed, before turning to look back at Colton who was done with the bottle and was trying to climb into my pancake stack. I fed him a small bite, his eyes lighting up.

The rest of breakfast we just talked and laughed. Reed mentioned needing to call his coach, so he got up and headed to the kitchen.

I placed Colton on the ground after cleaning him up, grabbing my plate and coffee mug heading into the kitchen.

While Reed was on the phone with his coach telling him about last night, Colton was sitting on the floor with his pucks in hand and I started to load the dishwasher. Not sure about Reed but I was feeling very domesticated at this time.

As Reed hung up, he leaned against the counter, "We have home games the next 3 games, so I will be around for the next week. If we don't hear anything by Friday night, I'm not going on the road trip."

I turned in shock to face Reed, "You have to go Reed. That's your job and your team needs you."

Reed ran his hand through his hair, "Yes they need me, but I need to be here with you 2. Plus it was Coaches idea."

"Okay, I'll trust your call with this. You're on Colton duty while I try to unpack. I brought diapers down if he needs a new one-this should be good practice for you when we move in together" I patted his chest while smiling at him, throwing in a wink as I walked away from him. He thinks he can just pause his life for us, then fine, he can change dirty diapers.

The look on Reed's face was photo worthy, I don't think he has changed a dirty diaper, so I already know the pure panic he is going to have.

For the next hour I sorted through my clothes and Colton's, I filled up the two empty drawers that Reed had available and used up the remainder of the closet space. I had made a list of a few things I needed from Summer when she made it to the house. For starters I needed a crib for Colton, I could not continue to sleep in bed every night with him, I love him but that boy spreads out.

I called Summer, giving her the run down on my morning and the list of items that I needed. Coach had moved up their departure so they should be landing by 3pm instead of 5pm.

Hanging up the phone I wandered into the kitchen to grab some water, trying to be as quiet as possible, wanting to hear the boys playing or talking, call me nosey. Yet, I couldn't hear a single thing.

Grabbing my water, I ventured into the living room to see Reed asleep on the living room floor, Colton was laying across Reed's stomach trying to grab a toy on the other side of him. As Colton went to grab the toy he turned to look at Reed's face, smiling his toothy grin, the look in his eye told me that he was about to do something, so naturally I waited.

Colton turned his body to line up along Reed's chest, taking his hand he grabbed Reed's nose, the other hand resting on Reed's cheeks. Then before we knew it, that hand was removed and came back down on Reed's cheek, "Dada Dada". After hearing the smack I ran forward, placing my cup down and grabbing Colton.

Reed, well he bolted upright, causing me to start laughing.

"Colton, we don't hit." I had grabbed his hand, getting his attention to look at me.

Colton started to bobble his bottom lip, the move he makes before he cries, especially when the word 'No' is involved.

Reed who was now sitting upright, reached forward for my water taking a large sip, "Don't get mad at him, I fell asleep to that damn toy that plays music. That kid lulled me to sleep, I needed the wakeup call" he reached forward taking Colton and hugging him to his chest.

"You are both ridiculous" I laughed taking my cup back. "I talked to Summer, they land at 3 now. I sent her a list of things I need, well all but one but that's fine. Also, what do we have so I can cook dinner?"

Reed placed Colton between his legs, Colton's back pressed to Reed's chest. Reed grabbed the toy Colton wanted originally, handing it to him before looking up at me. "What item can she not get?"

I let out a breath, "A crib. He usually stays in the pack in play, but the pack in play is bulky and honestly it's hard on me reaching down to lay him on the mat, plus he needs an actual bed."

"Why don't we run to the store together, let's get some food to hold us over for a while and then let's just pick up a crib." Reed offered reaching back for the cup in my hand.

"Reed, I'm not going to go out and buy a crib. It's fine. Plus he and I can stay in the guest bedroom so we don't have to worry about less room in the bed. I will go with you to the grocery store, but can we not be out long. I don't like the idea of being in public anymore."

Reed's hand came forward, tilting my chin to make my eyes meet his, "Umm not allowed. You have officially unpacked in my room, now our room, you are not sleeping away from me. There will be no guest room nonsense. Let's just curbside pickup. You pick it out I'll order it, we pull up, they hand it to us we move on. Same for groceries."

Have I mentioned how I can't win with this man. "Reed I can't make you pay for that. It's expensive."

"Chloe, you're lucky your car isn't here or I would be ordering another car seat so we don't have to keep moving this one back and forth, plus we will have to buy one anyways when get the new house." Reed's thumb stroked my cheek, my body naturally leaning into his palm.

"You are ridiculous, but fine. We need something, because I can't continue sleeping as his personal pillow" I laughed, leaning forward to peck his lips.

Standing up, I ran my hand through his hair, giving him some scalp scratches that I know he loves, "We are really lucky to have you."

An hour later, the crib had been purchased online, Colton was strapped in the car seat and we were off to the store. We spent more time going back and forth on what crib to order because I wanted the basic one and Reed wanted to more fancy one. I can sadly say that I lost that battle and Colton's new favorite person if it isn't already is Reed.

Reed helped the worker place the crib's box in the bed of the truck and then we were headed to the grocery store to once again, sit and wait for the items to come out. I'm not against this, but I used to love walking the aisles of the store, it was calming. Now I can't even do that.

By the time we got back to the house it was close to 2:30 in the afternoon. Colton hardly napped in the car so he definitely needed one, I needed to start dinner and Reed was probably going to be building a crib.

We got the groceries into the house, placing the bags on the counter. Reed ran outside and grabbed the box with the crib, maneuvering his way back into the house.

"I'm going to go place this in our room, and I'll come grab Colt so he can help build it or sleep. Is that fine?"

I looked up from rifling through the bags, "You sure you want him? Nap time is fussy time."

Reed smiled, "I want to do it all, good practice right?" He started rubbing the back of his neck, a sign he is nervous, I mean he should be he's going to be living with a mini terror and myself here on out.

"I think that's great Babe. Go put the box upstairs and I'll make his bottle and then I'll bring both of them up." I smiled at him, seeing the nervousness leaving his body.

He nodded his head, before grabbing the box and running upstairs, the best he could.

With the bottle made, I grabbed Colton placing him on my hip. Before leaving the kitchen, I went back and grabbed a cold beer out of the fridge, Reed probably needs this if he's building a crib with crappy instructions.

As I entered the room, Reed had all the small pieces up high on the dresser and everything else laid out. "I brought you a beer, and do you want me to feed him or you?"

Reed grabbed the beer, placing it on the dresser, "Nope, I got him you can go cook your little heart out my dear. Us men, we got his handled, right buddy?" Colton reached forward for him, grabbing the bottle out of my hand on the way.

All I can think of is, good luck to the both of them. When I see them next, I bet both will have shed tears.

Back to the kitchen I go, my happy place. I started pulling out the ingredients for dinner. I decided on making Chicken Parmesan with a Cobb salad and garlic bread.

Ever since Reed took me to Francesca and Lorenzo's restaurant, I can't get enough Italian food.

Summer and Matt had landed and were heading to the house to grab some things and scope out the house to see if anyone got back in. Summer offered to drive my car over since it was still there and they were in her car.

Around 4pm, Summer and Matt had entered the house, arms loaded with bags, dropping them by the stairs. "Chloe, please tell me we have beer in the fridge?" Matt asked dragging himself into the kitchen.

"I already had one out for you. Thanks for grabbing my stuff" I said while handing him the beer.

"Thanks. And no problem, you okay? Where's Colton and Reed?" Matt was looking around, almost like he was afraid I was here all alone.

"Well you might need to go check on them. I left Reed about 30 minutes ago in his room building a crib he had to buy for Colton. Colton should still be asleep, but I wouldn't be shocked if both are awake playing games or both asleep" I laughed turning back to the garlic spread I had been making for the bread.

Summer passed him on the stairs before entering the kitchen, immediately grabbing me into a hug. "I am so sorry I wasn't here. Are you good? He didn't touch you or anything right?" She held my shoulders, looking into my eyes trying to get a read on me.

"We're all good. I got us in the bathroom and locked the door and called the cops, they showed up not long after. He was in the house, he climbed in through your upstairs office window. I was so scared Summer. Now I've put all of you at risk" I started sobbing, falling into her arms.

"You didn't put us at risk. We wouldn't let you go through this alone anyways. Even if you were in California, my ass would have been on the next plane." She held me while I let the last of my tears out, quickly wiping them from under my eyes.

After we held each other a few minutes longer we went back to cooking dinner, Summer jumped right in, helping me prep and cook the meal. Not long after the chicken was placed in the oven, Reed and Matt came down stairs, Reed holding the baby monitor in his hand, a large smile on his face.

"Little man is passed out in his new crib, I feel so accomplished." He grabbed me by the hips pulling me in for a heated kiss.

I pulled back after a few seconds, "I am so proud of you for getting that built. What a man you are now" I giggled, kissing his cheek.

"Oh and look, I figured out how to work your monitor thing." He Smiled showing me the screen with a sleeping Colton, holding his giraffe.

"Thank you" I whispered.

Reed held me back, his hand gently squeezing my hip, "Anything you need baby, you have it" he said kissing the top of my head.

Matt stood by the stove looking nervous, "Can we eat or do we have to wait?"

Summer turned to look at Matt, "Since when do you ask?"

Matt's cheeks blushed, turning back around he started piling his plate.

18

Chloe: House Hunting

The next two days seemed to fly by between looking at the listings that Reed's Realtor friend sent over to discussing plans for Summer and Matts wedding.

"Can we aim for this summer, like May or June?" Matt asked pouring another cup of coffee.

Summer abruptly looked over to Matt, taking her eyes away from her meticulous planned Pinterest board on her computer, "Married like in 6 months from now? Of this year?"

Matt took a heavy sip of coffee staring at Summer with a flick of happiness spread across his face, "Duh. Like this coming year."

Summer looked back over at me before looking back at Matt, "That gives us no time to plan, we need a venue, caterer, photographer, dresses, tuxes-"

Matt interrupted Summer's rant by placing both hands on her shoulder and leaning down, "Summer, I love you and I know you want the wedding of your dreams, but I can't spend another damn moment not being your husband. Why don't we have a small ceremony with our parents and these 3 weirdos and then you can plan the big show without stress." Leaving a kiss on her temple.

"You want to just elope and then have a big ceremony later?"

"If you are good with that love, but I will do anything you want to do. I just love you to damn much."

Summer looked back at her computer before turning to look at Matt, "Okay, I can do that. We can plan something small and intimate and then I can go crazy with the big wedding reception. I like this idea."

Matt leaned down kissing Summer, while I took that as my cue to advert my eyes or even leave the room.

Talk about a saving grace, Reed and Colton sauntered into the dining room area, "Good news, but first stop making babies while I have good news." Reed shielded Colton's eyes.

Matt groaned in an annoyed way lifting his head to meet Reed's gaze, "Let me kiss my fiancé you douche."

Reed laughed moving to stand behind me, removing his hand from Colton's eyes, who was giggling the entire time, "As I was saying. The Realtor called, he made us an appointment for tomorrow morning at 9:30. He lined us up 4 houses. So we can go before I need to be at the arena for the game at 7."

I turned to face him, giving him a large grin, "Ooh which 4 houses do we get to see?"

Reed ran a hand through my hair, "I haven't seen the listing for 2 of them, he said they came up on the listings recently, but the other two were on our list."

Before I could answer Matt popped into the conversation, "So how soon can you move in once you buy? I'm thinking a nice office would look great in your room."

Summer turned and smacked Matt's chest, "Ignore him, we are excited for you guys to start this new chapter in your lives."

Smiling back at Summer, I am really going to miss our late night chats and our wine nights when we had gotten them, "Alright boys, isn't there a sports game on you need to watch, we have some elopement planning to attend to."

Reed leaned down kissing me, running his thumb over my cheek, "Yes ma'am. We will get out of your way, let me grab his nap time bottle and I'll be gone."

Once Reed grabbed the bottle he walked past Matt, nudging him to walk into the living room to leave Summer and I to the big decisions.

Summer scrolled through her Pinterest board looking for color inspiration while I looked at my laptop trying to find venues in our area, "So, what do you think will come first, an engagement ring for your finger or baby #2?"

I stopped scrolling, brining my eyes to meet her gaze, she had a smirk on her face and her eyebrow raised, "Umm, what?'

"Don't play dumb, you two are endgame. You think he will propose soon or knock you up?"

Luckily I wasn't drinking anything or eating anything because I think I would have either choked to death or spewed liquid across the table, "I'm going to say hopefully a ring. I would love a baby but I do not need 2 under 2 anytime soon. Plus we haven't even moved in together."

I went back to my screen, absentminded scrolling not even reading the venues description. I hadn't thought about marriage or another baby, well I have, but I haven't hyper focused on them. Now I will, thanks Summer.

"Didn't mean to make this uncomfortable, it's just that a man loves you and Colton. House is a good step, pretend I didn't say anything."

I let out a sigh of air and cradled my head in my hands covering my eyes with the palms of my hands, "No your fine. I just haven't really spent much time thinking of those things, especially lately. Honestly if I had to choose, I don't think I could, either sounds fine to me."

Summer gave me a soft smile, "Alright ignore what I said, what venues did you find for May or June?"

Just like that we were back on the train of wedding planning and that lasted the remainder of the day. Good news is that the boys kept Colton occupied and we figured out the much needed details for the impromptu elopement.

The following morning Reed and I had Colton in the truck and headed to the 1st house on the tour. Pulling up to a large gated community, the houses were larger than any house I had seen, "Reed, these houses are gigantic, I don't think we need something this big."

Reed parked the truck in front of a large home that had a large front porch and swing attached. The garage was large enough to house 6 cars and from what I could tell, I was going to hate cleaning this home.

Reed smiled after shutting the truck off, "We don't need anything this big right now. Let's just keep an open mind, sound good?"

I nodded in agreeance before exiting the vehicle while Reed got Colton out of his car seat. We spent the next 30 minutes touring the home which should have been classified as a museum. The kitchen was gorgeous, large open concept, stainless steel appliances, a wine fridge, in cabinet ice maker and even a large island and eating bar. Still too much for me.

Reed eyed me as I wandered around the kitchen taking it in, "Lay it on me. Is it a Yay or a Nay?"

I met his gaze, taking a second to collect my thoughts, "I love the kitchen, this is the kitchen of my dreams but we don't need 8 bedrooms and 10 bathrooms or even a 6 car garage."

Reed looked over at the Realtor, "What she says goes, we don't need anything else this big."

The realtor nodded, "Ill scratch house number 2 off, it has a similar layout. House number 3 is in a different gated community, a little smaller of a house but still very promising."

With that we loaded up and drove the 10 minutes to house number 3.

Pulling up, I was met with a beautiful, newer built farm house with a dark brown trim. The front door was a double door with the most beautiful stained glass patterns. The garage was normal sized and the front yard had the most beautiful raised garden beds and a walk way around the house. There was a smaller tree in the front yard that seemed to provide decent shade-or would in the summer months. Before we even got to the front door, something was telling me that this was our home.

I was right, the kitchen had all stainless steel appliances, a eating bar, island, 2 large sunken in sinks and granite counter tops. The oven and stove were industrial and there was a window over the sink that faced the back yard.

It was perfect.

The home was modest compared to what we had previously seen, it was 4 bedroom 5 bathroom and a space for an in home office. The master bedroom had its own master bath with a shower, his/her sinks, vanity and a jacuzzi tub. The walk in closet was glorious and perfect for Reed and myself.

As I walked to the sliding glass door that overlooked the large backyard, which had a pool and hot tub, Reed walked up next to me kissing my temple, "Well, what do you think?"

I grabbed Reed's hand in mine, turning to look at him with Colton laying against his chest, "I think we're home."

Reed squeezed my hand, "Good because the moment we pulled up I saw your eyes light up and I immediately put an offer in. We should find out by Friday."

My mouth hung open in shock, "You already put an offer in?"

Reed laughed, "Yeah, cash, definitely an offer they can't refuse. Plus the Realtor knows that they are fans of the team so he's slipping that bit in when he calls them."

I was shocked but also pleased, "We're buying a house."

Reed leaned down claiming my lips with his, "we're buying a house."

It was hard to leave the home, but knowing that there was a high chance that I would be returning back shortly, I willingly left.

Reed left at 4pm for the game, I decided that Colton and I were staying home tonight since we still hadn't gotten word from the detective and I wasn't wanting to go out in public by myself with my toddler.

Reed had been adamant about taking us with him, but having to be there 3 hours earlier was not something Colton was feeling-neither was I.

Summer and Matt had already left, so it left Colton and I to our own devices until later that night.

I had decided to cook dinner rather than order in due to the fact I was weary of strangers bringing my food now.

By 7pm, Colton and I were perched on the couch with the game on, both snacking on our version of dinner. For me it was left over spaghetti and for Colton it was a yogurt pouch and a pack of blueberries-we are really winning tonight.

The game had been a tough game, we were playing Vancouver and they were putting up a fight. By the start of the 3rd period we were tried 1-1. Luckily Reed had avoided what would have been a nasty hit and has remained out of the sin bin.

Matt on the other hand has been in the sin bin twice for minor penalties.

With a 1:50 left in the 3rd period, one of our defensemen sent the puck flying down the ice into the opponent's empty goal, giving us a

2-1 lead. At the same time the buzzer went off, there was a knock at our front door.

My heart dropped, who is knocking at 9pm at night and why my house? Colton had fallen asleep on the couch wearing his Collins Jersey, unfazed that his mother was not on the verge of sobbing thinking this is the end.

I slowly raised to my feet, tiptoeing to the front door, peaking through the peep hole. Luckily I didn't see a person but a note was slid under the welcome mat. I knew better than to venture out of the door, for all I know my ex was hiding around the corner.

I quickly walked back to the couch, picking up Colton and grabbing a kitchen knife before hurrying to Reed's bedroom and locking the door.

I grabbed my phone and called Summer, I was praying she had her phone.

With a click I heard the roaring of the crowd, "Chloe what's up, you okay?"

I couldn't hold the sob back, "No." "Chloe, what's going on?"

I took a deep breathe, "Someone knocked on the door a few minutes ago and there's a note under the welcome mat. I'm afraid, what if he's here, what if he found us?"

I could hear Summer yelling at people to move out of her way, "Where are you Chloe? I'm coming home."

"I'm-I'm in Reed's room with the door locked, I grabbed a large kitchen knife and I have Colton. Summer be careful, what if he's here when you get home?"

"Fine, I'm running to the locker room." I could hear breathing hard before she started yelling, "Reed! Matt! Chloe stay on the line, I'm going to grab them and let them know what's happened, don't hang up."

I choked out a sob while I held a pillow to my chest, "Okay."

I could hear her relaying to the guys what had happened, from what I could tell Reed had called the detective in charge of my case and he was meeting them here.

After staying on the phone with Summer the entire length of their drive, I was exhausted from the crying.

"Chloe, we're pulling up. The detective is outside, looks like he found the note. I'm going to hang-up and come inside, I'll knock 3 times okay."

I sighed, "Okay."

Hanging up the phone I ran a hand through my hair before cradling my head in my hands. There were 3 knocks to the bedroom door and I could hear Summer call my name.

I bolted off the bed opening the door letting her in, immediately engulfing one another in each other's arms.

Summer stayed with me until a disheveled Reed ran into the room pulling me into his arms, placing kissing around my face, "Fuck baby I'm sorry I wasn't here. Are you okay? How's Colton."

I took a deep breathe, reaching up to place my hands on either side of his face, "I'm fine, Colton's fine. Just shook up. What did the note say?"

Reed ran a hand through his hair, Summer met my gaze before getting up and exiting the room. "Umm, shit. It was him. Pretty much the note said he was back and wanted back what was his."

I felt speechless or that the air left my body, "Wants what is his? What the fuck?"

Reed pulled me into his arms, "He isn't going to touch you or Colton. He can't have what isn't his, last I checked he's a fucking criminal and sperm donor."

I took a large breathe, burying my head into his chest, "He was closeagain Reed."

Reed ran his hand through my hair to calm me but to also calm himself, "I know love. Good news is the directive talked to the neighbor who has security cameras and he thinks he caught his license plate, so they are running it now and they put a BOLO out of it."

I nodded my head, kissing his chest, "Did we win?"

Reed laughed kissing the crown of my neck, "Yea baby we won. Let's get you to bed."

I couldn't sleep, but that was expected, I also put Colton in bed between us so I knew he wouldn't vanish. I need this nightmare over with.

19

Chloe: Packing

The following two weeks passed by slower than a snail stuck in molasses. We were a week from Christmas and the only good news I had received was that our offer on the house was approved and we could move in this week.

Since the note was left that night I was home alone, Summer had taken time off work to stay home when the boys had their away games. Reed wanted to stay back and protect us, but I needed him to play hockey.

Reed's parents were called shortly after the incident as well as when we heard about the approval on the house, so they showed up yesterday to help me pack while also watching Colton. So even if Reed is gone, I feel safe with family around me.

I made a run to the shop yesterday morning but was accompanied by Summer, since I had finally opened I had decided to take on clients via appointments and only work when I felt safe to do so. Hopefully once this stalking crap passes I can open for longer hours.

Since that night when the note was left, nothing had happened further. The detective called saying that they found the car abandoned but they were able to lift fingerprints off the steering wheel. Confirming my worries that it was forsake James, my psycho ex.

I don't have many regrets in life, but without question he is number 1 on the regret list; although he gave me Colton.

This morning the 4 of us adults and Colton ventured to the old house to start boxing and packing items. Luckily most of my stuff was still boxed so that made it easier to move.

For the time being the boys garage gym was housing all of our items-a problem they can fix when they get home.

Dave was sitting in the living room, surprisingly on the floor pushing race cars around the carpet with Colton, while making car noises. Off and on you can catch Colton saying "no papa" or "Vroom Vroom."

Susan was being a doll and helping summer sift through the kitchen utensils and making sure whatever Summer was moving in there weren't duplicates, giving me and Reed free kitchen things. Win-win for us.

I wasn't sure how long Dave and Susan were staying for, with Christmas next week I was hoping they would stick around but I wasn't aware of their traditions. I haven't celebrated Christmas since I was 17 before my parents had died.

While I was labeling boxes in the garage I felt my phone vibrating in my pocket, a phone call for sure. Seeing our Halloween family picture on display I knew it was Reed, "Hello Love."

Let me tell you I was not prepared to find a shirtless, sweaty, messy haired Reed on the other end of this FaceTime, pretty sure I was drooling, "Hi handsome. Aren't you a sight to see."

Reed ran a hand through his hair flexing the muscles in his arms, "You're a vision of beauty baby, what you doing?"

A vision of beauty my ass, my hair was every way to Sunday, I had 2 day old mascara on, I was wearing one of Reed's long sleeve shirts and a pair if Christmas pajama pants. This man was blind.

Looking back up at my screen after assessing the mess I am I let out a laugh, "Honey I think you need to get your eyes checked when you get home. There isn't anything of beauty here."

Reed's smile dropped, "Babe you are beautiful, do you not believe me?"

Biting my lower lip and releasing it, "Not when I look like this. I've been moving all day, pretty sure I look homeless."

Reed ran a hand down his face, "Chloe listen to me and listen good" he growled. "You are beautiful, it doesn't matter what you're wearing or what makeup you have on, you could smell and I wouldn't care. You are the most beautiful person I know, please believe me."

"Okay, I believe you; I might disagree occasionally but I believe you. What are you doing?" I maneuvered my phone to stand up on a box while I moved to the next one.

"Just finished a killer workout, now I'm undressing you with my eyes-nice ass by the way" Reed wiggled his eyebrows.

"Reed Michael Collins, I know I raised you better than that" Susan berated her son. I guess I should have given him a warning that his mom had walked in with coffee for me.

I couldn't help but laugh watching the color drain from his face, "I'm sorry honey, I would have warned you she was here, but I didn't think you would have said that."

"Sorry mom, sorry Chloe. I promise to behave better." Reed hung his head down shaking it back and forth.

Susan shook her head hiding her laugh while handing me a coffee mug, "I'll leave you two, by the way Dave's gonna make dinner no idea what that will entail. Good luck tonight son."

"Thanks mom." Reed huffed. "Really Chloe, a heads up?"

I giggled holding the mug to my lips, "I didn't think you would go all naughty on me like that."

Another growl left Reed's mouth, "Don't say 'naughty' like that baby girl. I can't do anything about it and you're killing me."

I sat down in front of the box, crossing my legs, "Okay change of subject then, what day do we want to move in? I would like to be in by Christmas if that's okay."

Reed's smile grew, "Baby the keys are on the dresser, you can move in tomorrow, but I ask that you wait till I get home. How about Saturday? I won't have practice or a game and we can get settled."

Sipping my coffee, enjoying the taste, I locked eyes with Reed, "I'm happy baby, like really happy. I'm so excited even with the crap we are dealing with."

"I'm happy that your happy love. Also, are you cool if Mom and Dad stay through Christmas?"

"Yea, I was hoping they would stay. Colton hasn't really had a Christmas so this will be perfect, maybe your mom can help me prepare dinner in the new house." I loved the idea of cooking with Susan and learning different family recipes that I could use in the future.

"This will be the best Christmas ever I can promise you that. Also, I need to go, I need to get my shoulder taped up, I'll call tonight okay? I love you"

"I love you to Reed, good luck."

After hanging up, I stood up grabbing my phone and cup of coffee when I started to feel dizzy. Leaning against stacked boxes, I composed myself and caught my bearings before heading inside. Not sure what the fuck that was, maybe I need to eat and get some water. Or a nap. A nap sounds great.

20

Reed: Christmas in the New Home

Coming home had never felt so promising as it does now. My mom, and Summer were in the kitchen moving boxes while Matt and my Dad were taking boxes labeled 'bedroom' or 'nursery' to their rightful places.

Chloe was moving the box holding our brand new Christmas tree and the bags upon bags of Christmas items into the living room to be added up later.

I was trying to coax a fussy Colton to take a nap, but sadly moving day was way too exciting.

Thankfully Christmas isn't until Tuesday so this gives us 2 full days to really unpack and decorate.

"Come on little man, take a nap for dada so he can help mama unpack us, then we can stay up all night."

Chloe snorted trying to hide her laugh, "That's a loaded promise, I am not a part of that deal."

My dad came around the corner placing a box labeled, 'Living room' in very sloppy hand writing displayed on the side. "Give him over Reed, I need a break from boxes."

I willingly handed Colton over giving my arms a shake since they had been holding him for so long, "Thanks dad. Maybe you will have a better chance with him."

My dad laughed "He must take after you regardless if he has your blood. You were a pain to get down for a nap at this age."

Chloe came up wrapping her arms around mine leaning her head on my shoulder, "I'd rather he take after Reed than me then, I hardly slept through the night until I was 3. Talk about a tiny terror."

I leaned down kissing her head, "Not sure how he would take after me."

Chloe laid her hand on my chest, looking at Colton and looking back at me, her eyes soft holding so much love and compassion, "You know he isn't just my boy, I like to think he's also yours if you are okay with that."

I leaned forward claiming her lips, "I like that, he's our boy."

My heart grew I felt like the Grinch, I knew I had a heart but hearing her clarify that she sees him as my son warmed my body. He is my son damn it, since the day I first met him, there was a pull that brought us together.

By 5pm boxes were in different parts of the house, most of the kitchen was unpacked, bedding was on our master bed and the guest bed, the nursery was somewhat unpacked, we did end up storing the crib and going with a toddler bed since Colton had been wanting to start climbing over it.

I noticed throughout the day when Chloe would pause and lean against the counter or couch almost like catching her breathe, it seemed off but I figured she had been running a mile a minute, but it was something that worried me; something I'll ask about once we go to bed.

Mom and Dad went out to retrieve dinner and other food to fill the fridge, I made sure to send mom with my credit card telling her to buy whatever they thought we needed.

Chloe and Summer were decorating the kitchen with their Christmas items while Matt and I attempted to put the tree up-I'm making a reminder to buy an already assembled one next year or a real one.

Colton was playing in the now empty tree box, just laughing his little heart out.

I could hear the girls giggling in the kitchen, faint Christmas music was playing in the background, this is something I never imagined- me settling down.

If I ever need a resumé I am writing 'professional Christmas tree assembler' on the first line. Not only did this shit piss me off but holy fuck I never want to do that again.

Mom and dad returned with a carload of groceries and pizza for dinner; shortly after eating, Summer and Matt left to return home. Matt and I have a game tomorrow night so best to be rested before being pushed into the boards by Florida tomorrow.

My parents retreated to the guest bedroom while Chloe had put Colton down in his new room. Leaning against the door frame I was watching as she held him in her arms whispering sweet words to him and placing soft kisses on his head.

I loved seeing her in mom mode, there was something sexy about it but also something primal in me that couldn't wait to have more kids with her.

She placed him in the bed when I noticed her catching herself against the side. Her head hung low as I could hear her erratic breathing, her weight resting on her arms.

Rushing forward I pulled her into my arms while I placed her on my lap as I sat in the glider, "Baby what's wrong? You've been doing this all day, talk to me."

Chloe breathed out, resting her head on my chest, "I've been getting dizzy for a few days now. I thought it was stress, or moving, or my ex coming back, hell I even increased water and food intake and it hasn't let up."

Stroking my hand over her hair, kissing her temple, "Why didn't you tell me when you started feeling this way? Do you feel sick?"

I could feel her breathe through my t-shirt, and her hands holding mine, "I feel fine none the less, I think I'm just stressed and the lack of sleep. I'm good now, let's go to bed."

She tried to escape my grip but I stood up holding her in my arms, "You aren't walking down the hall love, not when you're dizzy."

"Reed I'm fine now. I just need sleep, if it gets worse I'll tell you, I promise." She huffed.

I refused to let her get up to even change, placing her in the middle of our new Cali King bed, giving her my best 'don't you move' glare while I grabbed her one of my t- shirts to sleep in. "Here love, get changed."

Chloe let out a frustrated groan, "Reed I need to do my routine like wash my face."

"Fine, go wash your face and do your routine but I swear the moment I see you getting pale and weak, I'm grabbing you and getting you to the car and taking you to the ER." I threatened. I hated seeing her not feeling her best and not knowing why she was dizzy was killing me.

Chloe carefully emerged off the bed retreating into the bathroom where she spent the next 10 minutes going through her routine before heading towards me.

"Look I'm good as new, nothing bad happened as promised." She smirked.

As she got in bed I pulled her to my chest, "If it gets worse, we're see a doctor. I don't care if its 1am, we're going. I love you and worry about you."

Chloe hummed in response, nuzzling her head into my neck, "I know baby, I'll be honest about it I promise. Now can we go to sleep?" she lazily kissed my neck.

I slept like champ, having a brand new bed with my girl in my arms, in our new home was mind blowing. Walking in to see all my clothes with her clothes and our shower with both his/her items was fucking earth shattering in a good way.

By the time I had made it to the kitchen my mom had pancakes on the counter while Chloe fed Colton at the dining room table. Dad was pouring coffee and putting juice in Colton's bottle before scurrying back to the table.

Kissing my mom on her temple and grabbing coffee I headed toward the table, stealing a bite of pancake from Chloe, "You know there are more than what's on my plate right?"

I smiled down on her kissing her forehead, "I know but I gotta run. Since the games at 2 I gotta get there soon. You guys all coming?"

My dad nodded yes while taking a bite of pancake while Chloe tried wiping the syrup off Colton's face, "Yes, we will be there, I think we are leaving at noon so we can be there early."

151

Taking another sip, I ran my hands through Colton's hair, "What do you think little man, should I wear our matching suit again or go with the dark green one?"

Colton clapped his hands together babbling his version of a conversation.

"Alright green one it is, good choice bud." Leaning down I kissed his forehead before running back up to get ready to head to the arena.

Well, we lost, shit happens but it's over with and done. I got my ass chewed after taking a 5 min penalty and being involved in 2 fights. The only thing calming me is that Chloe is currently straddling my back giving me her version of a deep tissue massage.

"Chloe" I growled

I could hear her hum in response, "Yes?"

"2 things. One, have you gotten dizzy today and two if no then I'm about to spin this massage into an early Christmas gift for you."

Chloe let out a sweet laugh. "I'm fine Reed I think it was the stress and packing. And how are you giving me an early Christmas gift?"

Without warning I flipped on my back making her wobble around my legs. Leaning up I grabbed the back of her neck plunging my tongue into her mouth, bring my other hand to her hip, before reaching under her shirt assaulting her nipples.

Chloe let out a seductive moan as I pinched her nipples and squeezed her tits. Removing my hand from her neck I flipped her over so I was on top, "Your early Christmas gift is a night of orgasms and the promise of not walking straight for days."

Chloe's eyes fueled alive with desire, taking her hands she shed her shirt throwing it across the room before attacking my neck with her pouty lips.

With only a pair of panties and my boxers between us, she could feel my cock pressing against her and I could already feel how wet she was, "Be quiet baby we don't want the house to wake up."

She let another moan out of her mouth, eyes closed as I rocked my hips into her. Leaning back I hooked my fingers into the top of her panties, removing them in a swift moment leaving her bare. Eyeing her bare body caused my cock to twitch in anticipation. Keeping eye contact, she bit the bottom of her lip as I stepped out of my boxers, grabbing my length in my hand, giving it a few strokes.

I grabbed her legs bringing her towards me, taking her lips with my mine, "Flip on all 4's baby and be quiet."

Her chest raised with anticipation as she flipped, her ass sticking straight up for my view.

Grabbing her I squeezed her ass before leaning down and biting one of her plump cheeks, eliciting a sexy whimper leave her mouth, "Be a good girl and say quiet."

She pressed her face into the comforter as I leaned down and licked her sweet pussy from behind, taking my tongue and fucking her sweet folds until I could tell she was close. Pulling the folds into my lips and biting down as I pulled back, her hips rocking with my movement needing more, "Tell me what you need baby."

Chloe moaned, "You, Reed I need you."

I leaned back in taking hold of her hips as I continued tongue fucking her sweet cunt burying my face into her folds.

"Reed I'm close."

I pulled her in more, sucking on her until I felt her body release and start to shake. Lapping up her sweet juices, nothing tasted better. Pulling back I took another bite into her other ass cheek, while rubbing the other one.

Stroking my dick with one hand, "You taste so good, I could eat you for every meal. But not tonight I'm going to bury my cock into you that you won't know your name. I want to feel you milk me baby."

"Fuck me Reed. Fill me up, I need you" she begged.

Without warning I push my cock into her feeling her body grip me so tight.

I continued my pace, increasing my thrusts, holding tight to her hips.

Reaching forward I grabbed her by the hair pulling her gently back against me giving me access to kiss her neck and whisper into her ear, my other hand finding her clit and rubbing back and forth.

Her breathing was more like panting, her eyes closed as her hands came up around my neck, holding the two of us in place.

"Fuck Chloe I'm close" I panted.

"I am too, cum with me Reed." She breathed.

I bite down on her shoulder as I felt her shutter against me, her pussy milking my own release, filling her up.

Both of us coming down from our highs, I released Chloe, pulling out of her, leaving a chaste kiss at the base of her neck, "Holy Fuck baby, you're amazing. I love you."

Chloe rolled onto her back, her blonde hair fanning around her face, her cheeks flushed and her lips parted, "I love doing that with you. Love you too baby. Let's get some sleep now."

Shortly after cleaning up, we both climbed into bed, arms finding each other and legs intertwining. Peaking at the time it read 12:34 am, "Merry Christmas Baby" I breathed out kissing her head.

"Merry Christmas Reed."

And a very Merry Christmas it was about to be.

Sleep, was all I needed and wanted but there was a small terror named Colton who had decided that 6:30am was the best time to wake up for Christmas. Opening my eyes, I was met with a pair of sleepy, yet awake eyes focused on me; his blonde hair disheveled and a pacifier in his mouth. Reaching out with one hand towards Colton, he walked closer, taking his pacifier out, "Dadda" he giggled.

As he got closer I scooped him into bed placing him in the middle. It was then that I noticed that Chloe wasn't in bed, which means she's either getting ready for the day or in the kitchen.

"Merry Christmas buddy" I kissed his head as he sat up playing with the comforter.

Watching Colton was one of my new favorite things, he was so into everything around him and watching the amazement in his eyes fueled me to always be great for him and appreciate every moment.

While watching him there was a knock at the door, my dad walking in with the most ridiculous Christmas pajamas on and a Santa hat, "Get your butt up and let's get started with gifts. The girls are already in the living room and Matt and Summer just pulled up."

Running my hand down my face letting out a groan, "Coming. Let me change into what I can assume are matching pajamas that Chloe got us and I'll be down with Colton."

Dad nodded giving me a large smile before heading back down.

I have never loved Chloe more, the matching pajamas are actually comfy and not ridiculous like dads, red plaid pants and long sleeve black Henley, my kinda look, matched with Christmas slippers. The best part is Colton and Chloe match me while mom is decked out in an ugly Christmas sweater.

The 7 of us ate breakfast together before handing out the gifts under the tree.

Colton had made out like a bandit between us, his new set of grandparents and his aunt and uncle, this kid was set for any game, event and activity you can think of. Which I need to make a mental note to get Matt back because apparently Colton's at the right age for a fucking drum set, and not shockingly, the kid fucking loves it.

Chloe had gotten me some new ties for games as well as a new watch since mine broke.

I had gotten Chloe some St. Louis sweaters, a diamond tennis bracelet and a pair of the red bottom heels she has been dying to get her hands on.

Summer and Matt made eye contact before leaning forward and handing Chloe and I a box, "This is for the two of you."

Chloe leaned into me more helping me unwrap it before opening it and pulling out 2 shirts. One of them read, 'Best Aunt Ever', and the other read, 'Best Uncle Ever.' Chloe and I both took the moment to process what this meant, Chloe beating me to saying anything, "You're? You're pregnant!"

Launching off of me she tackled Summer into a hug, rocking back and forth.

"Holy crap Matt, you're going to be a dad" I laughed, getting up to pull him into a much less aggressive hug.

Matt laughed, "I know, I'm freaking excited. We can do this dad thing together."

Chloe pushed us aside while she pulled Matt into a hug congratulating him, while I turned and did the same for Summer.

"Holy shit guys. How far along are you?" Chloe asked sitting back down next to me.

"6 weeks, I found out after we came back from the cabin. I guess when Matt was begging for kids, he should have been asking for forgiveness instead of permission" she laughed.

"Oh this is so exciting, Dave aren't you excited? More babies to love" my mom gushed.

The rest of the day passed, Colton played with all his new toys while we lounged and ate. First Christmas as a family man and I wouldn't trade it for anything else.

Kissing the top of Chloe's head, I leaned down till my nose graced the top of her ear, "Thank you for giving me this baby."

Chloe looked up, kissing my jaw, "I should be thanking you for giving me this. Before you, Colton and I weren't this happy."

Placing my hand on the back of her head, I guided my face down, capturing her lips with mine, "Love you."

21

Reed: This Fucker

T he time between Christmas and New Year's was grueling but also exciting. My parents had taken off, promising to be back during my week break later in January. Chloe and I continued to unpack and build the house into a home.

As I walked into the kitchen Chloe had Colton strapped in his high chair eating his late breakfast while she cleaned the dishes.

Coming up behind her I circled my arms around her waist "You feeling okay still baby? Any more issues with feeling dizzy?" I knew she was stubborn so knowing she wouldn't tell me was accurate.

"I'm okay. I'm just tired."

She turned in my arms giving me a soft kiss on my lips, "What times the game tonight again?"

Kissing her back, I pulled back pushing a piece of hair behind her hair, "7. If you're tired you don't need to go, it's okay."

She leaned against me taking a minute to answer, "I want to go, I think I'll just stay in the suite instead of being down by the ice. Do you want us to go with you today?"

"You can baby, I have post-game interviews so not sure what time they will have me out, I don't want you waiting around, but I also want to make sure you are safe since we haven't heard anything lately."

I hated that we still hadn't heard anything in regards to the bastard stalking my family.

"We can wait for you, this way nothing happens."

By 3:45 we were loading up in the car to head to the arena.

I dropped Chloe off in the family room so she could visit with the wives and girlfriends before the game.

Walking into the locker room I noticed a note sticking out of my locker. Looking around I noticed there wasn't a lot of guys here yet.

Carefully taking the note I unfolded it, reading over the words carefully, "I am coming for what is mine. You won't even see it coming."

My hand started shaking reading over the words.

Turning the leave to find Chloe, Matt came in noticing my demeanor, "Bro what's wrong?"

I handed him the note, "He's threatening me now. I need to call the detective and find Chloe. Shit, I need the camera footage to the locker room door to see if it was him."

I started panicking, shaking and running my hands through my hair.

Matt handed the note back, "Call the detective right now, I'll call Summer to find Chloe and I'll talk to coach. I got you bud. No one threatens you or your family."

I nodded my head grabbing my phone dialing the Detectives number, "Detective Brown its Reed Collins. I just walked into the locker room and found a note stuffed in my locker. I think it's from James."

I could here a deep breathe on the other line, "Okay I'm on my way, where are Chloe and Colton?"

I ran hand over my face, "They are here in the arena which now worries me, I left them in the family room. Summer is locating them now."

"Okay Reed, I'll be there in 5, I'm close by. I need video footage of anyone coming in and out of the locker room, can you get your coach and anyone else who would help together?"

Taking another deep breathe in, "Yea, Matt is grabbing the coach now. I will see if we can meet in his office. I'll have Matt come get you from the door."

As I hung up, a worried Chloe walked in holding Colton to her chest, "Reed what's going on? Summer seemed panicked and didn't say much."

I pulled her into me, handing her the note, "He was here. Left this note."

Chloe opened the note reading it over, pulling Colton closer into her chest, her eyes lifted off the paper meeting mine, "What do we do?"

"I called Detective Brown, Matt is going to let him in.

Lets' go grab coach."

We walked into Coach Benson's office, closing the door behind Chloe.

Coach's gaze swept over us, sensing what was yet to come, "Matt filled me in. Is the detective on the way?"

I nodded yes, pointing Chloe to sit down, "Yea he is going out to grab him now. Who has footage of the door to the locker room, he is going to want to see it."

Coach grabbed his cell phone before pulling it up to his ear, "I'm calling the GM and tech to get our stuff. We will stay in here so no one is aware of what's going on."

I sat next to Chloe, placing my hand on her knee that was shaking, "It's okay love. He came here because he doesn't know where we moved to. He isn't going to take you."

Within 5 minutes we had our GM, head of tech, Coach Benson, detective Brown, Matt, Summer and myself and Chloe. Colton was playing with some pucks Coach had given him, poor kid was unaware of the events taking place-I was envious.

Video footage was sent over to Detective Brown while the GM made some phone calls to secure more security and make sure to run extensive background searches to prevent breaches.

Since Matt and Summer were no longer in the path of being targeted, they were released to prepare for the game and gather themselves.

Coach didn't want anything to seem off to the media or fans so they were going to pull me out under the label of sickness, this way Chloe and I could get home. Detective Brown was sending a patrol unit to our house to wait for us but also clear the house and then they were going to be our security through the night.

This wasn't how I wanted to spend my evening, but leaving Chloe for 3 hours wasn't an option. Sadly my parents had left yesterday for Florida so I didn't have extra eyes on my family or the house.

Deciding we had better leave since it was 5:30 and game was at 7, my GM Frank wanted to personally walk us out with security and detective Brown, to make sure we got to my truck safely.

I had Colton in my arms who was playing with the pucks from coach, Chloe besides me, gripping my arm for dear life, "It's okay baby, we have a protection detail and we will have the house cleared before entering."

She took a shaky breathe, nodding her head to what I was saying. It was then that she collapsed into me, her head down and her body giving up. My GM lunged forward, securing his arms around her to prevent her from falling.

Stopping in our tracks, I could see the color drain from her face, "Chloe baby what's going on?"

No response

Everything blurred together, Chloe was conscious but pale and weak, she hadn't been dizzy unless she failed to say something. I should have paid more attention to her during this.

Detective Brown rushed over, "Ambulance is on its way. Let's get her to sit down on this bench until they get here."

As we got her to sit down, she leaned her head against me, "I'm sorry Reed, I got dizzy again but I was hoping it would pass."

I shifted Colton to my other arm, pulling my arm around her into my body, "Baby you need to communicate. If Frank hadn't been there you wouldn't be standing."

"I know. I'm sorry." She gripped my hand.

The ambulance showed up within a few minutes, they had taken her into the back to check her vitals while I stood next to the open doors with Colton, Frank and Detective Brown.

I was pacing back and forth wearing the pavement down when the EMT came over, "Her vitals are good. She doesn't seem dehydrated, it could be stress but I recommend taking her in to see her doctor first thing tomorrow. She needs rest right now."

Letting out the breath I had been unintentionally holding I shook his hand before heading over to help Chloe out of the ambulance, "Let's get home and get to bed and I'll cook us dinner."

Chloe willingly let me help her into the truck, after getting Colton strapped in I said our goodbyes with the promise to communicate if anything else were to happen.

Once we were home and the cops had done their search, Chloe settled onto the couch while Clayton played with his trucks on the play mat. I walked into the kitchen to prepare a quick meal before settling down with my family.

I was so over this shit, I gripped the edge of the counter hanging my head down. How could he have easy access to me, to my family? I felt like a failure for not keeping my head on a swivel, plus having no updates for days at a time has been stressful. Chloe can't even open her business because she's scared of being there alone, now we can't even go to the arena.

I must have been lost in thought because 2 arms circled my waist and a faint kiss placed between my shoulder blades, "Reed, were okay. I'm okay. We can go Monday to the doctor and I can get checked out."

I'm glad she's realizing that her practically fainting is not normal. I choked back a sob as I turned in her arms pulling her in, nuzzling my head into her neck. I let the tears flow, I didn't care if I looked weak, I'm stressed, upset, worried and frustrated; all during a time in my life I should be happy, excited and not looking over our shoulders.

I could feel Chloe rubbing my back and my head trying to calm me, peppering kisses around my cheeks, "We will get through this Reed."

After a few more minutes I pulled back, keeping her close to me, kissing her forehead, "I know I just hate the unknown of why now? What does he want? How can he be getting away with all this? I'm pissed at myself and him."

Continuing running her hands down my arms, reassuring me, "I don't have the answers Reed. But don't hate yourself, he's crazy and unhinged. I hate myself for bringing him into our lives."

Changing the topic, mainly to save my mental health right now, I focused on the task at hand, dinner. "Alright is frozen pizza fine because I don't have motivation to cook?"

Chloe laughed grabbing a diet coke from the fridge, "Frozen pizza sounds amazing, I'll be out there with the game on playing with Colton. Don't burn the house down."

I loved watching her walk away, it didn't matter that I legit bawled my eyes out seconds ago, her ass had me mesmerized and completely in a trance.

"Stop looking at my ass Reed!" She laughed.

22

Chloe: Doctor Said What?

Monday had finally ventured around and Reed was adamant to go with me to the doctor. Summer and Matt had been nice enough to watch Colton at our home while we were gone.

Waiting in the waiting room, I started feeling nervous, I had no idea what I was feeling dizzy and faint. I'm hoping the doctor can find the culprit and we can fix this because I honestly hate feeling this way.

Holding Reed's hand, I could also tell he was nervous; giving his hand a squeeze I leaned into his shoulder when a nurse emerged from behind the door, "Chloe?"

Looking back at Reed, we stood up following the nurse to a back room where she allowed us to settle, "It says here you have been dizzy and even almost fainting. Is there anything else that is a concern?"

I took a deep breathe, reaching for Reed's hand, "No, I've been pretty stressed with moving and Christmas and some personal issues that I think it could be my body just telling me to slow down."

Reed squeezed my hand, giving me reassurance.

The nurse smiled making some notes, "Okay we want to run some tests so I will need you to take a urine test and then we can move on to scheduling you a blood test and hopefully those can get us some answers."

Reed hung back in the room while I ventured into the bathroom down the hall to complete my test.

Once done the nurse led me back, "We should have some answers back here in a few minutes. I do have some further questions I would like to ask once we get back into the room."

Finding my seat back next to Reed, he leaned over giving me a kiss on the temple, "What are some things that you think could be affecting her to feel this way?"

The nurse smiled at Reed, liking that he took an interest in my health or she just thought he was hot; both are likely, "Well, for starters, dehydration but also pregnancy. Can I assume that the two of you are active?"

I almost choked on air, "Umm, yes."

Going back to writing notes, "And you are on birth control? Or using other forms of protection?"

I hate these questions, they make me feel so awkward, "Yea, I, um I have been on birth control for 6 months, but that's it."

Still writing her heart out, "Have you been pregnant before?"

Reed squeezed my hand again this time taking over answering, "Yes we have a year old little boy at home."

"Alright, I will be right back to get your results and I will have the doctor come back with me. Give us a few minutes."

As she left the room I let out a large breathe I had not noticed I had kept inside, "Reed."

This time putting his arm around me, one hand coming up to hold my jaw, turning me to face him, "Its okay. Whatever the results are we will handle together."

Leaning up I captured his lips with mine, pulling back I let out a shaky breathe, "What if I am pregnant, holy shit I think I'm pregnant. Holy fucking chicken tenders Reed."

I started to panic, Reed keeping his hold on me, "Okay and so what if you are? I'm not going anywhere. I'm in this regardless if it's positive or negative."

Finally getting my bearings together, a knock rang out through the small room, a round man with grey hair and wire rimmed glasses entered, "Hello you two. I'm Doctor McBride, I see you are here for getting dizzy and almost fainting Miss Murphy."

"Yes that is correct." I murmured.

"Well good news I have your urine test results, depending on them we can move forward with more tests as needed, so let's get into it shall we?"

It felt like years as he opened the folder he had carried in with him, his eyes scanning the results before looking up, "Well good news again, we can schedule you a blood test and I would like to schedule you with my OB, because it seems a congratulations are in order. You're pregnant Miss Murphy."

Speechless, fucking speechless. Another baby, another set of 10 tiny toes and fingers, another set of tiny footsteps on the hardwood, another bundle to love. Fuck I never knew how much I wanted another one, I turned assessing the state of Reed.

Reed's eyes were wide, mouth open, also speechless. "Reed, we're pregnant, we're having a baby."

"I take it that you guys were not trying for another one?" Doctor McBride asked letting out a soft laugh.

Reed finally found his voice, pulling me closer, "No with everything else going on we hadn't planned it, but damn, this is amazing. I'm going to be a dad...again."

Reed pulled me closer peppering kisses over my face, making me let out a giggle.

"When you two are ready head to the receptionist, she will have your paperwork for the blood work and then she will get you scheduled with my OB so we can get an ultrasound and a better idea at how far along you are. I would recommend cutting out unwanted stress, drink fluids and get some rest. Congratulation again to both of you." He turned, leaving the room allowing us to have a moment to ourselves.

"Come on Reed, we need to book those appointments so we can get me thoroughly checked out." I stood grabbing his hands dragging him out the door.

"Holy shit, we need to get more baby stuff." Reed started panicking.

"Calm down dummy, the baby isn't coming right away.

We have time, one day at time here please." I laughed.

We scheduled the ultrasound for Wednesday morning since Reed had a game that evening and didn't need to go in for optional skate. I scheduled my blood test directly after getting them both done the same day.

"Holy shit, we are having another baby" Reed breathed out, "What can I do to make things better, is there anything we need to go buy for you?"

I reached over grabbing his hand, "How about we go by the store and get some much needed groceries since we have the time and I could definitely go for a pack of powder donuts."

Reed laughed kissing my palm as he drove us to the grocery store before heading home. "We're having a baby."

Deciding that we were keeping quiet until we had more answers, we decided to not say anything to Summer and Matt and just make up a story about not eating enough. I hated lying to Summer but I needed to make sure me and the baby were completely fine and healthy before spilling the beans.

Later that night I laid in bed, my hands falling flat on my stomach. There was no bump yet, but in my mind I knew that life was in there. I was going to be a mom again and it was scary and exciting.

I knew what kind of mom I could be but now I need to be the best partner to Reed as he learns the new ropes.

Reed

I knew Chloe could keep the news bottled up, but I'm worried about messing up and saying something. After our surprise findings on Monday the only person I told, well accidentally told was Colton. I mean secret safe there he can barely talk so who will he tell?

It was now Wednesday, Chloe had already gotten her blood drawn so now we are waiting "patiently" in the OB's exam room.

"Reed stop pacing. We've been here 5 minutes calm down."

"What if she finds something wrong, what if there's 3 of them in there? I've never done this part before Chloe."

I could hear a laugh coming from the door way behind me, "New dad I see. Well I'm Dr. Strome or you can call me Melanie. How are you today mama?"

I watched Chloe adjust her seating on the exam bed, "I'm good. I've been dizzy off and on and almost fainted. Other than that I haven't felt sick."

I moved to Chloe's side, taking her hand in mine. "Well dizziness is common in the first trimester, so reduce any unwanted stress and rest. How about we check out this baby? Go ahead and lay down while I prep the wand."

My eyes grew as she grabbed this wand like machined and prepped it by placing a very large looking condom over it, "Umm, what is that?"

Dr. Strome turned to look at me giving a slight laugh, "This is how we do ultrasounds until the baby gets bigger and we can use the over the belly machine. This will go into her cervix and we can see the baby."

Chloe grabbed my hand, having already adjusted her body and her gown. She had her legs in these saddle looking straps. How can she be so calm spread out like that?

"Reed, come over here. It will be fine. I won't really feel it and the baby won't be harmed. I've had this done before."

"Are you sure?" This is why women are superior, legit being probed and acting like it isn't a big deal.

Dr. Strome inserted the wand, directing us to watch the screen while she located the baby, "Alright the baby should be right…. There they are."

Another reason I am not smart enough to be a doctor is because she pointed out the baby on the screen and I couldn't find it. "Where, I can't see it. Does this make me a bad father?"

"You are not a bad father, look right here to the left. You see this little circle, like a bean?"

My eyes latched onto the small circle/bean like item, "Yea."

"Mr. Collins, that's your baby."

The air left my body, I stared for what felt like hours at my baby on the screen. I could feel the tears threatening to spill over my eyes.

"Chloe, that's… that's my baby, our baby." "Oh wait hang on I see something."

My eyes jerked to Dr. Strome in a panic, "What is it?" "One second Mr. Collins. Okay there we go, do you see this other circle on the bottom left of the screen?" Chloe and I nodded our heads. "Congratulations, you are both having twins."

Twins, like 2 babies? Like 2 fetuses? How the fuck did we do that? I'm an only child, my parents don't have twins in their family. I don't think Chloe has siblings and she sure as shit only had 1 baby last time.

I could feel my heart racing, I could feel and hear the blood pumping through my veins. I was prepared for one baby but now two, can I handle this. I travel most the year, how will Chloe deal with 3 under the age of 2?

I was startled out of my panic by the whooshing noises coming from the machine, "What's that?"

Dr. Strome smiled at Chloe before meeting my eyes, "That would be their heart beats."

I must have been lost in the sound of my babies because I barely heard the doctor talking to Chloe, the only thing I picked up was she was measuring at 7 weeks pregnant. I started doing the math in my head. That would have been right after Colton's birthday. Probably the date night.

Turning to look at the doctor, I had questions and I needed answers, "Umm, how can we have twins. They don't run in my family and I don't think they run in Chloe's."

I squeezed Chloe's hand, needing to feel that she was there.

"It's actually quite common for parents to have twins without having family history. It seems that there could have been a factor of things such as Chloe could have more eggs being produced. If that's the case then more than one egg can fall and become fertilized."

So my girl was an over achiever, like I knew that but holy shit.

"Okay. I don't feel better but I guess I do at the same time. Umm, you said 7 weeks, are they healthy?"

The doctor had already pulled the wand out and printed the pictures handing them to me. Looking at the pictures and seeing the little beans, it's so real.

"Well Mr. Collins from what I can tell, yes they are all healthy, Chloe included. I would like to set up another appointment with you again at 12 weeks for another ultrasound."

Chloe sat up grabbing ahold of the ultrasound pictures before her eyes meeting mine, "Whatever life throws us we can and will handle."

My heart filled with love as I took her in, her hair was in a messy bun, a few pieces framing her face. She had little to no makeup on, just like I liked it. Her exam smock hung open to the side, and her eyes shined holding so much happiness. I loved her for a long time, but I think I re fell in love with her all over again.

I captured her lips with mine savoring her taste.

Forgetting we were in the presence of a doctor I pulled back placing my forehead against hers, "We can do this baby. I love you."

I wiped the lone tear under her eye before helping her off the exam table, Dr. Strome exiting to allow us our privacy and the chance for Chloe to change.

Fatherhood was just another challenge that I knew I could do. Colton gave me the job firsthand, but now I was needing to be on my best A game and be the best father for my babies and be the best partner for Chloe.

23

Chloe: Morning Sickness and Concussions

About a week after New Year's day, Reed and I decided to let Summer and Matt know about our pregnancy. This put me at around 8 weeks pregnant with twins none the less.

We were waiting to tell Reed's parents until they visited at the end of the month and we were refusing to post on social media. Mainly due to the fact that my ex hadn't been caught and we didn't need him becoming more violent or unhinged.

Detective Brown said they caught him on camera and they were able to use multiple cameras to figure out how he got in and out undetected.

Apparently he slipped by one of the new security guards, and when I mean slip I mean like handing him money on camera and sliding past.

He had entered the locker room about 15 minutes before we had entered the building which means he could have been around the hall corner or even in the parking lot.

Detective brown did say that they caught him getting into a car, a dark colored sedan, they did get part of the license plate. Which running the partial plate gave them good leads in finding where he is hiding or who he is living with.

The security guard was taken into questioning but I know for a fact he was fired.

Reed said he had talked to his general manager and that they were reviewing all new security guards within the past year and making sure that they were in the clear.

Reed was in the kitchen making our breakfast spread when Summer and Matt walked in. Summer being pregnant as well immediately made a straight line for the plate of bacon taking 3 pieces, shoving them in her mouth.

I had started getting morning sickness and my food aversions have been wild, so Reed did the cooking while I hid out upstairs or in the living room.

Walking in seeing Summer eating the bacon while Matt and Reed watched her was hysterical, they had the most dumbfounded looks on their face.

"Summer, Love. I get your pregnant but there are like 5 of us who want bacon" Matt directed.

Bless his heart for calling a pregnant lady out. "Matthew...I kindly do not give a fuck."

I snorted at Summer's response, placing Colton on the ground, as he walked to Summer he decided now was the best time to try new words, "Fuck".

No one could keep a straight face, "Summer I would love for my son to not know those words yet, shit" Reed laughed.

I loved that he started calling Colton 'His son', it warmed my heart knowing my son had a father in his life who wanted to be there and wanted to mentor him.

"I am so sorry. Colton we don't say that. That's a bad word. Auntie Summer is sorry" she pulled him into a hug when he decided to try the word a second time, "Fuck!"

My son was all giggles, he was proud of himself which made me proud of him, even it was for cursing.

Breakfast was eventful from Colton yelling his new favorite word and Summer eating all of Matts bacon.

It felt good to have friends that were more like family. Watching 2 people love my family like their own and vice Versa is a great feeling. Their love for Colton is almost at the level of love I have for my son as his mother.

I had been picking at my food, trying to not run to the bathroom to give away my pregnancy when I felt my foot being nudged under the table. Looking up, Reed's gaze met mine along with an eyebrow raise, almost like asking if we should tell them now.

I excused myself after giving Reed a head nod and walked over to the living room where I grabbed the small box.

Walking back in the kitchen I placed the box down in front of Summer and Matt, "We got you guys a little something."

Summer shoved the rest of the bacon in her mouth, wiping her hands before taking the lid off the box, giving me an eyebrow raise.

"Chloe, you guys didn't have to give us anything."

"I know, we just saw these and knew you guys would like them."

Chloe grabbed out a onesie that read, "My best friends are twins." Across the front.

"Twins? Best Friends? I don't get it." Matt furrowed his eyebrows reaching for the onesie.

"You guys know we are only having one baby and Colton is way too big for this." Summer kept her eyes trained on the writing.

I stood behind Reed, my hands hanging over his shoulders. We were both trying to not laugh.

Finally Reed cleared this throat, making both of them turn to look at us.

Reed grabbed my hands that were on his chest, giving them a squeeze, "Yea you guys aren't having twins, but—"

"Holy shit you're pregnant!" Summer exclaimed standing up from her chair. "And with Twins? Holy fuck."

I started laughing watching my best friend start to freak out, "Yea we just found out right after the new year. I had been dizzy and the doctor ran some tests and well- Surprise!" I held my hands up shrugging.

"Dude, twins? You are going to have your hands full" Matt laughed getting up and walking around the table.

Reed and I were both brought into a large hug with Summer and Matt.

It felt great having someone to go through pregnancy with but it also felt great to have major support along this journey.

My last pregnancy it was Colton and myself and Summer tried when she could to be around, but she needed to pursue her career and not give it up to help me.

These babies and Colton were going to be so loved and blessed to have the family that we have.

Reed pulled me into his chest, giving me a kiss on my cheek before turning to look at the other two, "We aren't telling my parents until they come out at the end of the month for our week break, and we aren't posting anything on social media since James is still out there. But we wanted to share with you both once we had confirmation that everyone was healthy."

Matt looked like he was about to cry, "You wanted to tell us first?"

I walked over to Matt giving him a hug, "Of course your uncle Matty."

Shortly after Reed and Matt left for the arena to prepare for their game tonight against Vegas.

Summer and I decided to relax and hang out with Colton and mainly discuss our babies and pregnancy.

We made it to the arena for the start of warm ups and decided to go down by the glass and see the boys.

I decided on my denim cargo jeans with my Collins jersey, having Colton's outfit match mine.

Being down on the glass and watching the guys skate by excited me knowing in a year we will have 3 babies down here watching their daddy play. I didn't think moving to Missouri would give me this life, I prayed everyday for a good man, but didn't realize changing one part of my life would give me all that.

The first and second period were brutal, both teams were playing hard, both wanting the win. Reed must have had some new motivation because he had 2 goals back to back in the first half of the second period.

The fans were eating it up.

By the middle of the third period we were tied 4-4, Matt had spent a few minutes in the sin bin for slashing on another player which allowed for them to tie the score.

For the most part our goaltender was having a good game besides the 4 goals, he was blocking most of the shots.

I was bouncing a sleeping Colton against my chest, taking a second to look at his sleeping face when I heard the fans erupt. Looking from the WAGS box down to the ice, I could see Reed caught a breakaway and his two defensemen were right behind him doing their best to keep his lane clear.

My eyes trained on his moving body across the ice, "Come on Reed, you got this."

Reed deked out the Vegas goaltender sending the puck through the 5 hole, giving us a 1 point lead with 15 seconds left in the period.

As Reed skated past the goal in celebration, he was hit in the back pushed against the glass head first by a pissed off Vegas player.

I watched in slow motion as Reed fell to the ground, his hands finding his head, his body not trying to get up.

I froze, "Reed get up, please Reed." I begged, I could feel the tears pooling in my eyes.

I watched as Matt came barreling towards the player who hit Reed, helmets, gloves came off and fists were flying. My eyes wouldn't leave Reed as the Sports Medicine team slide across the ice to be at his side.

My eyes met Summer's from behind the players bench, she had the same worried expression that I had.

I felt a hand on my shoulder, turning I noticed Candice watching my face before turning to the ice, "I got you."

I kept my eyes trained on the ice watching them escort Reed off to the locker room.

I wiped under my eyes the best I could, taking a deep breathe.

I hadn't noticed but Frank, the general manager was standing next to me, his eyes also trained on Reed. "Let's go see him and make sure he's okay. He probably wants you both there."

I nodded turning to grab the diaper bag before following him down the hallway, heading towards the unknown.

Walking into the team doctor's room and seeing Reed being assessed broke my heart.

I could see the dried blood under his nose and chin, his hair was a mess and then I noticed he was shirtless. Blame it on my hormones but I wanted to cry but also lick his chiseled abs. I love and hate pregnancy because now I want to jump his bones when I should be making sure he's okay.

I must have been staring a little to long because once I finally found his eyes, they were already on me and a smirk on his lips, "You like something you see?"

I could feel my cheeks flush, "Shut up, please tell me you're okay?"

Reed held his hand out for me to walk in between his legs while he sat on the exam table, "Doctor says I have a concussion, which makes sense because my head fucking hurts. I'm out the next few games. So no road trip for me."

I gently ran my free hand through his hair, "Well me, Colton and the babies will love having your all to ourselves for the next week then."

I felt Reed's hands on my back before snaking one to my stomach, letting it rest.

"Babies? Shit you have more on the way?"

We both stilled, thinking we were alone, Reed peered over my shoulder seeing Frank.

"Umm yea it's a secret through-twins."

I turned smiling at Frank, "We are just trying to help build you the next great team." I laughed.

"Well congratulations are in order. I won't say anything, this is awesome guys, also here are your 3 pucks from tonight Reed, besides the hit you did great out there."

We thanked Frank as he walked out leaving us to be alone once again.

"I forgot to tell you congrats on the hat trick, daddy." Giving Reed a heated kiss on his lips.

I pulled away, running my hand back through his hair. "Daddy? Hmm I kinda like that coming off your lips baby, and if I didn't have a concussion I would be showing how much I like that name tonight." He squeezed my leg with his hand, "Also" picking up the three pucks in his hand and looking at them, I saw love, passion and happiness dance in his eyes.

"These are for my kids, 1 for each one of them. Tonight I dedicated to my future legacies."

I felt my heart swell and a sob choke in the back of my throat, "That's beautiful baby."

He put them down, grabbing my hip in his hand and his eyes meeting mine, "When we get home, I'll write on them to commemorate tonight and when we know genders and names, I'll add those to them. Colton can have his tonight."

"That's sounds great hun." I kissed him again, pouring all my emotions and feelings into the kiss.

"How about we get home and relax a little baby. I have nowhere to be tomorrow. Oh, if you need to go into your salon this week, we will go with you, I'm free for a week."

I loved that even though he is in pain and probably upset with himself for allowing the hit and being out for a week, he still wants to support me and my dreams.

"Let's go home baby."

24

Reed: Laying it out

Chloe is currently 11 1/2 weeks pregnant and my parents are showing up today to spend the week with us.

Mom and dad don't know the extent to the stalking that we have been battling so not only will we tell them about the twins but also about that.

I'm hoping mom and dad will eventually move out here to help Chloe when I'm gone but to also be here to see their grandkids more.

I am their only child, so why not leave Florida, there is nothing there for them. I know I sound self-centered, but I am, they are my parents and these are my babies. I want my family close.

Speaking of the stalking, another note showed up the week I returned back to the lineup, this time on the hood of Chloe's car I drove to the arena.

"Times ticking" was all it said.

After practice and after dealing with the detective and finding video footage to confirm it was him, I drove to the dealership and sold Chloe's car for a newer model SUV in a different color.

I'm done having this bastard know her car and being able to locate her if she were to be driving it. Fuck him.

Chloe loves her new car, it has 3 rows of seats, its extended for more space in the back and full sun roof and her favorite part, the heated seats.

She did yell at me because she didn't want me to spend my money on her. Jokes on her, I won't stop. I've even been looking at engagement rings.

She didn't stay mad though when she saw the car, so win-win for me. She thanked me later that night by wrapping her pretty pink lips around my cock and milking me dry.

I need to shake these dirty thoughts before my parents walk through the door and see the semi hard on I have.

That would just be fucking embarrassing.

I snuck out of the house this morning before Chloe woke up to go by the store for another large bouquet of flowers for her along with her favorite pastries from the cafe she loves in downtown.

Quietly putting the flowers in the vase and setting them on the counter with her pastries and her 1 cup of coffee she's allowed, it was perfect.

As I was "Fluffing" the flowers, I don't know what the fuck it's called. She walked in and stopped, Colton running past her to the kitchen, "Daddy."

"Good morning to my beautiful family. Baby I have your favorites right here." Walking over I kissed her lips, running my hand through her hair.

Colton attached himself to my legs laughing. "Daddy" he exclaimed again.

Chloe and I pulled apart, her lips partially swollen and a smile on her face.

"Good morning to you to baby daddy. You didn't have to do all this but now it makes sense why your side was empty and cold."

She kissed my cheek again before walking to the counter, deciding what pastry to devour first.

Finally looking down at Colton, who was smiling showing me his teeth-to think this kid had like 1 when I met him.

"You hungry buddy? You think mommy will share her pastries?"

I could hear a laugh leave Chloe with her back to me.

After we ate, and surprisingly my baby mama shared her food with us, we decided to do some house cleaning before our guests arrived.

Colton was too busy playing with his cars in the living room to be bothered and Chloe was on laundry duty while I cleaned the kitchen.

By noon my parents let themselves into the house, catching us by surprise due to the fact we had all been napping on the couch as a family.

Luckily Chloe was wearing one of my large t-shirts because she had started showing and we didn't want to give it away yet.

My parents got settled while Chloe and I prepped lunch.

Colton had attached himself to my dad leaving us to finish lunch without stepping around the toddler or worrying when it got quiet.

Once we got settled for lunch, Chloe grabbed my hand giving me a squeeze, locking eyes and a soft smile. I decided now was time to rip off the major bandaid here.

"So, we have something we need you guys to be aware of." I cleared my throat.

Both parents eyed me weary, "Whats wrong?" My mom asked.

"Well Chloe's ex is back in town. And well he's been causing some issues-legal issues." I started.

"Does he want Colton? Because he's not a dad to that kid, we will fight." My dad blurted out. Causing Chloe to let a small giggle escape her lips.

"No he doesn't want Colton, that I know of. I wish that was it, but it's not." She spoke timidly. "He's been stalking me and Reed. Breaking into Summer and my home as well as leaving notes for Reed in the locker room and on my old car."

She let out a large breathe, breaking eye contact to look at her lap.

I know she thinks this is all her fault and she thinks my parents will hate her.

"He's stalking you guys? Have you called the cops?" My mom asked.

"Yea, we have been working with a detective. The fucker is keeping his distance at times to not draw attention. He says he wants what's his, but nothing here is his. It's another reason we moved to a gated community and why I bought her a new car." I explained.

"Do they have any leads on him?" My dad asked, looking at Chloe and myself.

"Yes, they know his partial plate on his car and they have seen him breaking into the stadium as well as paying off a security guard. They have eyes out everywhere and it's a matter of time he slips up." I took a large breathe, squeezing Chloe's hand.

"I'm sorry that I brought this on your family, I didn't mean for Reed to get involved or even for him to show up. After I woke up in the hospital over a year ago I never saw or heard from him." Chloe was fighting back tears.

My dad and moms face softened, "Hospital? What are you talking about?"

I leaned over to Chloe, "You don't have to talk about it baby."

She smiled at me before taking another breath, "No I need to." Turning to face my parents she took a second, straightening her shoulders. "When I was with him, he was abusive, verbal and physical. I had no family, no one. Summer tried to show me how bad he was, but once you're a victim, it's hard to get away."

She paused, wiping under her eyes, "The night I wound up in the hospital, he had decided to get drunk and beat me. He slammed my head into the tile floor of our apartment and proceeded to punch me. I guess after I passed out, he walked out. The neighbor knew about the abuse and called the cops where they found me bleeding on the floor. When I had woken the next day the doctor informed me I was pregnant."

She ran a hand through Colton's hair, "I knew I needed to get out of there. The cops came and talked to me and told me that they had him in custody. They placed me in protective custody and 2 weeks later he was let go. His lawyer was dirty, got him off without a trial and then he disappeared."

I faced my parents, pulling Chloe closer to me; both their eyes had unshed tears. My mom pushed up out of her chair coming around and pulling Chloe into her arms.

"Sweetie you are so strong. We don't blame you for this man's actions and you shouldn't either. We support you hun."

My dad walked around the side, gripping my shoulder with his hand, "Chloe I don't know if you noticed but we are family, we see you as our daughter and we see Colton as our grandson. We will not let anything happen to you."

That was my breaking point, I hung my head in my hands and bawled.

My mom moved from Chloe to holding me, "Oh honey it's okay, it's going to be okay."

Once everyone had calmed down and we had resumed eating our lunch, I excused myself taking Colton, under the cover that I was going to clean him up.

In all honesty I was changing his shirt to say "Big Brother x2". It didn't take long for Colton to get his new shirt on, picking him up, I stopped by the other bedroom we dedicated to the new nursery and grabbed the ultrasound pictures.

I'm not sure why I was nervous, I knew they would be thrilled, but it was still nerve wrecking.

Before walking into the dining room, I set Colton on the ground and kneeled down to be eye level, "Colt buddy, can you take these pictures to Meemee and Papa?"

Colton grabbed at the pictures, almost studying them before giggling and turning around.

I had to jog to catch up since he bolted, entering the dining room Chloe halted her conversation looking at me.

Colton walked to my dad, "Papa, Papa" waving the pictures in the air.

"Oh hey bud you all cleaned up? What is it you have there?"

My mom grabbed the ultrasound pictures, confusion etched across her face. My dad was unaware to the words on his shirt as he sat there playing with Colton.

"Dave, look at this." Mom handed the paper over before looking at Chloe and myself.

I stood behind Chloe my hands on her shoulder as her hands gripped mine. We were both nervous, I could feel It.

"You guys are? Pregnant?" My mom asked before turning to stretch out the front of Colton's shirt.

"Wait what?" My dad asked.

"You guys are pregnant, give me that ultrasound back Dave, holy crap!" Mom exclaimed.

Chloe and I both laughed at my parent's reaction.

Finally turning to face us for answers, Chloe squeezed my hand three times, "Yea, we umm, well I'm almost 12 weeks pregnant...with twins."

My mom gasped putting her hand over her mouth before looking between my dad and us.

"Twins? Dave did you hear that. 2 of them. Oh my goodness I'm going to be a grandmother…again."

"Twins! This is amazing news!" My dad gushed grabbing the ultrasound pictures again. "Colton are you going to be big brother."

"Bubbbba" Colton babbled.

In his defense we have been working on words, so that was pretty good for him.

"Bubba is right buddy." Chloe laughed, "Good job love."

I leaned down kissing the top of Chloe's head, "Since you guys are here this week, we were wondering if you would watch Colton tomorrow morning while we went to her 12 week appointment?"

"Heck yea we can! Maybe Colton and I can bake some cookies together. Babies call for a celebration dessert."

Chloe let out a large sigh, "Ooh cookies, those do sound amazing. Can you make a double batch?"

I laughed again, squeezing her shoulders, "Let me guess it what the babies want?"

"Yes you ass, it's what the babies want" she laughed. The remainder of the day was my mom gushing over Chloe while my dad Colton and I lounged around watching whatever we could find on TV while enjoying each other's company.

I really hope they decide to move here, I miss days like this with my dad and mom and could use more of them.

The following day Chloe and I were back in the exam room with Dr. Strome, this time, no use of the wand. Just over the belly ultrasound.

I hadn't noticed how much Chloe started to show, but then again with twins it makes sense. But seeing the bump made things so much more real.

"Alright guys, lets check out these babies. How have you been feeling mom?"

Chloe raised her shirt, allowing access to her small baby bump, "I've been good, morning sickness is kicking my ass. I did have some food aversion, but those have seemed to lessen."

Dr. Strome nodded, "Sounds about right. With 2 babies, it could be the reason, if it gets worse call the office and we can try getting you on medication for it. Alright here we go."

After a minute of moving around Chloe's belly, she finally located both babies, by locating it also meant two strong heart beats coming out of the machine.

"Your babies are here on the screen, their heart beats are healthy and strong. They are measuring on track. I believe we will stick with August 4th for due date based on their measurements." She removed the wand and cleaned off Chloe's stomach.

My babies were bigger than the bean that they were last time. I can easily see them on the screen and their heart beats brought me to tears.

The day we found out about the babies and even to this day, my love for them has grown tremendously and love for their mother grows with every day. I know in my heart she's it for me and I think it's time I make that a reality.

Dr. Strome picked up the newest ultrasound pictures handing them to me before leaving the room giving us privacy.

Chloe sat up, her arm grasping my forearm, her head leaning against me as she eyed the pictures in my hand.

I looked down studying the happiness and excitement that danced across her face, kissing the top of her head, the words tumbled out almost in a whisper, "Marry me."

Chloe's eyes went wide before she turned to look at me, confusion replaced the happiness on her face, "What?"

I had to commit to my words, I hadn't planned how I was going to ask, but now seems like the perfect time, "Marry me. Marry me not because I got your pregnant or because we live together. Marry me because you love me. I am madly in love and devoted to you. I don't want to spend a single day on this earth without you. So please, Marry Me."

Chloe's eyes filled to the brim with tears, "You want to marry me? After everything we have going on?"

I wiped under her eyes, "Of course baby. Marry me and let's make the family official."

"Yes, Reed. I'll marry you." The moment I heard her words, I laid the pictures on the exam table, taking her face in my hands and brought our lips together. "And if you will allow me, I would like to adopt Colton, make him legally mine and we can all share the same last name."

A sob slipped out of Chloe as she grabbed onto my shirt, "Yes, there's no one else I want to raise my babies with. And you've been his 'dada' for a while now Reed. But let's make it legal."

Over the moon, that's how I felt. My family was coming together. My fiancé, my kids, my career, everything was where it needs to be.

Fuck the stalker, fuck the haters, fuck anyone who tries to tear us apart.

25

Chloe: Why me?

I t was the Thursday of Reed's week off; having him home all to myself has been a blessing and a curse.

After we got back from the appointment, Reed pulled a very large engagement ring out of the bed side tabled and made our engagement official.

We invited Summer and Matt over for dinner with Reed's parents where we spilled the news that we were engaged and he would be adopting Colton.

Everyone was over the moon for us which made me so happy. I never knew what support like this was since my parents died when I was 18 and my only person who I have had in my corner was Summer.

She had been there when my parents had died, she had been there when I started dating James and she was there for the birth of Colton and now she is still supporting me.

Reed and I decided we wanted to do something similar to Matt and Summer's plan of eloping. Since Summer and I are due around the same time and they wanted a summer wedding this year, they decided to get married this spring with the intentions of doing their large reception in a year from now.

Reed and I talked with his parents and they supported our decision of eloping and not worrying about a large reception since we wouldn't have many people to invite. Reed wants to get married ASAP, which I'm fine with but I would still like time to plan and make it memorable.

We decided Memorial Day weekend since it was a 3 day weekend and the season would be over-we could do a small ceremony and then take a few days to spend on a "honeymoon".

Reed's parents also sat us down and explained that they had thought about it and they wanted to move near us to be here for us and the babies.

Knowing that I will have them nearby reassured me that a I would be okay when Reed was gone on games. It also was nice knowing I had help but also baby sitters who are trustworthy.

Reed and his dad were looking into houses and working with Reed's realtor to get a tour set up before they leave on Sunday.

Susan has been great with helping me with either cooking, cleaning or watching Colton for me when I was getting things done. She even went yesterday with me to see my salon and hang out while I met with some clients.

Reed still felt uneasy sending me and his mom in case something happened. Reed promised to keep his phone on him and truck keys in case I needed him there.

Good news, nothing happened. But I loved that he cared.

I was currently parking my new SUV in front of my shop with Susan sitting passenger.

Walking to unlock the front door I noticed a slip of paper tucked in the door. It was ripped and dirty looking.

Susan came to a stop next to me watching my face before turning to see the note, "Is that a note?"

I quickly grabbed the paper, "Umm yeah. I, I don't know why it's here."

Susan leaned into me as I turned it over, "You can't hide, you can change your car and address but I can still get to you. I can still take the boy."

Susan gasped reading the words, "I'm calling Reed, call the detective, Chloe."

Susan ushered me back to the car, once inside she locked the doors.

She had Reed on the phone in seconds relaying to him what had happened.

My hands shook as I dialed Detective Browns number, "Chloe are you alright. You never call."

"Hi Detective Brown, umm, uhhh" I let out a shaky breathe before I felt my breakdown, "I, umm, I found a note at my shop. Umm he threatened to take Colton and I don't know what to do."

I could hear the sirens of his patrol car in the background, "Are you at the shop now?"

I took another breathe trying to control my breathing, "Yes, my mother in law and I are in the car. I don't feel safe anymore."

"Where's Reed. I'll be there in 5, don't get out of the car."

I wiped under my eye, "I think he's on his way. I won't."

"Good, Chloe look around, is there a vehicle that looks suspicious or out of place?"

I turned around in my seat and checked my mirrors before noticing a dark sedan down the street with their lights on. "Umm down the street towards the west hand side, umm their lights are on. It's a dark sedan."

"If they drive by, take a picture of their license plate, do not get out and wait till we get there."

I could feel my body shaking, the tears have long spilled from my eyes and my breathing was erratic.

Susan grabbed my hand, "Chloe I need you to breathe, focus on me, what can I do?"

I felt like I was squeezing her hand to the point of breakage, "Umm, can you take a picture of the dark sedan parked behind us down the street. Don't get out, just zoom in."

Susan released my hand turning in her seat and taking the picture.

Shortly after Detective Brown pulled up behind me, sending the dark sedan to flee the scene, bypassing us all together. As the car passed I turned my head to see it pass by, locking eyes with the devil himself.

I watched Detective Brown radio in to his units and give the license plate number.

My breathing was erratic. Seeing his face again, the look in his eyes and knowing he was here to mess with me or hurt me, or worse kill me. I felt like I couldn't breathe as I started sucking in air.

Detective Brown was knocking on my door but I couldn't register unlocking it and began bawling but also gasping for air. I needed air, I needed to breathe but my body wasn't allowing me to.

Susan unlocked the doors before reaching across the center console taking my face in her hands, trying to get me to focus on her.

"Chloe, look at me, it's me Susan. You're okay, he's not here. You're safe. Focus on my voice."

I could hear her pleading and I could feel Detective Brown trying to help console me.

Meeting Susan's eyes, I could see the worry and panic on her face, I focused on her voice and getting my breath, "I saw him. That was him. He was here. He smiled, smiled at me. He's going to hurt me and Colton and, and, and the twins."

Detective Brown slowly turned me to face him in my seat, "I got the license plate, my units are on it, I had a few in the area waiting when you called. You and your family are going to be just fine. I promise you."

As my sobs came to a stop and my breathing leveled out, I saw Reed's truck come flying from around the corner.

Within minutes his truck was parked and he was running to my side.

I could see Dave with Colton getting out of the truck, walking over cautiously.

"Chloe!" Reed's eyes locked with mine seeing my makeup or lack thereof smeared around my eyes and the redness from crying evident on my face.

I slowly got out of the car, running into his arms, taking a deep breath of his scent to calm me. "I'm okay now. It was him, I saw his face Reed. He was waiting. He left when Detective Brown showed up. They got the plate and hopefully they get him."

Reed pressed me further into his body, one hand caressing my head, I could feel his lips on the top of my head.

"This fucker needs to get his ass beat, I am so over him doing this shit. I'm sorry I wasn't here baby. I'm here now. We're all safe. But let's go home." Reed leaned down planting a sweet refreshing kiss on my lips before his hands came to rest on my hips.

Turning to walk back to the car, Susan was bouncing Colton around, his laughs and giggles healing a little apart of what I felt was broken.

Detective Brown walked up shaking his head, "My officers found the car 2 blocks from here, looks like he ditched it. They are actively searching the area around the car, because he couldn't have gone far. I will update you both with more information as I get it. Go home and try to rest, I know it's hard but I need you to try and stay calm."

Reed shook his hand before putting me in the passenger side and shutting the door.

Reed talked to his parents before they walked to Reed's truck, keys in hand and Reed placed Colton in the backseat before hopping in the driver seat.

Once in, he started the car, grabbed my hand and gave it a squeeze. "Let's go home baby."

26

Chloe: Can't Wait

Tomorrow is Valentine's Day, I am almost 15 weeks pregnant and life had slowly started going back to how it was.

Reed's parents had extended their trip to see some homes and luckily for me they found a home 15 minutes away and purchased it.

Reed went back after the week break and was playing so much better than before, I think the stress of us doing so much so fast, plus the issues with James, had held him back from his full potential.

Matt and Summer had moved out of the guys old house and found one in our neighborhood, 1 so they could be closer to us and 2 they loved being in a gated community after all the shit we went through. They were still planning for their small ceremony this spring, the third weekend of April, just a small ceremony in their new backyard.

I hadn't told Reed, but with all the crap we endured and the battles we fought, I realized after they caught James that I didn't want to spend another moment without him being my husband.

I was moving our wedding date up, and moving it up like tomorrow. I had it planned with Summer, Matt and Reed's parents all I needed was a husband.

Reed and I were lying in bed, it was a little before midnight. Reed had a game earlier this evening and now we were basking in the post-game celebration.

My hand laid on his chest, drawing circles while my head rest on his shoulder. Reed had one hand caressing my baby bump and the other playing with my hair.

Peppering kisses along his chest, I lifted my head to smile at him, "Reed?"

His eyes were closed, but he was still awake, a small smile on his face, "Hmmm?"

I looked at my finger with my engagement ring, "Marry me?"

Reed opened his eyes, training them on me, "Baby we already established this, that's what your ring means."

I let out a little laugh, grabbing his hand that was on my belly, intertwining our fingers, "No, I mean, marry me tomorrow. Like let's make it official."

Reed continued to stare at me, his eyes trying to get a read on my face to see if I'm joking, "You're serious? In like 30 minutes tomorrow?"

I laughed again, kissing his chest, "Yes like 30 minutes tomorrow…"

He kissed my forehead, letting his lips linger before pulling back, "Baby I would have married you in the doctor's office when I proposed, I just have 1 question. Why tomorrow, what changed?"

I looked at our intertwined fingers before looking back at him, "I realized the day I saw James that I never wanted to go another day without being your wife. But also, him being so close made me realize that had something happened to me, I would have wished Colton had your name so he could remain with you, so he could forever have his father."

I took a deep breathe, closing my eyes fighting off the tears, "I love you Reed and I don't need a fancy wedding or reception. I just want to be your wife and the mother of your children."

Reed removed his hand from mine, bringing it up to wipe under my eyes, "I realized that same day that I wanted you to be my wife like ASAP. I just didn't bring it up because I didn't want you to think you needed to change our plans for me. Of course I'll marry you baby."

Reed leaned down kissing me harder, caressing my face.

Once he pulled back, I leaned forward, making myself nose to nose with him, my finger stroking the side of his cheek, "Good, because you had no say. I had it planned already."

Reed let out a deep belly laugh, tugging me down, our lips reconnecting before he pushed me back to lay on my back while he leaned over me. "Aren't you a sneaky little thing?"

I bit the bottom of my lip, watching Reed's eyes cloud with desire, I quickly moved my hand behind his neck, bringing us back together.

Tonight was my last night as a single woman, tomorrow night I'll be a wife and he will be my husband.

Morning came way too early. I knew Summer was coming over, same as Susan and I even invited Candice. Matt had planned for the boys which included a few guys from the team and Reed's Dad to have an early T time, so he was in charge of getting Reed.

When my eyes finally opened I found a bouquet of deep red roses and a note on the bedside table, along with my favorite chai latte.

I sat up, reaching for the note and coffee, bring the cup of holiness to my lips, tasting the sweet relief. Reading the note, I wanted to cry but tried my best to hold off.

'To my Bride,

Today we say 'I Do', today we start forever and combine our lives to form one. I had planned to go all out for Valentine's day, but it seems that you have stolen the show–I mean you always do with your smile. Thank you for giving a guy like me a chance, for allowing me to worm my way into your life and become the man I was always destined to be. You motivate me everyday to be the best man for you and the best dad for our children. I'm not sure what else you have planned today, but I am excited to end our day as husband and wife. I am beyond blessed to be able to call you my WIFE. I love you and I love our babies.

P.S. I took Colton with me, to allow you the relaxation you need before the day gets wild. See the bathroom for a relaxation getaway and check the kitchen for your favorite pastries.

I love you, forever and always

Reed'

Well fuck, here comes the water works. I tucked the note in the drawer of my bedside table before slipping on my brand new white fluffy slippers and making my way to the "relaxation getaway" Reed wrote about.

Entering the bathroom I found multiple candles, unlit thank goodness, all we needed was a burnt down house because I slept in. There were bath salts and a bath bomb on the side of the tub, a brand new robe and a heart shaped box of chocolates.

I ran the water before dropping in the bath bomb and climbing into the warm water.

I could instantly feel my muscles relax and the scent of Lavender and Eucalyptus candles surrounding me. I decided to dig into the chocolate-the babies want it, so whatever they want they get.

Closing my eyes, I allowed for my body to sink into the water while I rubbed my baby bump, sharing this moment with them, soon they would be here and I wouldn't get this time of relaxation-at least without help.

15 minutes later I had eye masks under my eyes, my hair tied into a top bun and my new robe and slippers hugging me. Walking into the kitchen not only was I met with the sweet sight of my favorite pastries but also Summer laying on the couch with her own pastry in hand and the tv on.

"Good morning Mrs. Collins!" Summer excitedly yelled from her comfy spot.

"Good morning maid of honor. What time did you get here?" Looking at the clock it was barely 7:30.

"Matt dropped me off when he picked up your boys, so maybe 6:55/7? I really don't know. I napped on the couch and woke up a little bit ago to eat." Summer patted the spot next to her as I walked closer, my pastry in hand and coffee in the other.

"Goodness you could have crawled in bed with me like old times" I laughed.

"I would have but those stairs make me winded." She took another bite of breakfast, turning back to the tv. "Are you excited about today?"

I leaned my head against her shoulder, I was about to answer when a laugh startled me. Turning around I see Susan carrying bags into the house, "She better be, it's not everyday you get an awesome mother in law."

I laughed standing up, walking over to help with the bags, "You are absolutely right, I am more excited about being permanently related to you – your son is just the bonus." She pulled me in for a tight hug, planting a large kiss on my cheek.

"That's what I like to hear. Plus I always wanted a daughter. So best day ever! Alright, you two finish up breakfast and I am going to get started in the backyard on setting up. What time is everyone getting here?"

"Ceremony is at 5:30. So I think makeup and hair to start at noon. We can come help you. Oh I invited one of the players' wives to come help as well, she should be here soon." I absentmindedly rubbed my hands over my bump.

"Perfect, also you have the stuff for your and Reed's surprise right?" Susan asked placing the bags on the kitchen counter.

Summer came into the kitchen to start helping when her head turned towards me, "What surprise?"

I gave get a large smile, "I may have gone to the doc last week for a checkup, Reed was pissed he couldn't make it due to a game out of town. So we wanted to find out the genders and well, I had my doctor put the results in the envelope and I may have sent them off to a business who makes them into pucks. So when you shoot the puck the color explodes out. I got them as a surprise and I am setting up a spot in the back for the reception for us to announce what we are having."

Summer's eyes went wide, "Holy shit we get to find out today? Holy cow your man is gonna have a heart attack from all the happiness."

Summer pulled me into her side, "Matt and I found out 2 weeks ago what we are having, but we are keeping it quiet. I'm so excited to watch our babies grow." Summer started choking up, tears filling her eyes.

Blame it on the hormones, I started to tear up, rapidly wiping them away before they fell down my face.

"Alright, I'm heading out, you two get yourselves together, my goodness it's not even 8am." Susan laughed walking out the backdoor.

The day seemed to pass in a blur, Candice had shown up shortly before 9, Brooke her 5 year old daughter in tow and all the makeup and hair items you would ever need.

Susan and Summer had the chairs and tables up in the backyard and they were setting up the small ceremony spot with an arch Susan purchased earlier in the week- she had snuck in when Reed was gone and hid it in the backyard.

Candice and Brooke helped prep the desserts and even made us all lunch, Brooke was super helpful and sweet, watching her run around and help made me wish that I get a chance at having a daughter. I think Reed would be such a good girl dad but I also want to enjoy having a little girl to do all the mommy me things with.

Before I knew it I was sitting in my kitchen on a stool while Candice did my makeup and Summer helped with my hair.

Reed had text me that they were having a good time and that he missed me. He had sent me a photo of Colton dressed in a golf polo shirt, khaki shorts and his new golf shoes. Colton had his ball cap on backwards, when did my little boy grow into a man.

More pictures came flooding in, Reed had even gotten him his own golf clubs when he found the shoes so my son was now trying to golf with the big boys.

The last picture to come through was of Reed sitting in the driver side of the golf cart with Colton on his lap. I guess not seeing my soon to be husband before he left, it didn't cross my mind what he would wear. But now I can see, the two of them were matching from the backwards hats to the shoes. Both boys beaming at the camera- smiling like father and son.

I could feel the tears filling into my eyes, but I couldn't cry. Candice saw me put my phone down and take a deep breathe before looking at my phone to see the last picture, a smile spreading across her face, "He loves that little boy as if he were his own flesh and blood."

I smiled looking back at the photo, "He's all I've wanted for Colton and myself. He's amazing and he loves us so much."

Candice gave my shoulder another squeeze before moving back to the makeup, I'm thankful for her to know how to read me and allow me the time to gather my emotions.

Friends like her and Summer are one in a million.

27

Reed: Holy Matrimony

I had slipped out of bed at 6 am to Matt calling my phone, "What Matt?"

"Dude I'm picking you up before 7am to go golfing with the guys and your dad. So get dressed."

"Matt, umm, Chloe and I are going to get married today I can't just leave her."

I could hear his sleepy laugh on the other end, "Dumb ass, I'm taking you out golfing as a mini bachelor party so the girls can get ready and get set up."

I ran a hand over my face, "You knew?" "Of course I knew."

"Well that's nice to know. I think I'll bring little man so Chloe can relax a little, but also I bought him clubs and a pair of golf shoes I've been dying to get him on the course with me."

"I can't wait to see him decked out. See you before 7." Before I could answer he had already hung up.

I had already purchased items for a relaxing bath for Chloe, along with getting her flowers, pastries and coffee delivered to the house. Least I can turn those into a 'Valentine's Day/ Wedding Day' gift.

Before I knew it I had a sleepy Colton dressed in a matching golf look to mine. He was sleeping against my chest holding his favorite wolf stuffed animal I had gotten him months ago.

Walking out the door I was met with a pregnant, sleepy and probably annoyed Summer trudging into my house. She stopped leaned in and kissed Colton's cheek before giving me a pat on the shoulder, saying nothing and passing me into the house.

"She's a delight this morning" I joked placing Colton in the car seat. "This was her idea, so she can hate herself for waking up early."

Pulling into the golf course, Colton had woken up and was munching on his McDonalds hash brown sitting in the golf cart waiting on everyone.

Luke Davies one of my defensemen walked over pulling me into a hug, "Congrats man. Who would have thought the team's lifelong bachelor would not only get married but become a dad."

"Thanks Luke. Glad you could be a part of this and thanks to your wife for befriending Chloe. From what I hear they talk all the time and have planned multiple outings." I laughed.

"I can already hear my wallet crying."

We talked a little longer before Colton walked over wrapping both arms around my legs, "Dada."

"What's up little buddy. You okay? You need some juice or food?"

I kneeled down to be eye level with him as he reached forward touching my hat bill and then grabbing his, a smile etched across his face. "Juceeee"

"You want some juice? Let's check the cart."

Picking him up I walked back to the cart and located his apple juice handing it to him.

"You're an awesome dad dude, you can tell how much he loves you."

Turning around I notice another teammate, Brent, our goalie. He and I were rookies together and had played a little prior to signing with St. Louis.

"I love being a dad dude. If I had to choose, I would choose him and my twins over hockey."

Brent smirked, looking back at Colton he raised his hand, "High five little dude. You ready to beat all of us?"

Colton gave him a high five and a large grin, "Yeah!"

Once everyone had shown up, my dad included, we jumped on the carts and headed out to the first hole.

Colton rode on my lap, his laugh turning into a deep belly laugh, causing my dad and I to laugh with him.

Golf went surprisingly well, Colton played with his clubs and even attempted at hitting the golf balls. When a few of the guys wanted to shotgun their beers, he stood with them with his water pretending to chug. This kid is going to give me grey hair when he gets older but I wouldn't have it any other way.

I had sent some photos to Chloe around noon before we headed to the club house for lunch, I wanted her to see her baby boy looking all grown up, I just hoped it hadn't caused her to cry too much. I never know anymore, last week I walked into the kitchen to see her crying because she opened a small bottle of orange juice and cried because it didn't taste like a freshly peeled orange. Yesterday she cried because she wanted a bag of skittles and when she opened them she realized she wanted the chocolate pretzels instead. So no doubt about it she probably bawled when she saw the photos.

After lunch we spent another hour at the driving range to kill the time. While standing around bullshitting with the guys we started talking about babies and families, "Reed, twins right? You guys know what you're having?" Luke asked.

"We were supposed to find out last week but we had that away game, so I think she scheduled us to go in next week sometime."

"Dude what if you get twin girls?" Matt cringed.

I let out a laugh, running my hand through Colton's hair, "I really don't care, my wallet might, but as long as they are healthy, that's all that matters. Plus twin replicas of Chloe- they will be cute as shit."

"You would make a great girl dad, but yea bring on your grey hair and empty wallet." The guys laughed.

"I'll spoil them regardless girl or boy, I mean look at Colton, what 14th month old needs a set of golf clubs? I couldn't help myself."

My dad walked over clapping a hand on my shoulder, "You beat me to buying them, that's all I have to say."

"Papa!" Colton raised his hands wanting my dad to hold him.

"Hey there bud, you ready for a party tonight?" "Perddii." He babbled "Close enough little man."

By 3pm we finished up and the guys headed home to grab their wives and girlfriends before showing up for tonight's ceremony.

Matt, my dad and I made it back to the house, Colton asleep on my shoulder.

Walking into the house there was makeup and a variety of snacks all over the kitchen counter-yup Chloe was here. Since this was a last minute thing for me, I forgot to ask Chloe about what traditions we were doing, minus to sleeping in the same bed the night before. So, no idea if I am supposed to see her, hell I don't even know what I am going to wear.

Dad and Matt headed out to the backyard where I could see my mom and Summer running around with Luke and Candice's daughter in tow.

I decided to put Colton down in his bed, removing his gat and shoes. Taking a moment to watch him rest. I kneeled down, resting my arms on the side of the bed. I know I never created him, I wasn't there for his birth and I wasn't there the first time he laughed or smiled. In the short time this boy has been in my life I have grown so attached. Watching his sweet face sleep, I felt the tears fill my eyes, it's not his fault his biological father is a psycho, he didn't ask for a man to leave them or not love them. Now I get to watch the twins do all the first things that I missed with Colton, life isn't fair, but I can appreciate what I have been given. And as soon as I can I am making him a Collins so that no one in this house is separated out by a name.

Chloe is not only giving me her hand, her love, her attention or future, she is giving me so much more than life itself-starting with this little boy.

As I was wiping my eyes, I felt a soft hand run through my hair, "What are you doing baby?"

Looking up, giving her a soft smile, "Just watching him grow up fast." I sniffled.

"Come on, let him sleep."

I stood up grabbing her hand, leading me out the door into our bedroom. Once inside Chloe turned studying my face, "What's wrong Reed?"

I let out a deep breathe I had been holding before kissing her forehead, "Nothing's wrong, I'm just so happy to have you in my life and I'm extremely blessed that I also get a son-even if I missed out on a lot. Today it was like watching a younger me run around, I just wish he didn't grow up so fast."

Chloe wrapped her arms around my neck, "He loves you a lot. I think he loves you more than he loves me." She brought our lips together giving me a short yet sweet kiss.

"Oh shit, shouldn't I not see you until the ceremony?" I quickly covered my eyes.

Chloe started laughing, removing my hands from my eyes, "Reed I think we are past those traditions" pointing at her growing baby bump.

"You sure? Also, your makeup looks really good. You're beautiful." I kissed her again be conscious of her makeup. "Thank you. Candice did it. Also, thank you for the gifts this morning and you didn't have to take Colton, but I do appreciate you taking him."

"I figured you didn't need him under foot with everything going on."

We held each other a little longer, both quiet, appreciating the peace surrounding us.

Chloe broke the silence after checking the time, "It's 4:30 I need to start getting dressed. Can you check the backyard and see what else needs to be done, and in the guest bedroom is your outfit."

I pressed her closer, leaving a kiss at the base of her neck, "Yes I can Mrs. Collins. I love you."

As I peeled myself off her heading to the door, I turned around to finally notice her whole being, her hair was tied up in a curled pony tail, her makeup done and she was wearing her new robe and slippers. If we didn't have our wedding in an hour, her hair and makeup would be smeared and there would be no clothes on that body.

I raked my eyes over her multiple times, "Can't wait to get my hands on your later baby. Call me if you need anything else" giving her a wink I headed out.

After checking with mom, the backyard was all set and it looked perfect. Summer and Candice headed up the master bedroom to get ready with Chloe while Matt and I headed to the guest bedroom.

Standing in front of the mirror I fixed my tuxedo jacket, giving myself a once over. Chloe had gotten me black slacks with a black button up and a black jacket with a white lapel. It was classy and nice looking-she definitely has good taste. Colton ran in almost wearing a matching look to mine only his jacket was solid black.

By 5pm I was out greeting guests along with Matt and my parents, Colton didn't stray far from me but would go back and forth to my dad or Matt. Summer and Candice were back and forth.

We didn't have a lot of people in attendance, I had some teammates with their spouses, my coaches, and agent. Total we had roughly 50 people since not every player could make it.

Sadly, there was no one from Chloe's side since she was on her own. The one thing in life I wanted to give Chloe was a large family, so that's what I will do. She will never feel alone again.

As I was mingling I looked at the backyard transformed, there were lights hanging from tree to tree, there was a wooden arch covered in greenery and flowers where we will say 'I do'. Long tabled were set out with a sage green table runner on each with eucalyptus and roses scattered.

There was even a bar that my parents rented and had a bartender working. Mom had also ordered a caterer so they were set up near the bar and from what I could smell it was going to be delicious.

There were 2 photographers snapping photos at guests and it he corner near the bar it looked like mom or Summer set up a photo booth area. A DJ was set up near the arch with a wooden dance floor.

These girls had been scheming the last few weeks for sure, it was beautiful and perfect in every single way. Plus I didn't think we could fit all this back here.

"Alright man, we need you up at the front of the arch. It's go time." Looking at Matt I nodded as the DJ came on the microphone asking everyone to find their seats.

I stood in the front, my hands clasped together in front of me. What surprised me was Luke standing in the center of the arch, giving me a smirk, "Did you have any say in today?" He laughed.

"Nope, she planned all this. Thanks for officiating man." He just squeezed my shoulder, nodding his head.

As the music started playing, Summer and Matt walked down the aisle together, shortly after Colton and Brooke came walking down, once Colton saw me he started sprinting. Making the entire crowd laugh as he hugged my legs, content with where he was.

Once the music changed I took a deep breathe before turning to look in the direction of the house.

I could feel all he air leave my body when Chloe emerged from the door way. She was wearing a tight fitting white dress with a slit in the side that went to mid-thigh.

She held the roses I had left her this morning in her hands.

Once she got to the top of the aisle she stopped turning to smile as my dad walked over to her side, placing her hand in the crook of his elbow, they began walking towards me.

I could feel the tears streaming down my face as I watched her, her eyes also clouded with tears, giving me her biggest smile, mouthing the words, "I love you."

I placed my hand over my heart, hitting my chest 3 times- my way of saying those 3 words when I physically can't say them.

Luke started welcoming everyone, but the second her hands were placed in mine, I couldn't focus on the world around me. Our eyes trained on one another, both in our own worlds.

Luke cleared his throat getting both of us to turn to face him, soft giggles coming from the crowd.

"I'll ask again" he laughed, "Reed would you please say your vows."

I took a deep breathe, letting a nervous laugh leave my lips, "I guess I can do that." Clearing my throat and locking my eyes with Chloe I smiled. "Bear with me, I was told less than 24 hours ago this was happening." More laughs coming from the crowd as Chloe tried hiding her laugh.

"Chloe, there are so many things I want to say to you to express how much I love you and appreciate you. I have a feeling I won't be able to do it justice. Thank you for trusting me with your heart, your soul-" Reaching down with one hand to place on Colton's head, "And your son. You have given me everything a man could ever dream of. You have shown love and compassion and you have been there for me through the good and the bad times. I promise to love you, our son and the twins with all of my being. You 4 come first in my life and you always will. I'm not sure what I have done to deserve this happy ending, but I am thankful that it's me up here, promising to be your husband and the best one I can be. I promise to always have the kitchen stocked with pastries, vases full of flowers and to always fill our home with love and happiness. Thank you, for being my light. I love you."

I reached up wiping my eyes, noticing Chloe trying her hardest to not cry.

Luke wiped under his eyes, "Shit man that was nice."

Chloe and I both laughed before he turned and have her a head not to start.

"I apologize for the delayed notice but that was pretty good and I'm not sure my vows will be as good." She took a deep breathe before looking at Colton, reaching out to hold his hand.

"Reed, the moment we met I didn't know that you would have this kind of impact on my life and Colton's. You skated into our life the first day I moved, immediately helping with Colton without even being asked. You have shown since day 1 the kind of man you have always been and are; you have taken someone who felt broken and alone and made them feel whole and loved again. You have been there through every accomplishment, every good thing and even the bad. You have been my rock to cling too when I have felt like my world was collapsing. I can think of no other person I would want to raise our children with or grow old with. I want to cheer you on at every game, be your top supporter and your number 1 fan. Thank you for loving not only me but Colton and giving us everything we have dreamed of. I can't wait to see the milestones and moments we endure together and I can't wait to raise these babies with you as my husband. I love you."

I choked back the tears, trying to not lose it in front of everyone.

Based on the audience's reactions, there were no dry eyes, even the people working were crying.

I started panicking the moment I thought about the rings, I hadn't picked out a ring for me or for Chloe.

I must have missed Luke calling for the rings because before I knew it, Matt was reaching around me and handing rings to Luke.

I turned to look at Chloe with confusion written clearly across my face.

She smiled shrugging her shoulders with a playful smirk on her face. She had it handled. She has all of this handled and I realize again for the millionth time how lucky I am.

Luke handed me her wedding band a simple silver band, following Luke's instructions and restating the vows I slipped the ring on her finger. Sealing its placement with a kiss.

Chloe held my left hand in her hand and the ring in her right as Luke gave her the same instructions, and her reciting the vows. Once the ring was slipped on I noticed it was a matching band to hers only thicker.

It was simple, they both were and they represented the two of us so well.

Luke finally made it to the end of the ceremony, making me more excited for what's to come. "It's without further ado, I now pronounce for the first time, Mr. and Mrs. Reed Collins. You may now kiss your bride big guy."

I stepped forward, one hand going around her neck and the other holding onto her waist. Her hands both holding onto my hips as I dipped down bringing our lips together for a heated kiss.

Pulling back I placed another quick peck on her lips before grabbing her hand and picking up Colton, heading down the small aisle of our backyard.

Everyone was clapping and hollering, making it halfway down I pulled her in for another kiss, "We're married Mrs. Collins."

"That we are Mr. Collins."

We had taken photos with the photographer while everyone went to eat appetizers and mingle.

Finally with pictures done we got to sit down and eat dinner, everyone was having a good time it seemed, Colton was having a blast with the attention and the promise of cake.

Chloe sat in my lap with her hands around my neck as Summer and Matt did their speeches. Caressing her small bump, I loved how she had started showing and the promise of 2 precious babies inside her- my babies. I loved seeing her pregnant, it made me want to fill every room in our house with our children-if she would let me that is.

Her hands absentmindedly played with my hair, a feeling I loved. Little movements like this, showed me how much she loved me and cared for me.

Once speeches were over, Chloe and I stood thanking everyone for coming. When I was done, Chloe took the microphone with another smirk on her face.

"I have one more surprise. Last week we were unable to find out the genders of the twins. But, the wait is over. On the far side of the yard there is a hockey goal with 2 pucks set up and one of Reed's sticks. I would love if we could all find out together what we are having. Reed, happy Valentines day, do you want to find out what our babies are?"

I was speechless, looking at her and then noticing the small hockey set up, I looked back at her. Grabbing her and kissing her, "Fuck yea let's do it!"

We walked over, the photographers in place as Matt grabbed my stick for me and Summer set out the two pucks on the concrete slab in front of the goal.

Chloe gave me one kiss before she stepped back, holding her belly while Colton held her leg.

I calmed my breathing before eyeing the puck and swinging. Pink powder busted out of the puck.

Chloe covered her mouth in shock and I ran over kissing her. The audience clapping and shocked laughs echoing around us.

"We're having a girl?! Holy shit Reed!"

"I know baby. I got one more. Let's see what the tie breaker is."

I got back into place, focusing on the last puck, taking another swing, hitting the puck I was met with blue powder.

I stood frozen as Chloe ran over. Holy shit another boy, I get another boy. I grabbed Chloe into another hug kissing her face all over.

"Our daughter has no chance at dating ever" I joked. "Are you happy Reed?"

"Baby I'm fucking ecstatic!"

Everyone congratulated us before walking off to enjoy the rest of the night full of drinking and dancing.

Chloe walked off to sit with some wives and Summer as I walked to the bar meeting up with the guys.

"Dude congratulations! But your daughter has no chance at dating. Not only with 2 brothers and you, but also us as her uncles." Matt said pointing at all the guys.

"Fuck I can feel the grey hair growing already. Shit I'm a lucky bastard aren't I?"

Luke laughed handing me a beer, "Welcome to the girl dad club. We meet once a week and sometimes cry. Glad to have you."

I laughed taking the beer, "What did I do to get this lucky?"

My dad walked up hugging me, "Don't ask the question when no one knows the answer. But also don't question it son. Congratulations."

By 11:30pm everyone was heading out, Colton had already went to bed. Brooke had fallen asleep on Luke around 10. Poor guy was probably exhausted holding her.

Once everyone left Chloe and I headed inside going into our bedroom.

Once the door was closed we were on one another. I helped her out of her dress, watching the fabric hit the ground while she stood in heels and lingerie that I didn't know she had on.

I walked over unbuttoning my shirt, my jacket had been shed hours prior.

Grabbing her around the waist I hoisted her to wrap her legs around me and I walked us to the bed where I laid her down. Her hair was out of her pony tail, leaving it to cascade around her.

She was biting her lip while reaching for my pants button. My shirt was off, my hands finding her face, bringing our lips back together, I bit the bottom of her lip making her let out a moan, allowing my tongue entrance.

Once my pants were off, I crawled onto of her, "Reed my heels."

I growled in her ear, "You're going to leave those on while I fuck you."

She let out another moan as I pushed my erection into her core. Even with her lingerie on and my boxers, I could have come instantly.

I removed her lingerie, throwing them somewhere in the room. Grabbing her legs I pushed them apart, my hand cupping her core, eliciting a pleasurable moan from her lips.

I bit at her collar bone before kissing down between the valleys of her breasts, circling her nipples with my tongue, giving them both the attention they deserve. They definitely have started growing due to pregnancy and I am not complying. Chloe's back arched pushing herself further onto my hand.

"You're eager aren't you baby?" "Reed please, I need you."

Biting down gently on her nipple, my name coming as a cry off of her lips.

"Tell me what you need baby."

"I need you Reed. Touch me please."

Fuck I loved when she begged. I would usually drag this out, but I need to be in her instantly.

I settled between her legs, kissing at the inside of her thighs.

I licked her core bottom to top, another pleasurable cry leaving her lips, her hips bucking into my face.

I circled my tongue around her clit before plunging my tongue into her.

Removing my tongue I spread her pussy lips with my fingers, blowing air onto them to drive her crazy, her hips bucking and her hands gripping my hair.

I licked all over her sensitive bud, nibbling at her pussy lips, when I could feel her getting close I plunged my tongue back into her core, sucking at her sweet juices until my name was a whisper on her lips and her body shaking.

As she was coming down from her high, I continued to suck until she couldn't handle it.

Finally releasing her, I kissed back up her body, leaving a kiss on her lips, letting her taste herself.

I rolled on my back, pulling her on top of me.

I grabbed her hips, as she moved her hair over her shoulder, "Ride me."

Chloe leaned forward kissing me hard before lifting herself and impaling her pussy with my hardened length.

Her pussy clenched around me as she started moving up and down. Her hands placed on my chest pushing her upright. "Fuck you take me so well. You feel so good wrapped around me."

One of my hands reached forward fondling her round breast, her head fell back as she bit her bottom lip.

"Reed."

"Eyes on my baby. I want to see you come undone." I continued watching her as she bounced.

I could feel myself getting closer, reaching between us I placed my thumb on her clit rubbing circles.

Chloe's eyes now locked on mine, "Reed I'm- I'm close."

I started meeting her hips with thrusts, pushing further into her.

"Touch yourself baby, I want to see you help make yourself cum." I growled.

Her hands leaving my chest to replace my hand on her breast and the other on her clit.

I grabbed her hips, thrusting harder into her, watching her bring herself to the brink of explosion.

"I'm not going to last long Chloe." I gripped her harder. "Cum with me Reed." She begged.

Within seconds we were coming down from our highs, Chloe slumped against my chest and my hands caressed her and held her close.

"Fuck Baby. That was…"

She breathed out a large breathe, "Amazing?" "Fuck baby more like mind blowing."

Chloe kissed my chest before moving to sit upright, removing herself from me and laying down next to me.

I pulled her close peppering kisses to her neck and shoulder.

"What do you say about going to sleep Mrs. Collins?"

Chloe's eyes shined with admiration and love, she reached up caressing my cheek, "Sounds like a plan hubby."

28

Reed: Officially Collins

A month had passed since our wedding day, Chloe was now 18 weeks and getting closer to meeting her 1/2 way mark. Her belly seemed to pop overnight-there's no hiding the fact she's pregnant anymore.

The team had been on a good winning streak, we were currently in Winnipeg heading to the airport to finally head home after 13 days being gone. We had won against the Winnipeg Bolts 4-1- I could taste the promise of playoffs in our future.

I couldn't wait to get back, Chloe knew that I had every intention on adopting Colton, only she didn't know that I had already started the paperwork. I was waiting on a phone call from my Lawyer with the date we had in court and to get the adoption of Colton done.

After sending Chloe a text as I boarded the plane letting her know we were about to take off- I closed my eyes hoping I could sleep the entire way.

I was woken by Matt shaking me, "Hey we're here. Let's go."

I rubbed my eyes before standing up and grabbing my bag, following him off the plane. It had to be 2 maybe 3 am, it was dark outside still and quiet.

Matt and I had carpooled to the arena prior to taking off on the road trip, so we jumped into his truck headed for home.

Matt was quiet for a while before he turned to look at me worry on his face, "Have you guys heard anymore on the ex whose stalking you?"

I ran my hand over my face, "No, they found his car after it sped away past Brown and Chloe. We haven't heard anything from the detectives or her ex in a while. It worries me that he's gonna do something here soon."

"Shit man, that's rough. I was just curious, it seems like he was full force on letting you know he was around and now radio silence. I don't like it man."

"I agree, I'm hoping he slips up and they can catch him. I don't want to worry about him being around any longer. I have babies on the way-I don't need him trying to harm them or Chloe or Colton."

I truly hated the feeling of not knowing. I couldn't hyper focus on the fact that it had been silent a little too long for my liking. Chloe had started returning to her shop but now with mom and dad close, one of them always went with her while the other watched Colton.

Matt pulled into my driveway putting it in park to let me grab my things. "See you tomorrow sometime. Come over for dinner or something. And tell Summer 'hi' for me."

Matt waved pulling out of the driveway as I made my way back into the house.

Before unlocking the door I looked down the street and noticed a beat up dark grey car parked facing me. I hadn't seen it before and I hadn't noticed any neighbors driving it- let alone all the people who live in this neighborhood wouldn't be caught dead in that thing. I fished out my phone pulling up detective Browns number as the car crept forward.

I kept eye contact on the car not being able to see the driver.

Pulling the phone up to my ear, the car sped up passing by. I noticed half the license plate numbers trying to remember them for Detective Brown.

"Reed it's early what's wrong?" Detective Brown had clearly been sleeping.

"I just got home from a road trip and noticed a car parked on my street that doesn't fit the neighborhood. I got half the plate before he sped off past me."

"Hang on let me grab some paper, okay what's the 1/2 you got?"

I rattled of the plate I had gotten, sitting down on the step of the porch. "I will talk to my neighbors tomorrow about security footage from their houses and I'll check our front door camera as well."

"Alright let me call this plate in and see if anything matched the description you gave me. Get some sleep and call if things get worse."

"Alright, good night and sorry for waking you."

After hanging up I made my way inside where I found Chloe sleeping on the couch.

I dropped my bags by the couch before removing my tie and suit. Instead of waking up my pregnant wife and going to bed, I decided to just crawl behind her on the couch and enjoy her being close. Especially with what had happened not long ago.

Lucky for me, we had purchased a large sectional couch when we moved in, so cozying up together was doable.

I crawled onto the couch trying to not wake her as I snuggled my body between the couch and my wife.

Finally comfortable I grabbed the throw blanket, placing it over both of us before I pulled her closer to me.

She started stirring, turning her body to face me, the bump becoming a barrier- these twins better not show up in the world and be destined to cock block me my whole life.

I pushed a strand of hair out of Chloe's face as she snuggled closer to me, "When did you get in?"

I leaned forward kissing her forehead, "Just a few minutes ago baby. Go back to sleep, I'm here now."

Chloe kept her eyes closed, nodding her head in agreeance with sleep.

Holding her, while she grows my babies, in our home with our son sleeping upstairs-nothing could be better than this.

The next morning, Chloe and I had awoken with our legs tangled together and our bodies pressed tightly against one another.

Didn't matter where we slept as long as I got to wake up to her smiling face.

We had breakfast as a family and I was cleaning up in the kitchen when my phone rang, my lawyer.

I quickly answered with my heart racing, last I had talked to him was when I asked him to draft the paperwork for adoption and get the process sped up.

"Don, what's up?"

"Good morning Reed. All paperwork is completed, I talked with the court and they can fit you in on Friday that gives you 2 days to bring Chloe in and read over the paperwork before we go into the court."

I sighed a breath of relief, I only had practice on Friday in the morning so I could make this work, "This is awesome Don, I appreciate you working on all of this. Let me talk to Chloe and I will call you back. Can we get the paperwork emailed over?"

"I can have my secretary send you a copy that isn't a problem. I'll see you Friday at 1pm. Don't be late and congrats again man."

"Thanks Don, we will be there."

I hung up the phone as Chloe walked in with Colton on her hip, his head on her shoulder.

I walked over reaching for Colton, "Baby you can't be lifting him all the time."

Chloe rolled her eyes as she handed Colton over, who was eagerly excited to come to me, "Who do you think holds him when you're gone? Also, who was that on the phone?"

I gave Colton a kiss on his forehead before looking back at Chloe as she sipped on a decaf coffee (which I knew she hated). "So that was Don, my lawyer."

Chloe put the cup down, eyeing me with concern, "Is everything okay?"

With my free hand I reached out pulling her to me, "You remember when I asked to adopt Colton a while ago?"

Chloe placed her hand on my chest, playing with the collar of my shirt nervously, "yea."

"Well, I have had him working on some paperwork and well, how would you feel about going Friday at 1 o'clock to make it official?"

Her eyes started tearing up, "You...you already had been working on this? Since when?"

I pulled her closer kissing her forehead, "Since the day before we go married. When you asked me that night, Don was my first call the next day. He has the paperwork done and the judge said he would see us Friday. So, what do you say baby?"

Chloe stayed quiet, her head leaning against my chest, her hand circling my neck and I could feel her fighting off her sobs. I was nervous, we had talked about it and she was okay with it then, but I went behind her back and started the process. I just want us to be a family already.

Finally she lifted her head, wiping under her eyes, "I would love for us to all share a last name. Of course we will go on Friday."

I leaned down kissing her with so much love and passion, my hand coming up to caress her cheek, pulling away I peppered a few last kisses on her cheek, "I may not have been there to make him, but I promise to be the best fucking father for all of our babies. And he's our first baby."

Later that afternoon, we had received the paperwork from Don's office and Chloe and I were going over it together.

Reading the words on the document put it into perspective how big of a deal this really was. It made things real.

The rest of the day we spent lounging around the house, I had yet to tell Chloe about her ex scoping out the house last night. How he got in I'm not sure.

I had gone over to a few of the neighbors houses and they were going to send me any footage they might have picked up of the car driving away.

I decided to not share that info with Chloe until I had more info. My next away series wasn't for another two weeks so hopefully we can get things settled before I have to leave.

Friday came rather slow, maybe it was the anticipation and the excitement, but finally it was here.

After talking with my coach, he gave me the day off to get ready to see the judge and be with my family.

Chloe held my hand as I held Colton on my hip as we walked into the judge's office, meeting Don in the hallways.

"There you guys are. Glad we could make this all work today. Chloe how are you? I'm Don."

Don stuck his hand out shaking Chloe's, "Hi, it's nice to meet you. This is Colton." She gestured to the little boy being shy in my arms.

"Hey little man, you ready for the big day?"

Colton continued just to look at him before turning to look at me, hiding his head in my neck.

I let out a laugh rubbing his back, "He's just a little nervous I think. He will warm up soon. So, we ready to do this?"

Don knocked on the door before opening it and letting us in.

The judge stood up from his seat, a large smile spread across his face, "Ahh the Collins family. Come in, come in take a seat." He gestured to the chairs in front of his desk.

I placed my hand on Chloe's lower back directing her to one of the chairs.

Once seated, Don standing behind my chair, the judge took a seat, looking between Chloe and I before his eyes landing on Colton who was still tucked into me. He was an older gentleman, he reminded me of my dad but with round framed glasses and a greying mustache.

"What a beautiful family you have here. So, today you both are wanting Mr. Collins to adopt Colton, is this correct?"

Chloe reached over holding my hand, giving me a squeeze before responding, "Yes that is correct."

"Perfect. Your lawyer has provided you with the paperwork prior to today so you were aware of everything correct?"

I nodded, "Yes, we have both reviewed it."

The judge smiled looking back down at the paper in front of him, flipping through the pages, before his eyes lifted to look at Chloe.

"Mrs. Collins, is Colton's dad not in the picture?"

Chloe took a deep breathe in, "Umm no. His dad almost killed me and that was when I found out I was pregnant. After getting out of the hospital he disappeared and never came around. He isn't or wasn't aware I was pregnant, but I was okay with raising Colton on my own."

I squeezed her hand showing my support.

"You said wasn't aware' is it safe to assume he now knows? And you said 'almost killed you', was he charged with anything?"

Chloe took another deep breathe, her free hand going to her baby bump, "He was abusive, the night I wound up in the hospital he had beat me to the point I passed out and my neighbor found me bleeding over the floor. I believe he now knows Colton might be his, umm, he wasn't charged his lawyer actually got him off and then he disappeared. He's been coming around now stalking and breaking into our previous home. We have detectives trying to catch him."

The judge watched her as she told every word of her horrible past with her ex.

213

He then took a deep breathe looking at me, "Has this guy ever threatened you?"

I looked at Chloe giving her a soft smile, "Yes, he has left notes for me at the arena. He has paid off security guards to get into the locker rooms. And umm, he has shown up at our previous home as Chloe mentioned and broke in while she was home with Colton. He actually figured our new home location, he was staking out of our home early in the morning on Wednesday when I returned home from away games."

Chloe abruptly turned to look at me in shock. "What?" "Sorry baby, I called Brown and we got footage of the new car. They are now sending patrol cars throughout our neighborhood more frequently now. I didn't want to worry you."

The judge looked between us before trying to steer the conversation, "So this man has no parental rights correct?"

Chloe looked back at the judge shaking her head, "He was never placed on the birth certificate. Colton has my maiden name."

"You feel confident in the fact that Mr. Collins will make a great father for your son then Mrs. Collins?"

Chloe smiled, "He has made a great father for our son and he will continue to be a good father to our twins as well."

The judge finally noticed the growing bump, "A congratulations are in order. I'm sorry I hadn't noticed earlier dear."

"It's alright." Chloe smiled back at him.

"Mr. Collins do you feel that you can provide for Colton? If so, please explain in detail."

"I believe that I have provided for both my wife and son. I have purchased us a larger home in a gated community, Colton has his own room where he will not have to share the space. I have provided child care if my wife and I are working. My parents have moved close by to also be there for Colton and Chloe. I have added him to my health insurance the moment I married Chloe. I have also started a college saving account in his name, if he chooses to not go to college that's fine, it's his savings."

Chloe again turned to look at me in shock, "You started a savings account?"

I laughed, "Yea, it was going to be part of your mother's day gift baby."

The judge continued to ask us a few more questions, during this time Colton started wanting down. Placing him on the ground he walked over to Chloe wanting a snack. Once the little boy was satisfied he walked back over to me, one hand in the air, "dada".

I picked him back up, placing him on my knee as he started warming up to Don, who was making faces at him. And then turning to look at the judge giving him a toothy smile.

"He seems to see you as his father Mr. Collins. This is a good sign that he is comfortable with you. I also believe if you weren't a good father, you wife wouldn't have married you."

I let out a laugh looking back at Chloe, "Her opinion is the only one that matters. I wouldn't be sitting here in front of you if I didn't feel like I had her support or confidence."

Silence fell over us as Chloe and I continued to look at each other.

We were both shaken out of our trance by the judge, "I have gone ahead and signed the paper work. Mr. Collins, congratulations. You are now a legal parent of Colton. We can process the name change documents and he will now be Colton Collins."

Chloe and I stood up shaking the judges hand and Dons before peppering kisses on Colton's face, making him giggle.

"Colton Collins has a good ring to it, don't you think?"

Chloe ran her hands through Colton's hair, keeping her eyes on mine.

"The Collin's family has a better ring to it".

29

Chloe: Cornered

2 weeks had passed since Reed found James outside the house and the judge had signed off on the adoption papers.

Colton was now officially a Collins and I loved knowing all my sweet babies were going to share a name. When Reed and I first started dating I never imagined we would be married, 2 babies on the way and Colton officially adopted, but here we are.

Detective Brown had called in regards to the footage and they believe that they have located where James has been staying-so fingers crossed this mess comes to an end before I bring two more babies into the world.

Speaking of babies, my belly is already larger than when I was pregnant with Colton. I am 1/2 way through my pregnancy and both angels are active 24/7.

Reed rubs my belly every night before bed and talks to them and I can tell they love their daddy as much as I do just based on how crazy they kick and move.

Due to my size now, I have refrained from booking any clients and with James getting as close as he has, I have had to really focus on my safety. I feel terrible for letting my shop sit there unused, but until things blow over, I really don't know what else I can do.

Today is the start of April, which means hockey season is about over-depending on if Reed and the team make playoffs. Plus, I am also 4 months from giving birth, at least this time around I have a family to support me and I won't be alone.

Reed and I have also not discussed baby names, and it's driving me crazy. I have nothing else to do with my day that I keep thinking of names but I haven't voiced them to Reed yet. I would like to pick names out so I can start figuring out their nursery.

Colton was with his grandparents for the day while Reed had a morning practice-leaving me to clean the house, catch up on laundry and enjoy the peace and quiet.

Reed hated leaving me alone since James stalked the house, but with all windows and doors locked I begged him to let me have a few hours to myself.

As I was in the living room, I could hear what sounded like the front door handle jiggling. My in laws and Reed all had keys, so why the door handle was moving I don't know.

I peeked cautiously through the peep hole and my whole heart dropped.

Standing at the door, completely unaware that I was on the other side was James. He was looking at his phone before looking around at the road and driveway. My car was currently getting new tires on it at the dealership and Reed had his truck, James probably thought no one was home.

I covered my mouth to prevent any sound to leave my body as I stumbled back. Panic set in as I located my phone before quietly running up the stairs to the master bathroom, locking myself inside.

I dialed Detective Browns number, tears filling my eyes. "Mrs. Collins is everything okay?"

I took an unsteady breathe, "No he's here. At my door. I'm locked upstairs now. I saw him. He was trying to get the front door open."

"Stay on the line with me, I will head over now. I will call backup. Where is your son and husband?"

"Reed's in the middle of practice and Colton is with my in laws at the zoo." I kept wiping under my eyes.

"I will have a detective retrieve your husband. Do you hear anything in your home?"

I stayed quiet for a few seconds before gingerly making my way to the window that overlooked the front of our house, "No, it's quiet and I'm scared. I can't fight back if he gets to me."

217

"He will not get to you or hurt you. You have my word. I am almost there. Pulling up now to the guard's booth."

I could hear him talk to the guard at the entrance to our neighborhood.

The door to the bathroom started moving before I could hear James voice, "Chloe I know your there. I can hear you breathing. There's no running from me now."

My breath hitched in my throat, he had gotten into the house. Detective Brown wasn't here yet, maybe another minute out. Anything could happen.

I hung up the phone opting to text Brown, "SOS he's at my bathroom door. Help please!"

The door handle continued to move, and with every second that passed I felt like I was coming to the end of my run.

I sent Reed a text in case something happened, the tears falling freely from my eyes, I curled up in the bathtub, nowhere to run, I had no weapon to use and being 20 weeks pregnant, I couldn't go out the window or even make it far on my feet.

"Reed, he's here in the house. He has me cornered in the bathroom. Detective Brown is almost here. I love you. I love you so much and I am so happy for the time we have had together. In case something happens don't forget how much me and the babies love you."

I hated sending the message, but it needed to be said in case I didn't walk away like I did last time.

I didn't peer out the window to see if the cops have arrived, I focused on the door that was getting worn down from James. It was a matter of time before he got to me.

I continued to hold my stomach, I couldn't protect my babies but I would try.

Then my heart sank, the door opened and James stood there with the most evil smile on his face.

He looked worn down and skinnier than last time I had seen him. His eyes were sunken in and his beard was scruffy. His hair was going all over the place and in dire need of a haircut. "I told you that you wouldn't get far from me. Stupid girl. Thinking you could leave California without me knowing?"

He stalked forward as I tried to make myself invisible, which was dumb, I had nothing to hide behind. "James, leave me alone. I want nothing from you and I have nothing of yours. Just leave please."

I begged and I didn't care at this point. My makeup was running down my face for sure, and I was shaking.

He continued to stalk forward until he came to the side of the tub, leaning his body forward, "You took my son from me. My child. My blood. You took him away and I want him back."

I shook my head in protest, "He isn't yours James. He was never yours. You're wasting your time." I spat.

I had somehow decided to fight back with what energy I had, when it came to my children, no one would touch them or threaten them.

James wheeled his hand back before it came in contact with my face.

I gasped as I placed my hand over my cheek where he had struck me.

"You're just a bitch Chloe, always have been and always will be. You need to be dealt with. Didn't you learn anything last time about talking back."

This time he lunged forward grabbing me by the arm trying to pull me to my feet.

I tried ripping his hands off me, but sadly I knew I was losing.

Once he had me on my feet he pulled me forward, causing me to stumble out of the tub.

I placed my hand over my bump, hoping to protect them.

"Look at you, knocked up again." He laughed spitting in my face. "You going to run off and take them away from their father to?"

I reached forward trying to push him back, "Leave me alone, leave my family alone. We owe you nothing. Just leave!" I screamed.

James' hand came around the side knocking me in the head, causing me to stumble to the ground, hitting my head on the edge of the tub as I fell.

My vision blurred as I laid there, my hands holding my stomach as the world around me faded. The last thing I could hear before darkness consumed me was yelling, by who I don't know.

30

Reed: The Unknown

Coach yelled for me to head to the locker room in the middle of practice which seemed off as we had literally just started drills. I was skating off the ice heading to the locker room when I noticed 2 officers waiting by the small door by the player's benches. Both had to have been early 30's and both wore the same emotionless look on their faces. Theirs eyes tracked my movement as I skated closer to them.

"Are you Reed Collins?" One of them asked.

I removed my helmet, shaking my hair out, "I am. Is everything okay?"

"I'm officer Andrews and this is officer Martins, we were asked by Detective Brown to come get you."

I stared at both of them as if waiting for more answers, "Okay, is my wife and son okay? What's going on?"

"Your wife is on her way to the hospital, there had been a break in at your home. Detective Brown was notified by your wife and he is with her now. Your son was not there as I believe he is with your parents. But we need to go now sir."

I took off sprinting to the locker room to change as fast I could, the moment I heard Chloe was being taken to the hospital I felt hopeless. I could feel the tears falling down my cheeks and my heart beating rapidly.

After changing I grabbed my phone, noticing a text from Chloe, 20 minutes ago.

Hopefully she was telling me she was fine, but the moment I read the words my world collapsed around me.

"Reed, he's here in the house. He has me cornered in the bathroom. Detective Brown is almost here. I love you. I love you so much and I am so happy for the time we have had together. In case something happens don't forget how much me and the babies love you."

I sucked in a large breathe, typing back, "I'm on my way, I love you. You hold on, I will not lose you."

I had no idea if she was okay, injured, or worse. I ran out of the locker room with the two officers pushing the doors open for me to the parking lot. I hopped in the patrol car as they sped off to the hospital, I dialed Detective Browns number.

"Reed are you on your way?"

"I am now tell me what has happened. Why is my wife going to the hospital?"

I couldn't hold the sobs back, I hated not knowing. "Reed, he broke in. I was getting through the guards booth when he got into the house and found her hiding. She's okay as of right now, he assaulted her and when she slipped she hit her head on the edge of the tub. Me and my officers were only seconds late, he's in custody and is being booked without bail at this time. But I need you to come into the hospital so I can fill you in with more."

I ran a hand down my face, trying to control my emotions, and breathing, "Is she awake? Are, are the babies okay? Fuck is she going to be okay?!"

"The doctors are running tests, from what they can tell and how we found her, she never landed on her stomach, the force was on head and back. It seems like she turned her body to save them. Doctors are hopeful Reed. I have informed your parents Reed so you can be here and not worry about Colton."

Within 5 minutes the officers parked in front of the Emergency and I ran through the doors looking for Detective Brown.

Brown was talking with a nurse when her eyes went wide and nodded in my direction letting Detective Brown know of my arrival.

He turned around giving me a soft smile, pulling me into a hug.

The moment I felt his embrace I started bawling. I only knew this man on a professional level but here he was allowing me to fall apart.

"Reed, she's okay. The doctor just let me know that there is only a little swelling on her brain but that was from the fall. She's breathing, she's a little bruised but she should be awake in the next hour. They are going to do an ultrasound to check the babies if you want to go in."

I pulled away wiping my eyes, "Can I? What room is she in?"

He placed a hand on my shoulder, "Come on, room 213. Lets' go. She might not be awake but you can talk to her and the babies."

I followed him with his guidance down the hallway before walking into a room filled with natural lighting and the soft beeps from the machines.

A doctor and nurse where both setting up the ultrasound, giving me soft smiles as I entered.

My eyes falling on my wife, she looked so small in the bed. A bruise cascaded down the left side of her head, some dried blood stuck to her blonde hair. Her hands naturally falling on the bump that held our babies.

I walked over, feeling the air hitch in my throat. I reached for her hand, it was cold, she would hate knowing that.

I pulled a chair up, holding her hands in mine, intertwining our fingers together. Bringing her hands up I placed kisses on the back of them before another sob broke out.

"Please come back baby. I hate this. I miss you and love you." I didn't care who could hear me. She was my lifeline, my everything. She was the only thing in this world that kept my heart beating.

"Mr. Collins, we are going to do a quick ultrasound to make sure the babies are good. How far along is she?"

"Umm, 20 weeks yesterday."

The nurse nodded, writing the note down. The doctor started the process as my eyes drifted from her belly to the picture on the screen.

There were 2 babies side by side, they could be holding hands for all I know. But the moment the words "The babies are perfect" left the doctors lips I started crying again.

I guess I nodded off for a while. I could feel someone's hand running through my hair as it laid on the hospital bed.

I groaned, pulling my head to the side to see my wife's face. A wife who was smiling and staring at me.

"Chloe." I whispered.

"Hi honey. I'm so sorry if I scared you." Tears started running down her face.

I reached forward taking her face gently in my hands, smiling at her, "You're okay, you're awake and our babies are okay. There is nothing to apologize for. This was not your fault."

I left a gentle kiss on her lips pulling away.

She started sobbing, so I crawled in next to her, pulling her to my chest, "He broke in and found me hiding. I tried my best to protect the babies. I knew I couldn't do a lot but I needed to try."

I continued to hold her, letting her sobs soak my shirt.

My hand gently rubbing her head.

"Baby. You did so good. You did nothing wrong. All that matters is that you are alive, I would have been lost without you."

We continued to lay there holding one another. The doctor had come in to check on Chloe before leaving us alone again. We decided to call my parents and update them and I also updated Matt and Summer.

Around 7pm a soft knock woke Chloe and I both up from an impromptu nap.

My mom was standing in the door with Colton holding her hand.

"Dada, Mama" Colton ran over to the side of the bed wanting up.

I reached forward grabbing him, placing him on my lap where Chloe could wrap her arms around him.

"Thanks mom, for bringing him." I planted a kiss on her head.

"He wanted to see you both. He wasn't sure why we couldn't go home. I'll stay until you need me to take him home for the night. Chloe, how are you feeling sweetie?"

My mom held Chloe's hand, giving her a kiss on her forehead, "I'm better. I'm safe and so is my family. Thank you for taking Colton today."

My mom stayed a few more minutes before walking off to talk to a nurse about Chloe's departure.

As mom left, a pregnant Summer with Matt in tow came through the door, both had red puffy eyes.

"Fuck, can you guys stop pulling this shit. I can't take it" Matt cried kissing Chloe and hugging me.

"Sorry man. Go beat the bastard up who did this then." I hugged Summer, eyeing Matt.

"Fuck I'll go see if the detectives will give me and a few guys from the team some time with him to 'talk'" he air quoted.

Chloe smiled, trying to hold back a giggle. She reached for Summer's hand, "Hey no crying. I'm okay. The babies are okay. It's over. I promise."

Summer nodded, wiping under her eyes, "I know, it just, it scared the fucking hell out of me."

"I know. I was scared to. But it's over."

Hearing Chloe mention she was scared made my heart drop again. I wiped under my eyes trying to prevent any tears to fall. I needed to be strong right now and not cry, she needed me strong not broken.

I could feel her hand rubbing my back, letting me know she knew how I felt but didn't let up on it.

By 9pm, my mom had taken Colton home for the night and Summer and Matt had gone home to rest. With the promise of bringing us breakfast in the morning.

Doctors said we would be able to leave tomorrow sometime, so hoping it was early-I couldn't stand being in the hospital longer than we were.

I held Chloe to my chest, my hand in her hair, her hands on my chest.

We weren't talking, just being. She placed a delicate kiss on my chest, "I want to choose names tonight Reed. I can't stand referring to them as 'the babies' any longer. They need names. Can we name them please?"

I kissed her forehead, "Yea baby, I've had some names picked out for a while but I wasn't sure if you were ready to hear the suggestions."

She lifted her head to eye me, "You've been thinking of them?"

"Of course baby, I'm fucking excited about them."

She let out a soft giggle. "Okay what's your name for a girl?"

I twirled a piece of her hair in my hand, "I love the name Amelia."

"That's beautiful, I like that a lot. What about a middle name?"

"Hmmm" I continued to twirl her hair, "Rose."

"Amelia Rose" Chloe repeated out loud. "Amelia Rose Collins, I love it."

"Our baby girl" I kissed her forehead, "Alright what about for our terror #2?"

Chloe giggled again, "He will not be a terror, well maybe a little." She took a moment to think, "I was thinking Carter Owen. Umm, Carter was my dad's name."

This was one of the first times she has ever let info about her parents come out. "Carter Owen Collins. It's perfect baby and I bet your dad would be proud."

I watched her wipe her tear away, "I know I don't talk about them ever. Umm, but when I was falling into the darkness I prayed for them to help me and I could almost feel like I had been in their arms again. It sounds crazy. But I think they were with me Reed."

I felt like bawling, knowing she felt her deceased parents and she didn't feel alone warmed my heart. "Because they were protecting their baby girl like you protected Amelia and Carter."

"They would have loved your Reed. They would have hated James and they would have loved Colton."

She paused, gathering her words, so I let her have this time to think before talking, I didn't want to push her after the day she had.

"Mom and dad died when I was 18, dad flew planes as a hobby, he owned a small plane and he and mom would go on trips all the time. The last time they flew they were heading on a weekend getaway to the dessert, they asked if I wanted to go but I had school and I turned them down. Promised to go another time. They called everyday and sent photos of the fun they were having. On their flight home, something changed, they think some mechanical failure, but I'm not sure. Dad lost control and they crashed. I never got to say good bye, but I saved the photos they sent me before heading home."

I held her tighter, "I'm sorry baby. It sounds selfish but I'm glad you are still here. You or Colton wouldn't be here baby if you had gone."

She nodded in agreeance, "It took me to finding myself holding a newborn little boy in my arms to realize why I was still here. I don't regret the 'what ifs' anymore. I just wish they hadn't gone."

"I get that baby. They are still here though, they watched your go to school, have a baby, move across country and fall in love. They will continue to be with you, Colton, Amelia and Carter. They aren't far baby." I kissed her again drawing her close.

After a few more minutes of silence, I leaned down pressing my forehead to hers, "Let's get some sleep baby."

She yawned holding the collar of my shirt as I pulled the blanket up over the two of us.

She kissed my cheek as our breathing slowed down and eyes were closing, as a whisper I heard her murmur, "I'm glad I'm here and that there is no 'unknown'."

Fuck, the unknown, the unknown of what would happen to me, too Colton, to everything. She's right, she's here and we're okay.

31

Reed: Relaxation

C hloe was released from the hospital the following morning with strict instructions to rest. She did have a slight concussion but nothing major.

My parents offered to keep Colton another night- making sure that he was treating it as a "vacation", and let me tell you, he was eating up the attention.

Chloe had willingly crawled into bed when we got home, and lucky we had my dad and Matt who changed the busted door locks that James had broken.

I offered to sell the house and buy a new one if it made Chloe comfortable and she argued with me that she was just fine. I just don't want her to feel the need to lie to me in order to make things seem easier. I want her to want to be home, to feel comfortable in our space and never worry about something like this happening again.

Yet, she was adamant that she was fine and that she loved our home and with James behind bars, she felt safer than she has in a long time.

I sat in the kitchen on a barstool staring at my phone, I needed to call my agent, GM and coach; there was no way I was going to feel comfortable leaving my wife like this for an away stretch.

We only had 2 weeks of regular season left before playoffs and we were still unsure if we would make the wild card slot. Deep down as much as I wanted the shot to win Lord Stanley, I wanted to be home with my family.

I dialed my GM Frank first; everyone was aware of why I left practice early, but I hadn't had that conversation with any of them.

After 3 rings he answered, "Reed, how is Chloe?"

I kept the phone close to my ear, my other hand playing with the pen in front of me, "She's good. She's bruised up, small concussion and the babies are healthy."

"Reed, that's good news. I'm glad that she's home. Look I know why you're calling, take this next week off and come back for the last week of home games. I have already cleared you with everyone. Take this time to be there for her and your son and rest up."

I felt like crying again, I inhaled a large breathe, "Thank you Frank. I feel guilty leaving my team but, you're right. I need to be here for my family. I'll be good to go next week and ready for when we get that wild card spot."

"Don't worry about calling coach unless you want to.

But call your agent- he deserves to know what's happening."

I realized that I really hadn't informed my agent of anything happening. Luckily no press picked up on the previous incidences but now that police and ambulances had arrived at my home, it was bound to make the news somewhere.

"Thank you Frank. I'll probably be in once a day to the facility to work out-Chloe will force me out or come with me. Thanks for everything."

"Anytime Reed."

Call ended. I continued to sit there my phone in hand. I dialed my agent's number and for the next 15 minutes I filled him in on everything that transpired the last few months.

By the time I was off the phone with him, Chloe had waddled into the kitchen with a sleepy smile across her face. She was beautiful, she was wearing one of my shirts and a pair of sleep shorts. The shirt was like a dress on her even with the bump. Her hair was in a claw clip with pieces framing her face.

Her slippered feet made their way to where I sat, she spun me so the front of my body faced hers. Her hands gently caressing my face, the pads of her thumbs rubbing back and forth.

"What are you doing handsome?"

I leaned into one of her hands, closing my eyes, "My GM put me on personal leave for a week to stay home. I'll return the last week of regular season though."

I opened my eyes to watch her expression change, she kept the same smile her face as her eyes met mine. "Usually I would argue with you-but call me selfish. I'll keep you when I can get you."

I gently brought my hand her cheek pulling her to me, our lips meshing together perfectly.

"We got a whole week to relax and be a family. Although I need to go in once a day and workout to stay in shape."

Chloe's fingers threaded through my hair at the base of my neck, "Hmm, I would say if I didn't have a concussion that we could find other ways for you to stay in shape-but the gym might be better this go around."

Her eyes held love, desire and happiness in them, her emotions swimming in the irises of her eyes. A playful smirk on her lips.

I squeezed her hips, pulling her as close as the bump would allow for her to me. "Baby, you can't start things like this when we both know we can't do anything about it. So, how about you go sit on the couch, put your feet up, put on one of your shows and I'll bring you some food."

She pressed her forehead to mine, snaking her arms completely around my neck, "How did I get so lucky to have a husband like you." Kissing me one more time she unraveled her hands, turning to head off to the living room.

As she turned I gave her butt a smack, causing her to look over her shoulder with an eyebrow raised, "Reed Collins, what did you just say to me?"

I laughed nodding my head to tell her to keep moving, "Love you baby."

Later that afternoon Summer and Matt stopped by with dinner; Colton had been dropped off by my parents a few hours earlier. He has been glued to Chloe's side. He's still to young to know what happened but he knows that Chloe isn't feeling great.

Chloe and Summer are lounging on the couch, Chloe's head resting on Summers shoulder as Colton lays next to Chloe, asleep, with his head laid in her lap.

Matt and I decided to work out in the home gym I had set up, reminding us of when we lived together.

Matt was doing arm reps in front of the mirrored wall, "How's Chloe been today?"

I was on the ground next to him stretching out my back, "She's been fine. She's actually listening to me when I tell her to go rest. Colton has been attached to her side all day. She hasn't let up that anything hurts, but I doubt she will tell me right away."

Matt dropped the weights, sitting down next to me, "How are you doing?"

I leaned back on my arms, "I'm okay I think. Yesterday I was a fucking mess. I'll be fine. Her and the twins are fine and I'm happy knowing Colton wasn't home."

Deep down I know I'm not doing good. I'm happy Chloe is home and that she is okay. I didn't sleep at all last night and couldn't even get a nap in because I kept having dreams where she didn't survive and it fucking broke me.

"Reed, you can talk to me. You don't always have to be the one putting others first. You can put yourself first right now. I know you aren't okay."

I ran a hand down my face, I hated that Matt could always read me like a book, "I keep having dreams and thoughts that she didn't survive and it hurts so fucking much. What if he had pushed her harder or had a weapon? What if the cops didn't get to her in time?"

Matt rested a hand on my shoulder, "But she's here, she survived and she protected herself and the babies. You can't focus on the 'what ifs'. If you do that then you aren't living in the moment. You need to stop focusing on the things that didn't happen and focus on the fact you have time off to be with her and your son, maybe prep the nursery, then end of season, possible playoffs and then bam! You welcome two more terrors to the party. Let's take it a day at a time and stop focusing on the things that didn't happen."

I let out a shaky breathe as the door creaked open and Chloe peaked her head in giving me a soft smile, Colton running past her legs into my arms, "He's right baby. I'm here still, we have greater things to look forward to."

Matt got up saying something about going to get Summer something to snack on.

Chloe waddled over, her hands caressing her stomach before she reached for my hand, helping her sit down beside me.

"I know I shouldn't focus on what didn't happen. It just scared me when I read your text and the cops got me. I just don't know what I would have done if you had left me."

I could feel the tears sliding down my cheeks, Colton looking up, touching my face, "Dadda."

I leaned forward giving him a kiss on the forehead, "Daddy's okay bud."

Chloe reached out wiping under my eyes, "If something did happen, you and Colton would have been just fine with time. You would have had each other and the support system of our family. But the good part, is that you don't have to live the scenario. Let's focus on getting Amelia's and Carter's nursery done."

She always knew how to make me feel better and for her I will forever be grateful. Deep down it will take a me a week or longer to really move past this memory but knowing she's here and well will continue to help me thrive and push forward.

I guess a week home is more for me than for her.

32

Chloe: Playoffs and News

Reed's back on the ice after a week off of playing, the bruising on my face has gone down and isn't as noticeable. The press released information on my accident and Reed's agent and Detective Brown willingly led the press conference on our behalf. The support we have been shown from St. Louis and the fans has been amazing.

When Reed returned to the ice for warmups, he received a standing ovation and like clockwork the tears sprang from my face.

The media team even did a welcome back for him and us, the love and support has been what we needed to heal.

I'm sitting in the family box at the arena with a very pregnant Summer to my right and Candice to my left.

My in-laws are sitting in front of me with Colton pressed against the glass window.

Reed was worried about me coming but even more worried with me staying home alone. I was adamant that this is where I needed to be and we can all agree that I won.

We were in the 3rd period with 5 minutes left and we were leading 2-1 over Vancouver.

Reed had gotten an assist and one of the goals, but also spent time in the penalty box for slashing.

Reed was playing amazing, the week off must have helped him because he floated down the ice with such speed and grace.

Colton was asleep on Dave's chest as we were all on the edge of our seats.

This game was the deciding factor on whether the boys made play-offs and I knew that Reed wanted a chance at the cup but I also knew he didn't want to spend any time away from me.

I prayed they made it to playoffs, he needs a win right now and I will be more than okay to spend my nights in the rink if it meant he had a chance at achieving a lifelong dream.

The time ticked down, Vancouver was out to fight, they were trying their best to tie the game up. With the last 15 seconds, Matt got ahold of the puck, passing it across to Reed as he weaved in and out of the other team's players, making his way pass the blue line. Vancouver had pulled their goalie and once Reed made it past the last defenseman he shot at the goal. The buzzer sounding as the clock hit 0 and as the puck hit the back of the net.

I stood up faster than I should have, reaching to the back of the chair in front of me for support. Summer, Candice and I were excitedly high fiving and clapping.

The boys had clenched a playoff spot, they had done it, they worked so hard and now it has finally paid off.

I pulled Summer in for a hug, our bumps colliding causing us to laugh harder. Tears were streaming down our eyes when we noticed that the camera had panned to the box and we were being shown on the Jumbotron. The guys were skating around the ice hugging each other and celebrating.

Reed and Matt caught Summer and my eyes as they celebrated with one another on the ice.

Later that night Reed picked me up as we entered our bedroom, placing me down on the bed. A giggle escaped my lips as he peppered kisses along my jaw and throat.

"You are my good luck charm baby" Reed voiced in between kisses. His voice was filled with desire and lust.

"You're just now realizing this?" I laughed. My hand grabbing the back of his neck and the other grabbing his jaw. Bringing his lips to meet mine.

Our lips fought for dominance, both wanting to gain control of the other. Reed's hands grabbed my wrists, pinning them above my head as he trailed kisses down my neck through the valley of my breasts and back up to my ear.

"If you weren't pregnant right now, you would be by the end of tonight" he growled in my ear.

"I need you Reed, like now!" I moaned.

Reed pulled back releasing my hands, but they stayed on their own free will, taking in the appearance of the man in front of me as he shed his shirt.

I pulled my bottom lip under my teeth, biting back the moan that I knew was bubbling up inside of me.

I tried to squeeze my legs together to relieve pressure, I could feel my core getting wetter as Reed trailed his hands seductively up my legs.

"Fuck baby, giving me that look is getting me hard." Reed hooked his fingers into the waist band of my leggings, pulling them off animalistic style.

I sat up, pulling my shirt off my torso leaving me in a Lacey blue bra. My breasts were pouring out of the cups as I hadn't gotten new bras since they've grown with pregnancy.

Reed stood taking his dress pants off before climbing back onto the bed, hovering over me.

Within seconds he had my bra off and thrown across the floor, "Fuck baby you're hot."

Reed took my left breast in his mouth, swirling his tongue around my sensitive nipple while his other hand played with my right breast. My eyes rolled back in my head, my hands falling at the base his neck, a moan leaving my lips.

Reed switched breasts, giving them equal attention.

Reed moved his hands, gripping my waist. Pulling back he had me flipped over on my knees.

His hands pulling me close, his hardened cock pressing against my ass, "I'm going to fuck this tight pussy baby. You think you can handle that?"

Another moan left my mouth, "Please Reed, fuck me."

Reed immediately pressed into me, both our bodies stilling as we feel the other.

Reed felt so tight as he filled me, he rocked his hips into me as I met his pace.

Our pace quickened as we both chased our release.

I reached one hand under me, caressing his balls with my hand, a gasp leaving his mouth, "Holy shit baby. Doing that is going to make me cum faster."

He reached his hand down, drawing circles on my clit, causing me to react the same way he had.

We continued to meet each other's pace until we started getting sloppier. Both breathing heavy.

"Reed, I'm close." I drawled out "Cum with me baby."

Hearing the words leaving his mouth and his touch on my clit, he had me unraveling.

His thrusts became harder until he stilled, falling forward, his chest pressing against my back. I could feel his lips kissing my shoulder blades, "Fuck baby, that never gets old."

I couldn't help but laugh, as I was the one pregnant yet he was the one more winded. "I feel bad, seems like you did all the work, baby daddy"

Reed pulled out of me, falling to his side, his hands falling to my lower back.

Reed laughed, "Can't have my baby mama getting too overworked now can we?"

Reed got up, coming back from the bathroom with a warm wash cloth, cleaning me up. Once cleaned, Reed joined me in bed, pulling me to his chest.

"I love you Chloe." "I love you Reed."

The next day I had worked up before Reed, I had snuck out of bed and waddled my way into my morning routine before checking on Colton.

I grabbed the baby monitor once I noticed that Colton was still asleep and made my way into the kitchen to find some food.

When I was pregnant with Colton I hadn't gained all that much weight, but now having 2 babies in the womb, I felt like a whale due to the amount of food and sugar I craved.

After an hour of making a feast of French toast, eggs, bacon and fresh fruit, I was greeted with the sights of my 2 favorite boys with their sleepy hair and smiles.

Reed placed Colton on the ground, allowing for my sweet baby to walk to me wanting cuddles and love.

Since my stomach was larger than before, it was harder for me to hold Colton for long periods of times. I hated not giving him that time like we used to have. He was my first baby and I couldn't hold him like I used to.

I snatched him into my arms peppering kisses all over his cheeks making him giggle.

"Mama. Unngry"

"Is Colton hungry? How about some bacon?"

I held a piece out, his little hand reaching out grabbing it and devouring it.

"Just like your dad little man."

Reed grunted from behind me, "I don't devour food like that, I enjoy and savor, duh. He must have picked that up from you love."

"Uhh, I don't think so sir." I leaned over giving him a quick kiss, "Good morning baby daddy."

"Good morning baby mama."

Breakfast was perfect. Reed had playoffs in a week and his coach decided to healthy scratch him for their last regular season game. Which was perfect timing because that game was away and honestly I didn't want to be away from him quite yet.

We hadn't heard from Detective Brown in regards to my ex, but we were both waiting for that phone call any moment this week.

As I was cleaning up Colton, Reed worked on cleaning the dishes.

After wiping the excess amount of food off my toddlers face-still wondering how he got more of it on him than in him I will never know. My phone started ringing, Detective Brown, coming across my screen.

I picked Colton up helping him onto the ground as I accepted his call, "Good morning Detective Brown".

"Good morning Chloe. How are you feeling?"

I grabbed the paper towels I had used, making my way to the trash can, locking eyes with Reed, "I'm better. I should return back to work here soon. The bruising is down, but overall I'm ok. Thank you for everything."

Reed came over pulling my back to his chest, his hand circling my waist as he placed his head on my shoulder. Giving me time to talk with Brown but also letting me know he's there for me. This will also save me the hassle of repeating the conversation.

I removed the phone placing it on speaker.

"That's good to hear Chloe. I take it Reed is nearby. So good morning Reed."

Reed let out a laugh, "Morning Detective. What news do you have for us?"

"Well for starters, congrats on clenching, I look forward to watching you bring that cup home. Second, the judge who approved your adoption is also the judge who received the new file. Your lawyer should be calling soon, they want to have a meeting. But from what I know, the judge liked you and well-I don't think he's going to walk. But be prepared for anything."

I leaned further into Reed, holding his hand with mine, "Thank you for the heads up. If this goes to court, will you- um will you come with and be near us?"

I can feel a soft kiss on my temple.

"Chloe, I wouldn't be anywhere else. I'll even go to the meeting if it makes you feel safer."

I could cry, I hadn't had support like this before.

Reed noticed my change in demeanor, noticed I was about to lose it, "Thanks detective. We will call you when we hear anything. You have been in this with us since the beginning. Thank you for protecting my family."

"I'm here anytime Collins family. Have a great rest of your day."

I hung up the phone after saying good bye before turning into Reed's arms. We just let one another be, didn't say anything didn't move. Not until 2 little hands found themselves on our legs, his head pressed against our thighs. Reed and I both let out a laugh, turning our attention to the little boy smiling up at us, "Mama, Dad, paayyy".

Reed kisses my temple again, "Let's play buddy. What are we going to play with? Dragons, dinosaurs, trucks?"

He chased after Colton as Colton stopped turning around shaking his head "no" with a smile, "dada Ockey." Turning back around he headed towards his little mini sticks and goal set Reed and Matt had set up for him.

Reed stopped in his tracks, looking back at me, "Did he just say 'hockey'?"

I rubbed my belly as I walked closer to my husband, "What can I say he loves his daddy."

Reed smiled kissing me on the lips before practically hurtling the couch to get to the spare stick on the floor by Colton.

I could watch them for hours hitting the ball back and forth and doing their celebrations or 'cellys' as I had been corrected.

Later that evening we had heard from our lawyer who informed us of the meeting with the judge and my ex's lawyer. He mentioned that my ex wouldn't be present but we were more than welcome to attend.

Luckily it was at the end of the week and Reed's parents offered to watch Colton.

Tonight I am focusing on the little boy and his dad in front of me running around the living room with a hockey stick in hand.

33

Reed: Prison and Game 1

It's finally the end of the week and Chloe, myself and Detective Brown are walking into the judges office-almost deja vu. My lawyer is already inside seated, staring at the other lawyer trying to smooze the judge.

Chloe and I make our way to the 2 open seats placed on the right of my lawyer when the judge notices our arrival.

"Mr. and Mrs. Collins, nice to see you. How is your pregnancy going Mrs. Collins?"

Chloe smiled wide looking at the judge, "Very well thank you for asking. They are kicking like crazy lately. I want them here already."

I smiled stretching my arm over the back of her chair.

The judge shooed away the other lawyer moving back to his chair, insisting everyone sit.

For the next hour our lawyer and Chloe's ex's lawyer went back and forth while the other 4 of us sat there watching it unfold-almost like watching paint dry.

Her ex's lawyer was wanting a shortened sentence for his client's behavior, stating that he only acted that way because he was still in love with Chloe. That made me scoff- had he loved her he wouldn't have almost killed her, abused her or abandoned her. Fucking prick.

Chloe and I both shared our sides of the stalking and how much it affected our daily lives and how when he was close to being caught he acted guilty and disappeared- well tried.

Chloe also discussed how he had found her, Detective Brown also standing guard behind her as she spoke about the time and trauma. I

239

liked knowing he was also there for her, hell he found her and saved her. He got her the ambulance and stayed with her. This man isn't just a detective who saved my family, he is family.

The judge abruptly stood up, running a hand down his face, "I am giving James 10 years in federal prison on account of stalking, physical harm, attempted murder to Mrs. Collins and her two unborn babies and breaking and entering. This is generous and I will have no problem extending the sentence if he can't get his life together in prison. I am also putting a lifetime restraining order, meaning James once out cannot come in contact with the Collins family. He cannot come within 1,000 feet of them, contact them or approach them without being arrested again. This is my final decision."

With that James lawyer grabbed their belongings storming out. I stood up buttoning my coat jacket before reaching for Chloe's hand, helping her out of her chair. Both of us shared a happy look on our faces, although we wished for a longer sentence, it worked for now.

Detective Brown walked over shaking both our hands before moving to talk with our lawyer and the judge.

We thanked them before heading out towards the car, grabbing her hand in mine, giving it a squeeze.

"Well mama, how about a celebratory ice cream?"

Chloe giggled leaning into me as we walked, "How about celebratory sex?"

I turned to look at her with my eyes wide, "Well then… get your cute ass in the car and let's go home pretty lady."

Once we were home, we celebrated the best way we know how. After about 2 hours of making love to my wife, I trudged my way into the rink for some ice time to prepare for playoffs. My parents were taking Colton over and were staying for dinner. So, I worked my ass off to be home with those I loved.

Today had went well, we got answers, we got support and the weight lifted off our shoulders that we didn't near to bare.

It was game one of playoffs, we were playing Los Angeles and the arena was packed.

I had arrived early as usual, my family in tow. Chloe was meeting the other WAGs so they could do their "Photo shoot" for their new jackets they had specially made for playoffs. Colton also loved playing with Candice and Luke's little girl, so he wasn't complaining about cutting the cartoons off early.

I could tell tonight was going to be electric. The fans were decked out, the game was 100% sold out and the vibe was something I had never felt before.

Matt and I were in the locker room mentally preparing like we usually do. Summer was no longer our physical therapist since she was further along in her pregnancy-I think Matt was missing her in the room. That's how they met and it seemed to be their thing, his good luck charm.

I could tell it was eating at him, I nudged his shoulder getting him to look at me.

"Dude you good?"

He hung his head down, rubbing his hand over his face, "Ever since I got traded here a few years ago, Summer was always here. Now that she's in the WAGs box, I'm afraid of jinxing myself ya know?"

I knew what he meant. When we both got traded, it was as if Summer was his missing luck charm. The moment he got here, his game changed the moment she helped wrap his ankle. Since then it's something they always did. Hell I kept a rubber band on my wrist because I had forgotten it one game and I ended up playing so good I left it.

"Call her, she will come down and go through the routine bud."

As if she read my mind the door opened and a pregnant Summer sauntered in with a shy smile on her face.

"Hi baby. You want me to wrap your ankle?"

Matt smiled nodding his head, "Please?" His voice cracking.

"Did you think I wouldn't show up?" She asked unraveling the tape in her hand as she pulled a chair up in front of him.

"I just, I didn't want to bug you."

Summer smiled giving his thigh a squeeze, "I'll go through this routine with you any day and any time, pregnant or not" she laughed.

I watched as my best friend watched his fiancé wrap his ankle, a dumb smile plastered on his face. I loved seeing him happy, it made me happy knowing we both found happiness that we never thought we deserved.

As Summer finished wrapping his ankle, she turned to smile at me pulling something from her back pocket.

"Reed I have something for you."

She handed me a folded up paper, another form of deja vu casting over me.

I unfolded the paper to see another one of Colton's drawing. I could barely make out the figures, but Chloe's handwriting helped me decipher the art.

It was us, a family. The words "mama, Dada" written near two figures.

At the bottom of the page in her delicate hand writing, in perfect cursive, "We love you daddy."

I thanked Summer, placing the drawing in my locker next to the other one he had made me.

My good luck charms.

The end of the second period, I was walking down the hallway, my head held down. We were losing 3-1. I felt defeated, I had chances to score but LA seemed to know where I would be when I didn't even know where I would be.

Luke was the only goal scorer, helping us get on the board. I felt useless. This is game 1 of 7 and if this was how we were going to play we might as well not show up again.

Sitting in the locker room coach walked over, kicking my foot.

"Let's go outside Collins."

I stood up, waiting to be yelled at or belittled for the way I was playing.

As we made our way out of the locker room, he gently pushed me against the wall.

"Don't take this shit on yourself. You're playing good. You're a team guy not a selfish player. You've had some shit months, but stop taking it out on yourself. Pull your head out of your ass, and notice that it's not just you that's off. I need you Collins. What do you need?"

I picked my head up locking eyes with him, "Chloe". The only word muttered, he nodded his head, mentally telling me to stay put while he walked off.

I placed my head back against the concrete wall for what felt like 5 minutes.

A small hand wrapped around my arm, "Now I was enjoying the Buffett upstairs, gorging myself on hot wings and ranch dressing when someone told me I was needed immediately. So, you wanna tell me why our son is enjoying the Buffett without me?"

Her hands reaching up to play with the locks of hair cascading the back of my neck. I moved my face down smiling at her, my eyes locking with hers.

"I needed you. I-I feel like I'm playing like shit Chloe. I feel like I'm letting my team down. Tell me I'm wrong baby."

Her hands coming to the sides of my face, "You are doing great baby, you guys aren't talking though, you guys need to communicate Reed. Talk. Once you get that going, it will be game over. I believe in you love."

I wrapped my arms around her waist, pulling her into me, "Thanks baby. I love you. I'm also sorry about taking you away from the food."

She let out a little giggle, "It's okay. It's all you can eat and I have one period left, my ass is getting a to-go-box."

We spent the next 3 minutes holding one another before I had to let her go and head back in. She's right, me and the guys aren't talking, we are expecting the others to read our minds. That all stops for period 3.

I watch as Chloe heads back towards the elevator. Her legs clad in black leather pants that hug her sweet ass, she's wearing her stilettos (how I don't know), and her black leather jacket with my name and number clad across her back. She's a breathtaking view.

Period 3 was game over as Chloe mentioned. After a quick pep talk, our game changed. Things were connecting.

With 4 minutes left in the 3rd period we were tied 3-3. Matt had a minor penalty for slashing and was finishing his time in the sin bin. Without him for the next minute I needed to be on my A game.

As we lined up for a face off, the guy next to me started taunting me. He had been on me most the night, but he was getting really aggravating.

"How's that slut wife of yours Collins?"

My eyes filled with rage, I gripped the stick harder, trying to pay him no attention.

"How's that bastard son of yours too?"

I stared into his eyes, trying to relay to him to shut up, a smirk plastered across his face, "How about you shut the fuck up Johnson."

"Come on Collins."

I could feel my blood boiling. As he went to open his mouth again the puck was dropped and I took off skating towards the blue line, the puck being passed to me by Luke. By passing the last defenseman it was just me and the goaltender. Shooting the puck it soared over his shoulder hitting the net. I slowed passing the goal when I was slammed into the boards, not hard enough to take me out but hard enough for me to want to kill the mother fucker.

Once I got my bearings I turned seeing Luke holding Jefferson by the collar of his pads. I skated over in hopes of separating them but instead I took over for Luke. Shedding my gloves I threw a punch, hitting Jefferson along the cheek.

"If you ever talk about my wife and my son ever again, I will end your career."

The ref held me back as the other grabbed Jefferson, skating him to the sin bin.

I nodded to the ref, locking eyes with Matt as I skated over to join him for the last 30 seconds he had.

Sitting on the bench, Matt nudged me, "Fucking sweet goal man and awesome hit."

I laughed nudging him back, "Welcome to playoffs, am I right?"

Game 1: done. Stanley Cup you are mine.

34

Chloe: Stanley Cup Final

Reed and his team are heading into game 6 of the series final against Edmonton. If they win tonight, they win the Stanley cup. I'm 28 weeks pregnant and honestly I feel like a beached whale.

Reed was walking through the house at 7am, with the inability to calm the fuck down.

Colton laid on the couch with me, eating a fruit bar and "reading" his book to me.

"Reed!"

Reed stopped pacing looking at me worried, "What? Are you okay?"

I laughed, ruffling Colton's hair, "I'm great, you're not. What's going on?"

He moved to sit in on the other end of the couch, "I'm just nervous, I've never been this close to taking the cup home."

"Baby, you are going to do great tonight. You always play well, just remember communication and have fun. Just go out and do what you do best okay. And regardless for of the outcome, there's still 1 more game after if you don't win. But you will." Rubbing my belly, locking eyes with my husband to reassure him, "WE believe in you."

Reed got up, walking over to kiss me, "Thanks baby. I think I am going to head in. Are you sure you're good?"

I caressed his cheek, "Of course, Colton needs a nap before we go and your parents are going to come get us, this way you can drive us home."

He kissed me one more time before kissing Colton. "Colt say bye to daddy."

"Bye bye daddy" he waved at Reed.

"Daddy loves you, all of you" throwing a wink my way he headed out, going to the rink.

4 hours later Colton and I were seated in the WAGs and family box with Reed's parents snacking on the best Buffett I have devoured.

It's like Dave can read my mind, because the moment I think about getting more, the man places another plate in front of me.

I dressed Colton in his "Collins" Jersey for tonight while I was sporting my "Collins" playoff jacket. I was hoping tonight would be the last game for different reasons, 1: I wanted my husband home, 2: these babies were killing my back and 3: I was tired of putting makeup on.

I could easily stop trying with my appearance but that's not the kind a girl I am. So, call me selfish I don't care.

Summer was seated next to me, eating off the latest plate that was delivered to me. She was due early to middle of July, so her date was sooner rather than later. I think she is 33 weeks but honestly with pregnancy brain, I wouldn't count on it being correct.

They still hadn't announced what they were having and they refused to show anyone the nursery. For once in her and Matt's life, they could keep a secret.

The start of the third period was electric, the game was 4-4 and it was the most exciting game I had ever watched. Edmonton was not letting anyone get away with anything and St. Louis was willing to fight when needed.

Reed and Luke had spent time in the sin bin for jumping into a fight not intended for them, but together they helped their teammates. Something I admired.

I was on the edge of my seat, Colton asleep on Dave, Summer holding my hand as the time ticked down.

All the wives and girlfriends were quiet, holding onto one another and holding our breaths. We all wanted the win, the boys worked so hard we knew they needed this. Especially after the year Reed and I had, we needed something good.

With 30 seconds left, one of our young players, Jones, caught a breakaway and slung the puck flying into the back of the net. The crowd erupted as the buzzer sounded.

We had won.

We all made out way to the ice as the guys celebrated with each other, wearing their new Stanley Cup winner hats and taking time to kiss the Cup.

Summer and I waited on the player's bench, knowing we couldn't be on the ice being pregnant. Reed's parents took Colton out to celebrate with him and the players while we sat back, recording and capturing the moments on our phones.

Reed caught my eye as Matt skated over, holding onto Summer helping her on the ice, letting her hold the boards.

I stood up smiling as he skated closer, grabbing my face he slammed out lips together.

"Congratulation baby." I muttered in between kisses. "Thank you baby, I couldn't have done it with you." He kissed me again. "I'll hold you so you don't fall, but come out here with me please?"

I nodded, a little nervous about being on the ice, luckily I wore my sneakers instead of heals.

I trudged my way to the door, as he grabbed me by the waist, he held me as we made our way to his parents, he took Colton into his other arms.

"I didn't want to celebrate until all my kids and my lovely wife were with me." He leaned down kissing my head.

A reporter walked over asking to interview Reed, he accepted not letting me or Colton leave his arms.

"Reed, Congratulations on the win, now that you won the Stanley Cup, what's next for you?"

Reed let out a laugh, catching my eyes with his, taking a breath he looked back up at the reporter, "I'm going to be a dad."

The reporter continued to ask a few more questions before moving onto the next player.

I grabbed Reed's jaw in my hands, bringing his lips to mine, "How about we head home here soon and we can celebrate in your favorite way."

Reed's eyes swam with desire, "Well let's go home baby."

35

Epilogue: 6 months later

R eed kissed me goodbye as he headed out of the house heading to the rink.

Summer and I were taking the kids to the home game, the only new thing was we were taking all 4 kids-this was the twins first game and Summer and Matts little girls first game.

Summer and Matt had welcomed Ivy on July 18th, a month after they eloped and were finally married.

I had welcomed the twins on July 28th, Amelia Rose beat her brother out by 2 minutes and sweet Carter Owen took his sweet time exiting my womb. I have a feeling their arrivals will mirror their personalities.

Reed has been the best dad I knew he would be. He has helped with the late night feedings, taking them when he's home and being present with Colton as well. Colton has loved being a big brother, he will bring me diapers for no reason but he thinks he's helping-so we have a pile on the side table in the living room now.

Reed's parents have been life savers, taking Colton when he gets overwhelmed or just to get him out of the house.

Once Reed started the new season I was scared that I would be doing everything on my own again but I was wrong. My family has been the best family.

I had started back at work, taking on certain clients and only working a few hours a week. It felt good to be back in the salon and good to be doing what I love.

Reed's parents were currently getting Colton and Carter dressed for the game while I finished changing Amelia.

Reed and Matt didn't know we were bringing the kids, we were going to surprise them during warm ups.

I had ordered Amelia and Carter matching onesies with Reed's number on them with "Daddy" Across the back.

Colton was wearing his jersey to match them.

I grabbed the ear muffs for the kids and their little jackets that were gifted to us by the GM, they were St. Louis jackets with Reed's name and number on them.

Warm ups had started when we got there so we made our way to the glass meeting Summer and Ivy.

"Have they come out yet?" I asked her as I shifted Amelia in my arms.

Reed's dad had taken Colton and Reed's mom had Carter in her arms bouncing him slightly.

"Not yet. Luke saw us and waved, then skated off. Give them a minute."

As if she was a mind reader, our husbands came barreling out of the tunnel, they skated a large circle not noticing us at first.

I watched Reed, his hair hanging over his ears, his eyes hooded with concentration- I loved my husband but watching him in his element made me want to jump his bones.

Reed halted on the ice a few feet in front of us smiling wide, taking his helmet off, he shook his hair out before skating over to see us.

His face puzzled but excited.

Colton started laughing yelling "Daddy!!" Causing everyone including the social media team to notice our arrival.

Reed tossed 3 pucks over, 1 for each kid-something he has done since Colton started coming to games.

Matt met up with him cooing at his daughter through the glass.

I held Amelia up showing Reed her onesie and then pointing at Carters, smiling.

Reed laughed pressing his hand to the glass mouthing the words, "I love you." Before tapping his heart 3 times.

My world was complete. I have an amazing husband, 3 beautiful babies, wonderful friends and amazing support. Life seemed so bleak before, but now I know it was only missing key pieces. And standing here, holding my babies, watching my husband skate around with the C on his chest, I know I am where I need to be.

Who knew moving across country with a 9 month old would allow me to fall in love the first day I saw Reed. Life has a funny way of going about things, but I'm not complaining.

www.ingramcontent.com/pod-product-compliance
Lightning Source LLC
Chambersburg PA
CBHW031451260626

47154CB00016B/883